12/01

THE HARVARD LAMPOON'S™

GUIDE TO COLLEGE ADMISSIONS

—— CLIP & SAVE ———— CLIP & SAVE ———

THE HARVARD LAMPOON'S™

GUIDE TO COLLEGE ADMISSIONS

The Comprehensive, Authoritative, and Utterly Useless
Source for Where to Go and How to Get In

— CLIP & SAVE — — — — CLIP & SAVE —

By the Editors of the
Harvard Lampoon™

WARNER BOOKS

A Time Warner Company

ARTWORK AND PHOTO CREDITS
Yvette Blonski—vii; **Elizabeth Phang**—pages 5, 56, 58, 63, 101, 106, 122, 134, 135, 136; *Harvard Lampoon staff*—9, 28, 32, 59, 60, 68—71 (9), 74, 75, 76, 91, 103, 104, 108, 109, 111, 126—130 (10), 162 (bottom), 163; **Chess Stetson**—16, 72, 142 (2); **Emily Harrison**—18, 27 (5), 95, 139, 141, 159, 162 (top); **Amanda Burnham**—20 (5), 61, 140, 145, 146, 147, 150; **AP/WIDE WORLD PHOTOS**—20 (photo), 81 (bottom), 87; **Digital imagery © copyright 1999 PhotoDisc, Inc.**—30, 81 (top photo), 85, 99; **Jed Wahl**—66; **E. D. Bennett**—92; **Deirdre O'Dwyer**—116; **Fabiana Kulick**—118; **J. D. Brancato**—158.

Warner Books, Inc., 1271 Avenue of the Americas, New York, NY 10020

Visit our Web site at www.twbookmark.com

Ⓦ A Time Warner Company

Printed in the United States of America

First Printing: September 2000

10 9 8 7 6 5 4 3 2 1

Library of Congress Cataloging-in-Publication Data
The Harvard Lampoon's guide to college admissions : the comprehensive, authoritative, and utterly useless source for where to go and how to get in / by the editors of the Harvard Lampoon.
    p. cm.
  ISBN 0-446-67616-0
  1. College students—Humor. 2. Universities and colleges—Admission—Humor. I.
Harvard Lampoon
PN6231.C6 H37 2000
378.1'61'0207—dc21   00=042349

Cover design and art by Carmen Vecchio / Anagram Design Enfield
Book design / art and text composition by Spinning Egg Design Group, Inc.

This book is a parody. None of the characters or incidents described in this book are real. The names, test questions, and facts have been fabricated, and following any of our hints will likely get you smacked, kidney-punched, or rejected from your safety school.

Contents

🦆 Preface to the Book We Wrote

Hey! What's up? I really gotta thank you for picking up this book. I know that they probably have us sitting next to the latest Danielle Steel tear-jerker or Sue Grafton alphabet mystery. So, by choosing this book, you have proved that you are not a forty-year-old woman. Or maybe you're the janitor in the Time Warner warehouse, dusting the enormous pile of unsold *Lampoon* books next to *'N Sync Cooks with Santa*.

But chances are you've found us in the college prep section mixed in with the Barron's and Peterson's guides. Between you, me, and the lamppost, those guys don't give a damn whether or not you get into the college of your choice. All they want is to make sure that you go to Northwestern University. In fact, Northwestern is the only college ranked in most other college guides. So if you want to go to the University of Chicago or even the University of Illinois Urbana-Champaign, your chances are nil unless you do your own personal research. As a result of the scams perpetrated by the likes of these "First Sources for College Information," the small Chicago suburb of Evanston holds fully 85 percent of the college population in the U.S. And Mr. Barron is sitting back in his mansion, rolling in thousand-dollar bills, drinking an alcohol-containing beverage. Meanwhile, due to horrid overcrowding, Joe College Student is forced to share his Dickensian one-room dorm suite at Northwestern with four hundred other freshmen. I can almost hear his cry as he suffocates under a sea of unwashed flesh: "Why did I buy the Peterson's and Barron's guides? O cruel harlot Fate!! They said Northwestern has really great advising . . . Can't take it . . ."

"Ha!! Ha!! Ha!!" says Barron as he eats money.

Well, we're not going to tell you where to go. The people at Barron's just want your money. Their books are lifeless—statistics, charts, and "facts" to give you stone cold information. Our book is soft where they are hard, tender where they are tough. Our book is playful. Snuggled by a roaring fire in your spacious den, you might say to this book, "C'mon, champ, stop that. That tickles. But seriously, I love you. Let's cuddle."

Most importantly, however, our book will help you in a variety of ways. Many readers of this gem you're holding right now have already benefited immeasurably from our words. Consider the case of Jessica H., who was inspired by our book to drop out of high school and enroll in a remedial English course. Had she never purchased our book, she may never have known that she was unable to read. Had the copy she purchased not been printed in Portuguese, she might still be in high school today, and not hawking hot dogs on the side of the freeway. Bad example.

But how about little Max K., who, after a long and ill-fated international flight, used our book as a flotation device to stay alive in the freezing waters of the Baltic Sea? Today Max is celebrating his eighth birthday, as he will tomorrow and the day after. Unfortunately, Max and his frozen brain will never attend an American college.

Still skeptical? How about Bryce J.? Yesterday Bryce led his high school football team past rival Madison High with a fourth-quarter comeback. Way to go, Bryce!

Perhaps we should mention the case of Zoe P. After purchasing our book, Zoe recycled our fibrous pages, turning them into pulp. She then used this recycled paper to publish a wildly successful fanzine for Matchbox 20 frontman Rob Thomas. Check it out!

Nora T. read our book and thought it was okay.

Sawako H. made 1,000 origami cranes out of our book, and brought good luck to the proud people of Japan.

Gerry B., a clever little one, used our book as a Halloween mask. It's so funny . . . it's *scary*!

This book will not be the most useful book you will ever read. That distinction lies with Nicholas Evans's haunting fable *The Horse Whisperer*. But it might make you forget the frustrating process of college for a short while. *The Horse Whisperer* will also do this, but come on, that guy doesn't need any more money.

Introduction

Getting into College: This Is Not Hard

What is the big deal? You know and I know that getting into college is not hard. Every year, millions upon millions of astoundingly dumb people get into college.

Do you remember Lance Austin? Yeah, the kid from first grade who used to always see if he could squeeze his whole bare butt into the paste jar? That's right: He got into college. Or Michael Bolero, the boy who only wore cardigans and always smelled a little off? He would always stick his foot in the toilet and laugh and laugh until you wished he would stop laughing. He's laughing all the way to college, that crazy, stinky bastard.

SATs, college essays, the admissions interview: These all sound scary until you realize that Alison Jenkins, the girl without a nose, did just fine. Do you remember how she had a really hot body and you were all like, "Damn, if she only had a nose, she would be such a hotty"? Well, Alison had an hour-long interview as the interviewer stared at her horrifyingly noseless face, and then he recommended her for admission. If she can get in, how do you think you are gonna do, Dr. Von Nose-on-Face?

Don't even tell me you are sweating about the essay. Do you think Chuck Mengold from homeroom sweated when he wrote a four-sentence essay about how he loves taking shits? Now that guy loves dropping a load at—you guessed it—college! Do not even get me started on SATs.

Ryan Etzel took the SATs while he was totally making out with Becky, the cheerleader with the hairy pits. No, dude, it's true—Gilman told me it's all true. He was totally kissing her and doing the test AT THE SAME TIME. Ryan Etzel is now in jail. Regardless, the only math you have to know is *SAT=ain't no thang*.

Oh, what is that you say? Did you want to get into an elite college? Good luck, fancy pants—you'll need it.

Starting Early

Ideally, all of the children of the world would be able to receive the best education, leaving their doors of opportunity wide open. Unfortunately, Harvard College admits less than 2,100 students every year.

In this ridiculously competitive world, parents have only one choice: make their child the best college applicant he or she can be in the eyes of admissions committees across the country. Sure, we'd all like to be more altruistic, and raise our children to be do-gooders, confronting the social, environmental, and economic ills facing our world today. But a degree from, say, Northwestern won't even get you into Greenpeace.

Preparing a child for the college admissions process is a long, rigorous effort. If you think you don't need to start worrying about your child's college applications until his junior year of high school, you might as well just get him that job at the gas station he's always wanted. Wake up, parents; this is the new millennium, for Chrissakes.

With that in mind, we offer this chapter mainly as advice to parents smart enough to get ahead of the admissions game—a game not unlike Yahtzee, backgammon, or Australian Rules football.

Before we continue, a word of warning. If you're not yet in high school, and you're reading this because you're already worried about the college admissions process, you need to stop. Take a look at yourself in the mirror. Take off your glasses. Put your books down. Take your calculator out of your pocket. Remove the compass from the chain around your neck. Put this book in one of the 9-by-12 envelopes you keep in your closet next to the plants you're studying. Write on the envelope, "DO NOT OPEN UNTIL SOPHOMORE YEAR OF HIGH SCHOOL. AT LEAST."

Now shut up and learn how to play hockey.

Advice for Parents before Conception

Many parents feel that the college adventure doesn't begin until a child's junior year of high school. These parents are not only wrong, they're ignoring new scientific findings coming from our nation's leading research institutes. And their children will only get into crappy schools. A child's getting-into-college adventure begins far before high school; in fact, the college adventure begins far before a child is even conceived.

"I admit," Dr. Evan DeNoon says, "I didn't even think about where my child might go to college until she was in eleventh grade. Boy, do I wish I knew twenty-five years ago what I know now! I tell you one thing—I certainly wouldn't have conceived a child in late May!" Dr. DeNoon is referring to the findings of a landmark study he and his colleague, Dr. Lucille Harte-Hart, have carried out over the past thirty years at the University of California at Los Angeles Center for Pre-Fetal Education. In short, their study shows that the time of year, and, believe it or not, even the day of the week that a child is conceived can have a profound effect on a child's chances of getting into a good school. Their study involved collecting data from hundreds of America's finest and crappiest colleges and universities, as well as tracking children born in 1970–1980 from conception through their college application process. Says Dr. DeNoon, "This is the product of many years of hard labor, hard numbers, and soft bodies. What did I just say?"

Looking for an Ivy League child? "Best to plant the seed in early fall," advises Dr. Harte-Hart, noting that fully 16.3 percent of Ivy League students are conceived between September 20 and October 20. Other conception times that seem to leave children with a good shot at the Ivies include later winter (February 15–March 1) and the odd days in July.

What's the worst time to conceive a child? "August!" Doctors DeNoon and Harte-Hart both ejaculate in unison. Indeed, the numbers don't lie. More than 60 percent of children conceived in August don't even make it to college. Another 30 percent were only admitted to what Dr. DeNoon has categorized as fourth- or fifth-tier colleges or junior colleges. An additional 4 percent of August babies proved to be downright retarded. "When we first got this data back, it got to be a joke around the lab," Dr. Harte-Hart remembers. "If someone said something dumb, or spilled their drink, or forgot the 27-digit access code to the lab's computer files, we'd be like, 'What were you, conceived in August or something?!' That always cracked us up. We're very lonely." When asked if she thought the accuracy of the study might have been compromised by the fact that both Dr. Harte-Hart and Dr. DeNoon were conceived in August, Dr. Harte-Hart replied, "I don't think that's funny," while wiping a small tear from her eye.

The UCLACP-FE has also uncovered valuable information about other conceptual conditions. "Don't let it get too hot in the bedroom," warns Dr. DeNoon, pointing to a Magic Marker–drawn graph illustrating the dangers of high-temperature conception. "Realistically, once the sexual environment exceeds a temperature of 78 degrees, you're looking at a state school baby at best."

Dr. DeNoon and Dr. Harte-Hart's story does not end here. You see, the two researchers are not only colleagues, but husband and wife. Their first child, Aurora DeNoon-Harte-Hart, was conceived, according to their parents' estimations, on May 27, an inadvisable conception time. "Not surprisingly," says her mother, Dr. Harte-Hart, "Aurora dropped out after one semester at a community college."

For their second child, the couple put their findings into practice. Their second child, Bryan Harte-DeNoon-Hart, was conceived in a 68-degree room on October 3. Unfortunately, Bryan never even graduated from high school. Says Dr. DeNoon, "I guess some kids are just stupid."

Do's and Don'ts for Parents Raising a College-Bound Embryo

So you've successfully conceived a child, hopefully following the guidelines presented by Dr. DeNoon and Dr. Harte-Hart. If you had already conceived a child before purchasing this book, without following the advice presented in the first pages of this book, you should seriously consider starting over.

The human embryo is a strange, wonderful, gooey thing. What can parents do to ensure that their embryo won't end up at some community college? Here's a quick checklist:

Do ✔

Lecture the embryo on a variety of academic disciplines, ranging from spelling to numbers to the humanities to the biochemical sciences.

Don't ☠

Coddle it with cutesy phrases. The only thing this will serve to do is to develop a strong parent-child bond, totally worthless in the college application process.

Do ✔

Spend at least 30 minutes going over SAT flashcards with your embryo when you go in for an ultrasound. Although the embryo won't technically be able to see/hear the flashcards, both because of its lack of eyes/ears and the dense uterine wall separating it from you, it's still a good habit to get into.

Don't ☠

Allow your embryo to grow genitalia. Physical deformity is just one more way to separate your child from the normal, happy, sexually adjusted masses.

Do ✔

Punish your embryo if it refuses to use the Kaplan SAT prep books you swallowed for it. Heavy drinking or drug use will usually do the trick.

Don't ☠

Allow the embryo to sleep for more than 5–6 hours a night, lest you want an undisciplined, lazy infant who'd rather sleep than study.

Do ✔

Force your embryo to involve itself in at least 2–3 extracurricular activities, like captaining the varsity hockey team or being editor of the high school yearbook. If it protests that this is impossible (which it won't do as it has no mouth or brain), remind it that you didn't have an embryo just so it could sit around all day in your uterus doing nothing!

Don't ☠

Emotionally pressure your embryo into doing anything it doesn't really enjoy. Starving yourself is a much more effective way to make your embryo change its mind.

Do ✔

Encourage your embryo as it takes its practice SATs by shouting phrases like, "Don't screw this up, embryo!" and "When I was your age I was pulling down 1400s!"

Don't ☠

*Ever show your embryo that you love it. Remember, love the embryo's **achievements**, not the **embryo** itself.*

Your child is born, the miracle of life, etc. etc. But how are you going to get this kid on the Ivy path? It certainly wouldn't hurt to start planning college visits early. However, you don't want to intimidate your child; that's why we don't recommend starting looking at colleges until at least age seven.

The first step, therefore, is finding a reputable elementary school that will not only prepare a child academically for the rigors of a top-notch university, but look good in the eyes of admissions committees. True, nowhere on a college application are you asked to list which elementary school you attended. But admissions officers are hired for their savvy—if your child has attended an elementary school like the Dalton School, they just *know*.

Unfortunately, getting into one of said elementary schools is no simple matter. The application process can be quite a challenge for your youngster.

Dalton School for the Academically Gifted

1134 Central Park West, New York, New York

Admissions Test for 6-year-old Applicants

1. Finish this picture:

$

2. Mommy is standing in your bedroom. Your nanny comes in to wake you up. The housekeeper enters your room to clean up. The cook comes in and brings you some cereal. Another nanny begins to read Dickens to you out loud. Mommy leaves to laugh with the pool man. How many people are in your bedroom?

3. Cross out the mistake in the picture.

4. Daddy opens a bottle of Johnnie Walker Black Label and has three sips. After talking on the phone with Nana Winslow he has seven sips. After looking at the newspaper he has one sip. After telling you that your mother is an icy bitch he has ten sips. How many pairs of squash shoes do you own?

5. Which of these phrases rhyme?

◯ Money, Tommy
◯ Hispanic, Bad
◯ Public School, Hispanic
◯ Daddy invests money, Outlook sunny

The Recommended Book List

Your child's education, contrary to the belief of stupid people, does not end at school. It is a parent's responsibility to continue to read to children and feed their brains with a certain food called knowledge. This food grows on the tree of responsibility, in the forest of parenthood. Find it on a map, and half of your parenting problems will be solved.

Synapses. Neuropsychological pathways. Corpus callosum. Any good parent should be able to identify all of these developmentally crucial terms, know their interactions and their role in a child's well-rounded educational development. We at the *Harvard Lampoon*, however, have no idea what these terms mean. We can, fortunately, offer a list of books available in such stores as "Smart Kidz," "Brainy Totz," and "Books for Smarty-Pantz." The following are recommended for children ages 5–8. But you don't have to take our word for it! Well, I guess you do.

 *The Little CEO That Could*

Jungle Gym: A Story of Leadership

Building Blocks, Building Partnerships: A Playtime Guide for Tots and Their Parents

Mrs. Peek-a-boo Visits the Land of the Savants

Check Please!

Davey the Dinosaur Dunks a Doughnut: Calculus for Children Ages 5 to 8

Don't Bite the Doorknob!

Eat Your Vegetables, Invest in Mutual Funds

Othello

Yolanda Bolanda's Guide to Classifying Animals by Phylum

Randy Likes What He Sees

And Baby Makes Four! Helping the Older Sibling Understand the Birth of a Newborn, and Consequential Ramifications of Birth Order, Sibling Rivalry, and Relative Social Perceptions

Putting the Fun in In-fun-tile

Milton Berle's Private Collection of Jokes

Wizzy the Wampet Wishes for Woozles

Eat Me

Helpful Tips for Parents

Playtime is a great opportunity to introduce novelty in a child's life, showing the possibilities of a creative mind. One great idea is to rename popular games. This not only increases your child's brainpower, but might also trick them. That's always fun. For example, "Simon Says" might change into "Louis Says" or "Whatever Maria Says Goes" or "Phillip Is Currently Holding the Authority Stick."

Or you can change around the rules of games. This keeps kids' brains on their toes, if brains had toes. You understand, silly! Instead of using the board or game equipment as part of the game, have your child eat it instead! Those high-fiber game boards will certainly help form valuable synapses in your child's all-too-fragile cerebrum.

Music is a vital part of your child's preschool education; it is the universal language, more so even than Mandarin Chinese. No—just kidding. Make homemade instruments: Rubber bands and a shoebox make a great little guitar; a broom and some bigger rubber bands make a fantastic bass; a glue stick, some plastic gloves, and a deck of playing cards make an awesome flageolet! No, not like *that!*

Smart parents raise smart kids. Be proud of how smart you are in front of your child, and your child will be excited about the prospect of improving his brainpower. And, hey, don't forget to inject your child's brain with MensaMilk®. To prove that being smart is cool, try to get a celebrity to tell your child how much they love reading, learning, and being a braniac. Troy Aikman and Stanley Tucci are usually happy to oblige.

Children need to know the value of perseverance. "Try, try again!" goes an old saying which my uncle used to hackle as he "pitched" baseballs alarmingly close to my neck. I finally caught up to that fastball, and look where I am today! Here. In my parents' basement, playing Atari baseball, secretly taking bong hits when my mom runs to the grocery store.

Always perform a skill for your child as you're teaching it to him. Do you think Ken Griffey Jr. would have learned to swing a baseball bat if his dad hadn't showed him? If you said "No," please remove your crazy-pants and don a more suitable pair of commonsense trousers.

Use sensible rewards after accomplishments. If your child wins a spelling bee at school, buy him a book he's wanted. If he learns to play a song on the piano, get him a classical music CD. If he memorizes the order of the planets correctly, take a family trip to the grave of Johannes Kepler.

High School
Extracurricular Activities

With the waning importance of standardized tests and the increasing number of students with immaculate academic records, the importance of high school extracurricular activities is growing. It's a way of separating yourself from the thousands of other students applying to the same schools that you're looking at. "Hey," you can say, via your activities, "look what I did! Look at me, admissions officer! It's me, Phil. I was editor of my school newspaper!" If your name isn't Phil, then you really won't be separating yourself from the other applicants, because everybody else was editor of their high school newspaper as well.

So you should probably change your name to Phil.

Well, Phil, let's say you haven't yet started your high school journey. Or maybe you've got a couple of years left. We're here to tell you how to best spend your time—or at least how to make it seem like you've best spent your time. And we've also pointed out some extracurricular pitfalls to watch out for.

Whatever you do, Phil, please, do not participate in any sort of marching band. And, to be quite honest, this is not even so much college application advice as it is good common sense. In fact, colleges might like to see that you had enough spirit to spend time in the marching band. But Phil, this is the straight dope: All members of any marching band, past, present, or future, have always, and will always, die as virgins. It is a self-selective curse. Beware.

Anyhoo, remember that academics come first. There's nothing that colleges want more than good grades. If your homework is being sacrificed because you just don't have time after all your extra curricular activities, you might want to think about quitting the curling team.

Although extracurricular activities are important, you don't want to let them compromise your academics, especially if you've got a chance to be ranked at the top of your class. If you spend too much time practicing for the National Origami Championships, or something equally useless, you might end up like this guy:

Transcript of Salutatorian Address
by Aaron Watt
Amity High School, June 9, 2000

WHILE YOU WERE OUT

Congratulations, fellow classmates. I want you all to remember the good times of the past but always look forward. And congratulations to our parents, s who have helped us through these hard formative years. I would like to start off on this glorious day by telling a parable that can help us in our endeavors in the real world.

When I was only knee-high, my grandfather explained the difference between people who are "ha-ha" funny and "strange" funny. He went on to tell me there was also a difference between "cold, heartless, and obese" smart and "straight-up American" smart. My grandfather then continued to explain this distinction with a little story:

Let's say there was a feminist English teacher who taught, let's say, I don't know...the twentieth-century American novel and preferred the company of women. The "straight-up American" smart person would write an insightful paper that did not pander to any feminist or sexually alternative political stance. That person would get three points lower than a hypothetical "cold, heartless, and obese" smart person who would go to the weight room with the aforementioned sexually alternative English teacher. Maybe the fat smart person would agree with her ungodly Amazon freak of a teacher that doing squats made her feel "too girly" and so she preferred doing military press. And in the end those three points on an English paper would separate "straight-up American" smart guy from a cold, heartless smart girl who earns her grades in a lesbian sweathouse.

In closing, I would like to wish Susie, this year's Amity High School valedictorian, the best of luck at Yale. And I would like to wish Ms. Carlyle luck in her uphill battle in finding an acceptable place in our God-fearing society. As for me, I'll have a good time next year. A good time alright...at Davidson! My heart is black.

Peace out, go Cougars!

Signed

Of course, most extracurricular activities are rewarding, fun, and educational. We'll be the first to admit that they look great on college applications, but you should really do extracurricular activities for the activities themselves. Even some of the most seemingly horrid activities can prove to be exciting. We asked the members of the Wheelwright High School Math Team to look back on their season to help prove our point. Unfortunately, all the students at Wheelwright assured us that the Math Team was, in fact, the worst thing imaginable. So we went to Sherwood High, where we got the following quotes:

✳

"Math Team was the best thing I did at Sherwood High. I lived it, breathed it, and pissed it out at night. Know this: It's not for any old math-liker. You gotta have the love. Do you have the love? You probably don't."

✳

"Math Team was where the big boys came to run. Practices were the hardest thing I ever had to do, but they were also the most rewarding thing I ever did. But don't think that competitions were any easier, because they weren't. They were actually harder. Competitions were the hardest thing I ever had to do, along with practices. Fuck yeah."

✳

"The life of a Math Teamer is paradise. Wake up, sleep through class (Coach will bail us out if we get in trouble), skip half of the day to watch videos in his office, go to practice, then go home and have sex with hot girls."

✳

"My younger brother came out for Math Team when he was a freshman and I was a senior. By tradition, all freshmen get taped down and paddled by the seniors. All during that first day of practice, Mike stuck by my side, trying to get protection. That made it all the easier for me to snatch him and give him a beating. Brother or no brother, Math Team traditions must not die. I whacked him extra hard, in fact. Then he whacked me back, right in the gut. I just stood there, trading blows with my brother. It was awesome."

"My old man says I need to pay for my own college education. That's why I joined the Math Team. I know I have a natural talent, and maybe I can get a scholarship. If not, I will always have the memories, and also free rulers."

✳

"Have you seen my Math tattoo?"

✳

"There is nothing like a Math Team game day. Coach huddles you up, the team prays together, our captain gives us a pep talk, and we get all excited and start bashing stuff. Then we usually find Erik's little brother and give him a pinkbelly. Finally, we tie up our math-pads, put on our math-helmets, and go whup some mathematic ass."

✳

"Then there was the time that we had lots of sex with hot girls, ruled the school, and earned $800 for the March of Dimes walkathon."

✳

"If you talk smack with another Math Team member, I will fight you. If you insult our coach, I will fight you. The Math Team environment makes me a very belligerent young man."

✳

"Then there was the math."

✳

"Yeah; we did math."

Sometimes, students are simply unaware of the sacrifices that extracurricular activities demand. The National Honor Society is a prime example. Consider this constitution of one high school's NHS chapter, and think about whether the commitment described is worth the prestige that membership will bring. Sure, the prestige is valuable: Many NHS inductees go on to four-year college programs (you heard me) and some occupy the highest ranks at major American accountancy firms and have offices in New York City. It isn't easy for the average high schooler to prove himself to the Society. Only through acts of courage and valor can you truly demonstrate Honour. (You also need at least a 3.25 cumulative GPA.)

NHS

*L*eadership. Character. Citizenship. Service. These are the pillars of our student organization, the National Honor Society. The path to the NHS is not to be taken lightly and requires sacrifice and sometimes otherworldly commitment, but the rewards can be great. The National Honor Society Code (adapted from Ye National Honoure Society Code of 1977)

Article the First.

The Initiate must serve his masters faithfully. Death comes only before dishonour.

This is very important. An NHS member must remain faithful to his God, the Westview High School Cougars, and his country. If the principal asks a member to stay after class or to engage in gladiatorial combat with "divers Tygers and Sphynxes," he or she must comply unless he or she has band practice.

Article the Second.

The Initiate must provide his tithe to the coffers of the Organization.

Every member of the NHS has to sell at least two boxes of Crunch bars for the fall fund-raiser or else we don't get to go to the science museum.

Article the Third.

The Initiate always treats a lady with due courtesy.

Always provide female classmates with a decorative umbrella when standing in the sun. Provide them with a hand when they get out of a motor-carriage. Never refer to a lady as a ho-bag. Instead, offer her your seat when all are taken. If you see someone say something rude to a lady in the cafeteria, you should kill this person. The girl will then be your chattel. This only works if you are an attractive and athletic male.

Article the Fourth.

The Initiate must bathe in the blood of the Saracen hordes before the harvest celebration.

Yeah, we really don't do this one so much anymore.

Article the Fifth.

The successful Initiate is rewarded with a plot of land, title, and a proclamation.

Free refills at basketball games. NHS rocks!

For some students, extracurricular activities can be frightening not because of their impact on admissions officers, but because of activity-related trauma.

For example, you might be a huge nerd or have some sort of debilitating physical or social flaw. You've got the grades, the debate team stuff, the other stuff. But there's one thing left: You cannot flunk gym class. Though it's technically part of the high school curriculum, any sort of physical movement is completely foreign to you. But you have to take "physical education," and, if you fail, you might even end up at Brown or Pomona. But no need to worry, brother; we got your back.

Nerd Rule #1: Wear what everyone else wears

If your school does not have a school uniform, make sure that your gym class outfit is a normal pair of shorts and T-shirt advertising a sports team. Explaining your "If It Ain't Baroque, Don't Fix It!" shirt to Coach Ass-Face isn't going to be productive. "But Coach," you say, "this is a caricature of Oscar Wilde!" I just punched you in the face.

Nerd Rule #2: Pretend to be a girl

Girl gym class is easier. They do a badminton unit instead of weightlifting. And you can check out the girls in the shower room. This scheme only works for guys with no male anatomy. Like they need any more luck! If you are a girl, continue pretending that you are a girl. Check out the guy without genitals in your shower.

Foreign Exchange Student Rule #1*: Act dumb

If you accidentally shoot a basket for the opposing team, shrug and tell the coach that that's how they play "hockey" in Canada.

Foreign Exchange Student Rule #2*: Be from Sweden

Those guys are tough. You won't have any problems.

*Attention international students: Getting into college in the U.S. means more than just having good grades. High school students must participate in a variety of extracurricular activities. *Ex-tra-cur-ric-u-lar*. To stay on par with your American competition, you should consider your country's equivalent student activities.

American football	=	Outside North America, soccer; in Canada, arena football
Classic American baseball	=	Tokyo Giants. Alternately, Cuban cigars, or cricket
American swimming and diving	=	Foreign, not shaving one's legs and drowning
Spanish/French Club	=	America Club
Debate Team	=	Math Team (China)
School musical, cast or crew	=	Math Team (South Korea)
Boy/Girl Scouts of America	=	Math Team (Japan)
School newspaper	=	Skül MewçpØper
Church/religious organization choir	=	Pope-back riding
Community youth orchestra	=	Kangaroo wrestling; malaria
Junior Varsity tennis	=	Junior Varsity tennis…in **Belarus**!

One art you should learn to master is properly listing your extracurricular activities. Sure, plenty of people have played for their junior varsity tennis team, but how many high schoolers have spent fifteen hours a week doing "physics research: effects of various levers on trajectories of spheres." Advantage: you, am I right! Tennis! The point is that you need to phrase things the right way, especially when it comes to volunteer activities. For example. . .

Right ✔

Database Manager, Frederickson Senior Citizen Center
Maintained nutrition database for over 1,500 residents of Frederickson Senior Center. Computerized existing system, created daily printouts for nurse's reference. Developed personal skills by reading to seniors. 8 hrs/week.

Wrong ☠

Database Manager, Frederickson Senior Citizen Center
Revamped nutrition database. Replaced arcane alphabetized system with more applicable system based on adult diapers/no adult diapers. Personally maintained and administered over 4,000 kinds of medication, often on own initiative. "Read books" to Deaf Archie. Covered up accidental death of Deaf Archie. Named executor of Deaf Archie's will. 8–150 hrs/week.

Right ✔

Volunteer Tennis Coach, UpStart Inner-City Extension Project
Brought disadvantaged youth from the inner city to the White Bear Country and Yacht Club each Saturday for free tennis lessons. Taught basic tennis skills, as well as conflict resolution and life skills. 6 hrs/week.

Wrong ☠

Volunteer Tennis Coach, Todd the Loser
Forced by Dad to teach idiot little brother tennis as punishment for crashing the Jeep. Made out with Tiffany the lifeguard while Todd pooped in the locker-room showers. Gave Todd five beers, made him drive the golf cart into a tree on purpose, gave him his T-shirt to wipe the vomit off his mouth. Awesome. 15–20 minutes, May 13, 1999.

Right ✔

Grounds Assistant, Beckerstead Estate
Mowed lawns, maintained gardens, cleaned pools for elderly widow. Cooked meals, developed personal relationship with valuable member of community. Worked after school every day at no charge. 10 hrs/week.

Wrong ☠

Sweaty and Muscled Pool Boy, Beckerstead Estate
Hello there, Widow Beckerstead. Why hello, Rex, what are you doing here? I'm just gonna clean the pool. But Rex, today's not your day to clean. Maybe you could find something else for me to do, ma'am. Maybe you could come over here and I could make a man out of you. I'm sure I don't know what you mean . . . . OH! 15 hrs/week.

Right ✔

Marketing Consultant, Private Adoption Agency
Found homes for unwanted children. Managed massive overhaul of way in which potential adoptees were recruited, found, and stolen from homes. Successfully placed over 10,000 babies in care of Milo the Illusionist, chief executive officer of Glogon's Circus of Fun and Fancy, Inc. Assuming babies have all had happy childhoods and are successful in their chosen profession, whether law, business, medicine, or circus performance. 40 hrs/week.

Wrong ☠

**Black Marketeer, "The Baby Shop"
(formerly Glogon's Asbestos Warehouse)**
Stole helpless babies. Sold them. Left a pile of babies in open field for Glogon to pick up at his convenience. Assuming babies have all had happy childhoods and are successful in their chosen profession, whether circus performance or being eaten by Glogon and his traveling band of baby-eating gypsies. 40 hrs/week.

Some of you out there might be thinking, "I don't have any extracurriculars at all! I'm home schooled! Mom!" Well, home schoolers, just because you lead an educational existence destined to make you a horrible social pariah doesn't mean you can't participate in some sort of extracurricular stuff. Check out these two home-schooled applicants, both of whom were accepted to very prestigious colleges, and both of whom have zero in the way of friends, social skills, and lives.

Home School Application Form

Name: ___Jimmy Bengan___

Age: _18_

Home-schooled GPA: _3.11_

✓ Volunteer at a children's museum

✓ Community Tennis Team

✓ Cleans the closet regularly

✓ Massages Mom's feet twice a week

✓ Data entry for father's business

✓ Church Youth Group

✓ Cooking for Mom and Dad

✓ Does minor repairs to clothing for Mr. Davis's (a friend of Dad) laundromat

✓ Helps brother stitch sneakers together from assembled parts

✓ Pushes parents' Ponzi scheme door-to-door

✓ Continues to garden, even in the hot sun

✓ Delivers nondescript packages from one end of town to another, avoiding police on the way so as not to bother them

✓ Scrapes charcoal from own chimney, others' chimneys

Home School Application Form

Name: ___Daniel Felton___

Age: _18_

Home-schooled GPA: _5.11 (all honors curriculum)_

🏆 Winner, Felton Award for Perfect Attendance

✓ President, Student Council (9th-12th grade)

✓ President, Honor Society (9th-12th grade)

✓ Quad-Varsity Captain (Tennis, Soccer, Lacrosse, Feltonball)

🏆 Winner, Felton School Award for Student Leadership

✓ Volunteer: Felton Baby-Sitting Little Brother Club (10th-12th grade)

🏆 Winner, Felton Award for Excellence

✓ President, Felton Forensics (9th-12th grade)

✓ Editor in Chief, Felton Daily (published four times every four years)

✓ Volunteer: Felton Kitchen Dishwashing Program (9th-12th grade)

✓ President: Felton Driving Club (11th-12th grade)

AP Scores

Calculus AB: 2

European History: 3

English Literature: 2

French Language: 1

Latin (Iliad): 1

SAT: verbal _400_   math _550_

🏆 Felton Award for Super SAT scores

Part One

The SATs and the Standardized Testing Racket

Cool guys, start here:

All right guys, we're gonna level with ya. We took the SATs without studying much, and survived. We even got into a good college. This probably doesn't sound true, but the SATs, or Scholastic Aptitude Test (the 'tude test, as we call it while surfing), can be no sweat if you just take it easy and relax. Remember, this test is only one small part of your life, taking about six hours total. That's it. That's about the time it takes to Rollerblade from the CD store to the pizza parlor, with time left over to catch some waves in the afternoon!

Our buds would tell you that we are the *last* guys they would expect to do well on a standardized test. "You got a 1600 when you were ten years old and major in Applied Math at Harvard," they would say when talking about our less-than-bodacious academic habits. But no matter how well or poorly you do on this test, gravity still exerts a force that accelerates bodies in a vacuum at 9.8 meters per second squared on all test-takers, even during the test! Rad!!!! Now we're no physicists (biotechnology is more our speed, dude), but that's pretty awesome and bodacious!

The rest of you (yes, you), start here:

Well, the SATs are going to rake you over the coals, buddy. You take a two-thousand-dollar course to get spoon-fed vocabulary words by a twenty-six-year-old Ivy League dropout, have to wake up at seven in the morning, give Grandma a bath, and then take this six-hour-long exam on a Saturday. The average score is around an 800. I know that 800 sounds like a big score, but it's total crap. I mean, God help you. It would at least help if you were cool. Look at yourself: Paunchy around the gut, skin's a mess, three eyeballs, and BO like a shit farm on a hot day. If you really want to take this exam, you'd best start taking care of yourself. You might as well start here, with these helpful SAT tips and suggestions. If you follow these instructions to the letter, not only will you be the coolest person to ever score a 1560 on the SATs, but you will also be in jail for arson. Go for the gold!

SAT Horror Stories

You've probably heard a lot of urban legends about how your cousin came to the SATs naked or there was an alligator or Sasquatch at the exam. These kinds of stories are a dime a dozen, but not one of them is ever true. All of these stories below, on the other hand, are completely factual. You should read these horror stories carefully so that you can learn from the horrible mistakes of these stupid, stupid people.

The most embarrassing part of the SATs was when I realized that the girl in seat L53 was wearing the exact same blouse and skirt combo that I was!

I took the SATs twice. The first time was fine, but the second time this weird guy was sitting diagonally two rows away. I tried to figure out where I had seen him before, but could only see him out of the corner of my eye. Eventually, he caught me looking at him, and it was at that moment that I realized he was none other than the feared Boston Strangler! I think I did fine on the test and all, but it was just annoying because he rubbed his eraser so hard it squeaked.

Once during the verbal portion of the SAT, I forgot the difference between the words "uninterested" and "disinterested." Needless to say, I got that sentence completion wrong *right in front of my crush!* He said he wasn't looking over at my desk, but I know he was, because he later commented on the fact that I had a large booger hanging from my nose during the test. I'll never forget the definitions of "uninterested" and "disinterested" again!

Once when I was having my period, there was the SAT. Yeesh!

I had to go to the bathroom about ten minutes into the test. What was I to do? I ask you, what was I to *do?* I did what I had to do: I finished the exam and went *to the bathroom*.

I opened the first page of the test, picked up my sharpened pencil, took a deep breath, read the first question, and realized that I was stupid.

☕ I got the math and verbal sections mixed up, and so for like "What is the circumference of this circle?" I'd be like "halcyon is to calm" and for like "obstinate is to stubborn" I'd be like "24" or something. I probably should've noticed or something, but I was strung out on coffee from the night before when I stayed up eating lead paint.

☕ I was sitting there, doing fine, getting the questions easily, and for some reason I completely lost my confidence and couldn't go on. I think most of the kids in the room had the same feeling. There was no reason for the proctor to yell "Twenty minutes left till you fail" like that.

☕ I got a 1560!

☕ So right before the exam I'm reading this copy of *US* magazine with Meg Ryan on the cover. Then one of the passages we read was about people returning from the dead . . .which is just like in *City of Angels* with Meg Ryan. But the most ironic thing in the whole story is that I am Nicolas Cage.

☕ The day of the SATs I wake up and the power had gone out the night before. I panic because I think I missed the test after setting all three of my alarms to wake me up. So I run to the exam and find out that it actually doesn't start for another couple of hours. Then I burned my school down.

☕ Well, I'm doing the first math portion of the exam, and I happen to be peeling and slicing potatoes. I move my hand to pencil in an answer and the slices fall into my campfire. I get them out pretty quickly. "Hey," I say. "These are pretty good." This was when I got kicked out of the SATs for having a bunch of crib notes stored in my calculator.

☕ Me and my girlfriend were doing the SATs late at night out on Lovers' Lane. This message comes on the radio that the Hook Killer had escaped from the asylum. We started to get a little scared and then we heard a scratching sound on the side of our car. The exam proctor took the psycho Hook Killer and sat him down to take the test. He copied off of me the whole time. But it's not like I'm going to tell on the psycho Hook Killer!

☕ I was in the exam room and the kid next to me lets out a *huge* fart. It was really smelly and the exam proctor comes over and asks us which one of us did it. He immediately pointed at me. I was hauled off to prison to await my execution or internment. Never take the SATs in Cambodia.

☕ I don't read English too well. So when I take SAT, I make sure to sit next to someone to copy off. I get there take my seat and look over. The person next to me is a monkey! I accidentally went to zoo! Monkeys usually just guess "C."

SAT *TIPS*
The SATs do not represent who you are. Your worth as an individual comes from something much deeper: degree of approximation to an ideal body type.

SAT Verbal Flashcards

As we just saw, learning all of these words for the verbal section can be quite a drag. One interesting way to build word-power is to imagine the word in question being acted out. The word "stevedore," for example, could be pictured as my friend Steve walking through a door. The word means "dockworker," so I guess the door leads to a dock. Now look at these pictures and try to figure out the word they depict:

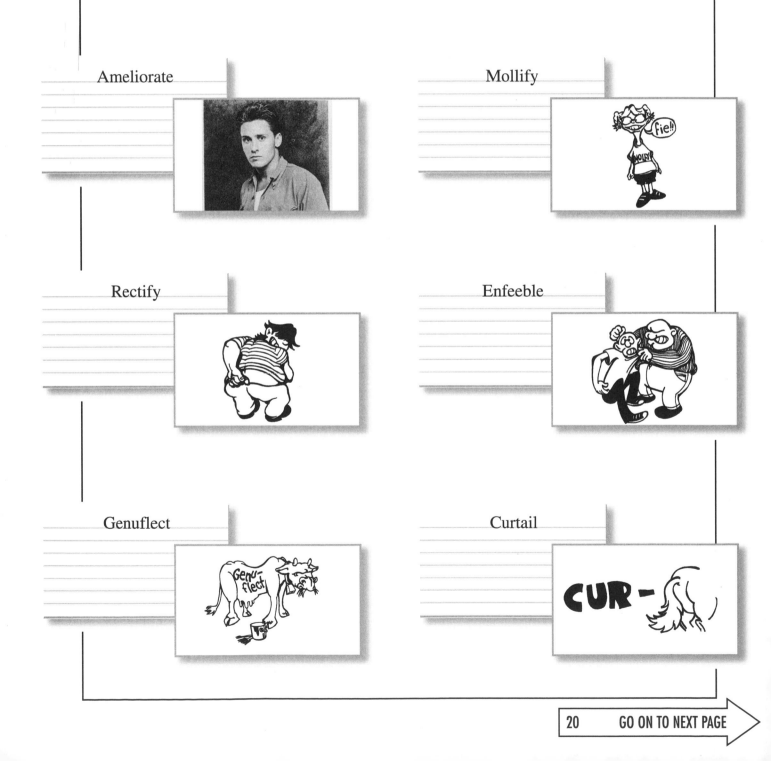

Ameliorate

Mollify

Rectify

Enfeeble

Genuflect

Curtail

Math Review

The nice thing to remember about math is that every question has a correct answer. It's not like the verbal section where you get a score based on handwriting and how you look in a skirt. Yes, the math section is the great equalizer; every person, no matter their skin complexion or use of hip slang terminology, gets a fair shake. This is your chance to show those "normals" with their fancy haircuts and their less-than-twenty-inch-long fingernails that you have what it takes. This will be the only such time, however.

Problem solving

Consider the following problem:

Eric goes out to a restaurant and orders three doughnuts and a glass of milk. Sally orders one doughnut and a glass of milk. He pays $3.75 and she pays $1.40. What do three doughnuts cost?

a.) $0.22
b.) $1.34
c.) $1.55
d.) $0.75
e.) $0.87

The first thing you have to do is read the question completely. I know, it's very long and boring and has numbers in it. Or you could just read the last part and try to figure out the rest. "What do three doughnuts cost?" Well, if you go to the store, you will find packs of six Hostess brand doughnuts for 49 cents. But you have a coupon from the paper for 30 cents off, so it's 19 cents. Half of this (three doughnuts) is about ten cents. Since you are in Africa you have to mail these doughnuts to America, so that comes to $5.67 if you send them third class. Now, if they haven't melted or been smashed up, chances are you will accidentally eat one of them at some point. So now you have two doughnuts that cost $68.99 to have platinum-electroplated, and you still need one more. If you find a doughnut that costs negative $68.24, you will find that the answer is d.). But it would have been much easier to have read the entire question.

Once you have read the problem carefully, you need to decide whether or not to do it. If the question is way too hard, you want to go on to another one. In this case, you should definitely skip this question. If you are taking the exam, you don't want to be reading some story about these two fat hogs stuffing their faces with doughnuts. This may bring an unsavory image to mind which will make you barf. You should skip this question and go on to all those questions about romantic love or triumph over the odds. If you have time left over, come back to the two fatties getting their oral lard injections. But then you may realize that this question has no correct answer.

If you decide to continue working on the problem, the first step is to eliminate a couple of choices that are clearly wrong. Choice c.) for example is $1.55, which is more than the fat lady paid for her entire order. Choice a.) can't be right. Three doughnuts for 22 cents? It is also doubtful that this enormous fat hog could subsist on three doughnuts and a glass of milk. She probably ordered a half-slab of baby back ribs too. That's going to run you an extra 10 bucks (even at Chili's) so 22 cents is really unrealistic. And e.) $0.87? When was the last time you ordered three doughnuts at a restaurant and the total was $0.87? Answer: The last time you went to a restaurant where the waitresses don't know algebra.

This is great: We have narrowed our choices from five to two. We are left with b.) and d.). To determine which is correct, apply logic. You should now learn to do all of these steps eight times faster than before.

Gearing Up for the Big One:
The Night before the SATs

Okay, buddy: This is it. You've been over our tips a thousand times, committed most of it to memory, executed your will, now it's time to go. The night before the Big One. You've gotta get in the right frame of mind for this. Here's five quick ways to prepare.

1. Relax. You're as ready as you're going to get, and you know a lot more than you think you do. Unless you've grossly overestimated your intellectual capabilities, as studies show about 60 percent of high school students do.

2. Have a good dinner. Be sure to continue your five-week program of carbo loads and protein shakes—remember, the SAT is not only a three-hour mental test but also a seven-hour Iron Man Triathlon, a fact many people overlook every year.

3. Chill out, buddy! Dude, just kick back with one of your favorite movies, like "Derivative Calculus Made Easy" or "Common Vocabulary Words of the Scholastic Aptitude Test"!

4. If you have one, break up with your boyfriend/girlfriend. Although it may be a painful and devastating loss, your mind shouldn't be distracted by *anything* when you go into the SATs.

5. Go to bed early. Enjoy a deep and relaxing sleep. You'll need it.

Oh Crap!
The Morning of the SATs

Okay. Time to get it on. Time to rock and roll. Time to shake and bake. Time to show 'em what you got. Time to get out of bed, put on clothes, and go to your testing location.

1. Get up early. Allow yourself at least an hour to sit on the toilet, purging your bowels of the horribly overfilling carbo load and protein shakes you had for dinner. What were you thinking?!?

SAT *TIPS* One great way to remember vocabulary words is through understanding the roots of words. For example, "phlegmatic" derives from the same word as "phlegm," and so one can extrapolate that a phlegmatic action is one that is covered in snot.

2. Take a shower. Now get out! Put on your clothes! No time to dry yourself, just get dressed! Hurry! Skip the underwear! Hurry! No! Not there! Go!

3. Eat some food! No, don't cook anything! Here, eat this banana! Now drink this juice! Hurry! Your pencils! Take them! Run! You call that running? Sprint, you fool!

4. Leave early for the testing location. Too late! Go! Speed! Drive! No, don't let your mom drive! That's it! Wrest the wheel from her control! Now go! Skip that red light! Don't slow down, just honk! Run over those squirrels! I can't believe you broke up with your boyfriend/girlfriend! That's all you're going to be able to think about during the test!

5. Arrive at the testing location at least twenty minutes early, carrying a photo ID and at least five number 2 pencils, wearing running shorts and a T-shirt with your race number pinned to it, ready for the SATs and a grueling Iron Man Triathlon, an event that will probably not be taking place today.

SAT Time Restrictions

This here is probably the best advice we can give you and it's easily worth the price of this book. As you no doubt know, one of the most galling aspects of the Scholastic Aptitude Test is the time restriction. Students the world over are left with combined scores of 900 or 910 when they would have gotten 1600 if they only had 5.2×10^3 hours. However, a little-known secret of the SAT is that some students are allowed to take the test with no time restrictions *at all*. The only restriction is completing the exam before you starve to death or are a victim of a natural disaster. But the catch is you have to have some sort of disease (like faceworm, hoof-and-mouth, or poopyfaceia, or whatever). It has been said that this SAT is the same as the regular test, but the *Harvard Lampoon* has found a marked difference between the two tests. Put on your laughing face and take a gander.

SAT *TIPS* There are a lot of good test-taking strategies out there. Choose which one is best for you. If success, wealth, and happiness are important to you, then choose the one leading to that outcome, whereas if you want to fuck everything up for all time, then choose the strategy leading to that outcome.

SAT *TIPS* If you want to do well on the SATs, then you should, I don't know, whatever, I guess you should study words and whatever, fuck it, I don't know. I don't really want to give SAT advice, I just want to dance!

SAT (No Time Restriction)

1. Is....................It.......................O...........K   Name: ○ ○ ○ ○ ○
.................If..............................We...............Begin.........   ⊂⊃ ⊂⊃ ⊂⊃ ⊂⊃ ⊂⊃
................Now?   ⊂⊃ ⊂⊃ ⊂⊃ ⊂⊃ ⊂⊃

   ○ a.) Yes.   ○ b.) No.   ⊂⊃ ⊂⊃ ⊂⊃ ⊂⊃ ⊂⊃

2. So, how is it going?   ⊂⊃ ⊂⊃ ⊂⊃ ⊂⊃ ⊂⊃
   ⊂⊃ a.) I am a little nervous.
   ⊂⊃ b.) I am a lot nervous.
   ⊂⊃ c.) I am a lot relaxed.
   ⊂⊃ d.) I am a little relaxed.

3. Some people say that it is impossible to say "toy boat" five times fast. Prove them wrong by saying "toy boat" five times fast. Do not go on to question 4 until you have completed this task. Well, you don't have to say it fast-fast, just be reasonable. Don't take all day. Unless you have to.

4. Do you want some lunch?
   Just let us know.

5. Feel free to go to the bathroom at any time. If you don't have to go to the bathroom, a fun thing to do is to go out into the hallway and spin around really fast for a few seconds. Then try to run down the hallway as fast as you can. Once you have done this, go to the bathroom.

6. Who are the six hottest guys/girls in your class?

   1. _____
   2. _____
   3. _____
   4. _____
   5. _____
   6. _____

7. Take a nice nap.

8. Write down the lyrics to Hanson's "MMM-Bop" without making a single mistake. The tape and headphones are under your test.

9. Thank you for taking the SAT. If you can sit without moving for the next ten hours, have your proctor sign your test sheet and get an 800.

The ACT:

Not Just for Fieldhands and Man-Children Anymore

Most of you reading this book are probably gearing up for the SAT. It seems like everybody's doing it—the smart kid who took it in eighth grade, the charming basketball phenom who has taken it upwards of eight times just for fun, and the Sumatran immigrant who was forced at gunpoint to take it. If you follow the crowd, you'd probably end up sharpening your pencil on some Saturday morning with plans to take the big S.

Apparently you don't live in the Midwest. In that portion of the country, which you may know as the "Heartland," the "Breadbasket," or "Injun Country," there is a different college test that's shaking up the calculators and rockin' the test-taking scene to its core. It's called the ACT, and it stands for All-American Knowledge Tryout. And the word on the Midwestern street is that if you're taking the SAT, you're just not hip to it, "it" being the ACT.

The ACT differs from the SAT in several fundamental ways, ways that make it (a) a different test from the SAT, and (b) a much more fun test than the SAT! For example, you may make the mistake of bringing a number 2 pencil to the ACT. Wonder why the Nebraskan in the seat next to you is laughing? The ACT doesn't use pencils.

So once you're seated, bingo marker in hand, you'll notice that the room is a lot less, say, academic than the testing rooms of the SAT. In fact, you may notice that the other testers are chitchatting with each other, scarfing Doritos, or even chugging the occasional Bud Light. Did we say that the ACT was more fun? I do believe we did! The people at ACT Headquarters want to make your test fun and carefree. So feel free to ask that Asian in front of you for answers—it's what's expected! Just remember to arrive early to claim one of the sweet beanbag chairs, because it makes the ACT a much more comfy experience. And here's an inside tip: don't fill up on chips—you'll need room for the ACT ice cream cake.

So do you think you have what it takes to sign up for the ACT? All you need is your love of fun, and you're in for a Friday night of social and "academic" sweetness. Sounds like you're gonna ace this baby.

Try these sample questions:

Reading Comprehension

Passage 1: The deliberate violation of the law as seen by most is an affront to the operations of a complete society. The action of "civil disobedience" comes by definition as such a violation and takes into account the necessity of the punishment of said act. Nonetheless, throughout modern history, civil disobedience has been performed as a form of dramatization used to call attention to the inability of the laws (as extant) to fit the needs of society as seen by the transgressor. It is as such a critique that the moral agent can justify illegal activity.

1. What is an appropriate synonym for civil disobedience?
- a.) Uhhhh . . .
- b.) Gawrsh!
- c.) Shee-IT!
- d.) [*spitting*]

2. Which of the following cases would *best* serve as an example of civil disobedience?
- a.) D'you check the almanac today, Maw?
- b.) Lumbago's acting up, feels like rain.
- c.) Staging a sit-in at a restaurant that practices discrimination.
- d.) I'll take a side order of home fries and a coffee. And how's about a slice of that pie?

3. Wei-Lin considers himself a moral man, but engages in protest activity in his native China. How might Wei best justify his behavior according to the logic presented above?
- a.) What's that name again?
- b.) Did you say China?
- c.) Wait a minute, who's doing what?
- d.) Stop hollering at me! I'm tryin'.

Mathematics

1. If Cy has twelve chickens and Steve takes away a prime number of them, which of the following is *not* a number of chickens Cy might have left?
- a.) 3
- b.) I know that Cy fellow but I didn't know he had any chickens. Well, 7, I guess.
- c.) Steve!!! You get back here with my chickens or you're going to be wearing an assload of buckshot!
- d.) Is Steve a Mexican?

2. If sin^{-1} represents the inverse of the sine function (ex. sin^{-1} (1) = pi/2), define the following expressions of the tangent in terms of. . .You know, you should probably just skip this one.

3. A plane takes off from Dulles Airport in Washington, D.C., and heads directly for New York City's Kennedy Airport two hundred miles to the north. The airplane is traveling at two hundred miles per hour. What is the total flight time?
- a.) Zzzzzzz. . .
- b.) . . .
- c.) Camptown races sing this song doo-dah, doo-dah
- d.) . . .

4. A plane takes off from Memorial Airport in St. Louis and heads directly for Hopkins Airport in Cleveland four hundred miles to the north. The airplane is traveling at two hundred miles per hour. What is the total flight time?

- ○ a.) 1 hour
- ○ b.) 2 hours
- ○ c.) 3 hours
- ○ d.) 4 hours

Science Reasoning

For questions 1–3, please refer to the diagram below:

1. Which of the above pictures best depicts your mama?

   ○ a.) A   ○ b.) B   ○ c.) C   ○ d.) D   ○ e.) E

2. D is a picture of:

- ○ a.) Some manner of plow
- ○ b.) Knitting needles and thread
- ○ c.) A machine that will help me do the washin'
- ○ d.) Don't know, but I recall seeing something like it in the War.

3. Don't a cool glass of lemonade just take the cake in the summertime?

- ○ a.) A
- ○ b.) B
- ○ c.) C
- ○ d.) D
- ○ e.) E

SAT II
Achievement Tests

Well well well. Look who's the hotshot. You just finished the SATs and you think that you're all done. Well, wait a second. Okay. If you have any desire to go to a competitive college, you'd better sign up for the hyperspecific SAT II tests. These will examine your ability to regurgitate information from all of those classes you skipped to get the high score on Arkanoid at Pizza Hut. Most schools require that you take three of them, and we suggest that you take the SAT II in Pizza, Arcade-style Action Games, and Writing. If you don't you should practice on these sample tests.

SAT II
For People Who Know Paul Berens of Edina, Minnesota

1. Paul Berens of Edina, Minnesota's middle name is:

- ⃝ a.) Bob
- ⃝ b.) Rob
- ⃝ c.) Dave
- ⃝ d.) Frank
- ⃝ e.) Kevin

2. Paul Kevin Berens of Edina, Minnesota's eyes are colored:

- ⃝ a.) azure blue
- ⃝ b.) bewitchingly hazel
- ⃝ c.) opaline green
- ⃝ d.) gray like the sea before a storm
- ⃝ e.) poopy-colored brown

3. Paul enjoys:

- ⃝ a.) Nora Ephron films and popcorn after a long day
- ⃝ b.) A soak in a tub with some light FM on the dial

SAT *TIPS* For God's sake, calm down. It isn't like the SAT is the ACT!

c.) Listening, listening, listening

d.) Face-stomping hobos by the train tracks

e.) All of the above (except d.)!!!!!!

4. Paul is looking for:

a.) Someone to grow old with

b.) Someone from AP English Lit to grow old with

c.) Mindy Zubrovski

d.) Kelly H.

e.) c or d

5. Paul Berens of Edina, Minnesota, is:

a.) One solid dude, Kelly

b.) One solid dude, Mindy

6. Going on a date with Paul Berens of Edina, Minnesota, is likely to bring:

a.) Happiness and possibly marriage and stuff to Mindy if she wants to go out

b.) The same stuff from a.) except with Kelly (I really like you, Kelly!!!!)

c.) Please don't be offended that I am asking you both out but I am just trying to cover my options. I fully expect that at least one of you will be offended and that is why I asked two.

d.) I am sorry that I am using the venue of a nationally administered standardized test to ask both of you out.

e.) But consider that you are getting a really easy 800 on this test whereas the rest of the country is probably very confused by this exam at this point.

7. Okay. That's it. Mindy and Kelly, if you want to call me, my phone number is:

a.) 865-3453

b.) 865-3453

c.) 865-3453

d.) 865-3453

e.) 865-3453

SAT *TIPS* Please make sure that you bring at least three pencils the day of your SAT. What would happen if you didn't have anything to write with? If your school is constructed entirely of lead graphite, consider yourself lucky.

SAT II
for God

So you're God and you want to go to college? Well hold on there, buster, you're gonna have to pass a little thing called the "SAT II (for God)" before you enroll in Harvard . . .

1. If you, God, are truly omnipotent, then the answer to question 2 is going to be (close your eyes and circle one):

  ○ a.) a
  ○ b.) d
  ○ c.) None of the above
  ○ d.) b

2. Did you cheat on the last question?

  ○ a.) Yes, I cheated.
  ○ b.) No, I never cheat. I am God. Stop asking silly questions.
  ○ c.) I may or may not have cheated, but you shall never know as I am God and can do pretty much whatever I want.

3. What was around before you, God, created the universe?

  ○ a.) This question lacks any logical basis.
  ○ b.) Strom Thurmond!!!!!!! That guy is old, right!
  ○ c.) I, God, existed in a vacuum with only my cat and a couple of Clive Cussler novels to keep me company. It was a lonely, difficult three years.
  ○ d.) A bathtub full of beer, a full bar, a kicking dance floor, and two weeks of Cancún spring break on the beach!

4. Can you, God, make a rock so heavy, even you can't pick it up?

  ○ a.) Of course! I'm God, I can do whatever I want.
  ○ b.) No way! I'm God, I can pick up any rock, even one I've created specifically to demonstrate that I am capable of creating a rock which I cannot pick up. Also I'm on this weight-trainer stuff and can put up like 350 and squat 230.

SAT TIPS   Worried about analogies, bucko? Consider this: Determination is to Success as Sleeping with your SAT Proctor is to 800.

5. If you, God, really like a girl, but you didn't know if she liked you, you would:

   ⚬ a.) Ask her on a date and allow things to progress normally from there.
   ⚬ b.) Telepathically force her to go on a date and allow things to progress normally from there.
   ⚬ c.) Telepathically force her to go on a date and telepathically force things to progress normally from there as you telepathically force her to perform lewd sexual acts.
   ⚬ d.) Not talk to her, let destiny pass you by.

6. If you, God, were stranded on a desert island, the CD you would bring is:

   ⚬ a.) Every CD in the world because I own them all. Awesome!
   ⚬ b.) A mix of my favorite MP3s.
   ⚬ c.) I have some Talking Heads imports, but those are on LP. Does that count?
   ⚬ d.) *Led Zeppelin III*.

7. Being God is like:

   ⚬ a.) Being Bruce Springsteen.
   ⚬ b.) Being Bruce Springsteen's wife.
   ⚬ c.) Being Bruce Springsteen's children.
   ⚬ d.) Being Bruce Springsteen on cocaine.

8. God, have you ever met Bruce Springsteen?

   ⚬ a.) Yes. I created him as I created all of my children.
   ⚬ b.) Yes. My spirit lives inside his soulful music.
   ⚬ c.) Yes. I opened for him once in Brussels.
   ⚬ d.) Yes. I bumped into him once at the Viper Room in L.A.

9. God, what is the secret to a happy life?

   ⚬ a.) All-knowing omnipotence.
   ⚬ b.) The power to cleave mountains with mere thought.
   ⚬ c.) Existence in heaven, the most ruling place ever.
   ⚬ d.) Being able to see through walls.

SAT TIPS If you are worried about not having enough time for the exam, remember that people with reading disabilities do not have *any* time restrictions. A surefire tactic: Walk into the test room and say, "Here I am for the TAS! Where bo I sit bown?"

SAT II

Obsessive-Compulsive Disorder

Please remove your exam booklet from the sealed bag. This exam has not been touched by human hands, so relax. You are allowed to bring two (2) number 2 pencils to the exam. If you need more utensils you will be unable to complete the exam. Wash your hands. Good luck!

Part 1: Verbal

Passage 1: The first names that spring into most people's minds when speaking about dictionaries are Samuel Johnson and Daniel Webster. After all, their contributions to the science of lexicography began the movement which led to the volumes with which we are familiar today. But the history of the dictionary goes back still further. The first dictionaries were bilingual, helping translation of Sumerian into Akkadian and vice versa. Today's books owe a great debt to these forebears.

1. Two languages that benefited from early dictionaries are:
- a.) English and Greek
- b.) Sumerian and Akkadian
- c.) English and Sumerian
- d.) Greek and Roman

2. When you first think of dictionaries, you immediately think:
- a.) Of Samuel Johnson and Daniel Webster.
- b.) Did I remember to do number 1?
- c.) I know I wrote my name on the exam, but what if the pencil mark wiped off?
- d.) The guy next to me has really gross fingernails.

3. Once you start thinking about dictionaries:
- a.) I just keep thinking and thinking and thinking about it.
- b.) I have to stand up and sit down thirty times really fast.
- c.) I write a dictionary of words that don't exist (yet!).
- d.) I engage in compulsive behavior.

Passage 2: Cecil B. DeMille was one of the world's all-time most successful filmmakers. His historical epics, however, have a dated look to today's sophisticated moviegoer. There are millions of centipede-like creatures that live in your eyebrows to eat your dead skin. DeMille produced his first feature, *The Squaw Man*, out of a barn in Hollywood. His first international success was *The Cheat*, they say that the paper was never touched by human hands, but what's "human," a film in which a female socialite sells herself to a Japanese businessman to discharge a gambling debt. DeMille is best known for his biblical epics, none of which touch on the fact that if you let your pencil lead touch your skin you will get cancer.

4. Cecil DeMille began his career:
- a.) At a major studio.
- b.) In a Hollywood barn.
- c.) In a really dirty public bathroom without any towels.
- d.) In a pile of dirt.

5. If I were to start a Hollywood studio, I would start it:
- a.) In a gross, poop-filled barn where there are rats.
- b.) Inside of a toilet.
- c.) Inside of someone's large intestine.
- d.) None of the above.

Note: Make sure that you fill in the circles dark enough because the machine can't pick up light marks. But if it's too dark, the lead will seep through the paper and mess up your answers on the reverse side.

6. DeMille's first studio release was:
- a.) *The Squaw Man*
- b.) *The Cheat*
- c.) Think about it. If you walk down a street and smell some poop on the ground, that smell is actually a little microscopic piece of poop that went inside your nose.
- d.) This exam is not very helpful to people with my disability.

7. Please recopy your answers to 1–4 67 times.

I'm really sorry but my pencil is a number 2 I think but it doesn't say number 2 on it. I'm pretty sure it is but I don't know.

SAT *TIPS* Eating a meal of Pop Rocks and cola before the exam will not necessarily help you on the SAT, but it will make your stomach explode.

TOEFL

The Test of English as a Foreign Language is an alternative to the SAT for people who no speak-ee the English. You can imagine how this is going to go.

☞ **1.** Do you understand what I am saying? Do you speak English?
- ○ a.) Yes.
- ○ b.) No.
- ○ c.) ?

☞ **2.** ¿Habla español? Parlez-vous Français? . . . DO YOU SPEAK ENGLISH??!!
- ○ a.) Yes, I speak English.
- ○ b.) No.
- ○ c.) ?
- ○ d.) ". . ."

☞ **3.** Can you hear alright!? Do you want me to speak louder?
- ○ a.) I can understand the language and am thus suitable to live in America, but I have a hearing impairment.
- ○ b.) I can hear fine, but I am the speaker of a foreign language and not the King's English.
- ○ c.) Both of the above.

☞ **4.** Policemen carry guns _____ protect themselves from criminals.
- ○ a.) can so they
- ○ b.) so can they
- ○ c.) so they can
- ○ d.) 屁扶考试屁屁

SAT *TIPS* Don't take prescription pain medication before the exam. There'll be time for celebration later.

5. The professor always _____ before every _____.
- ◯ a.) lambada-ed, mambo
- ◯ b.) prepared, exam
- ◯ c.) took a shower, leap year
- ◯ d.) superstar America #1 Cowboy Race, fantasta-terrific!

6. Pedro walked up to Al-Fariq and said, "The Americans pronounce the word 'cough' like 'coff' and the word 'tough' like 'tuff' and the word 'dough' like _____."
- ◯ a.) 'doe'
- ◯ b.) 'duff'
- ◯ c.) 'd'oh!'
- ◯ d.) 'Eat my shorts, man,' says tiny television yellow person to me!

7. Al-Fariq walked up to Pedro and said, "The Americans say 'elevator' but the British say 'lift' and the British say 'water closet' but the Americans say instead _____."
- ◯ a.) 'shithouse'
- ◯ b.) 'What is up, home-boy-ee?'
- ◯ c.) 'Speak to my hand, lady, because I cannot hear you!'
- ◯ d.) 'MMM-Bop skinny dinny bippity doo-wop!'

8. Selma walked up to Louie and said, "Flarken Blarken Oomla Tinga Ringa," and Louie knew immediately that she was speaking _____.
- ◯ a.) Dutch
- ◯ b.) Swedish
- ◯ c.) Dutch-Swedish
- ◯ d.) Swedish-Dutch

9. If I do not ever want to fit in this country I will neglect to _____.
- ◯ a.) learn English
- ◯ b.) wipe

SAT Practice Exam

Verbal

Analogies

This question : Hard :: You : _____
- ○ a.) Capable
- ○ b.) Confused
- ○ c.) Unhappy
- ○ d.) Dumb

Stan Musial : Stan the Man :: Shaquille O'Neal : _____
- ○ a.) The Shizzah
- ○ b.) Shaq Diesel
- ○ c.) Shaq Daddy
- ○ d.) Sha-quille a Mockingbird

Love : Amorous :: Yellow : _____
- ○ a.) Yellowish
- ○ b.) Colored yellow
- ○ c.) Yellow
- ○ d.) Yellowey
- ○ e.) Yellowrous

Hava Nagila : Hatikvah :: Mayim Bisasov : _____
- ○ a.) Maoz T'zur
- ○ b.) Shalom Chavayreem
- ○ c.) Or Chadash
- ○ d.) Tangled Up in Blue

Stuffed animals : Wussies :: My fist : _____
- ○ a.) Your face
- ○ b.) Your nose
- ○ c.) Your mouth
- ○ d.) All of the above

SAT TIPS Make sure to wear layers of clothing to the test. But also coordinate the layers of clothing such that, with any possible permutation of outfits, you look fly.

"I had to work late" : "That's not lipstick on my collar" :: "Your invitation must have gotten lost in the mail" : _____

○ a.) "Please come to my party"
○ b.) "You can still come. Oh, your ex-girlfriend is going to be there."
○ c.) "You didn't know we decided to have it last weekend?"
○ d.) "Have some cheesecake, friend."

Mistake : Correction :: Pregnancy : _____

○ a.) Reproduction
○ b.) Shotgun marriage
○ c.) Dropping out of high school
○ d.) An unfortunate end to a promising Olympic career in gymnastics

Translated from Japanese:
"The spirit of humanness makes in the believing" : "Pocari Sweat: Go the farthest distance, Grandma" :: 100% USA Cowboy : _____

○ a.) Kyoto: a modern city student joyous place
○ b.) The happy Italian eating loving tomato bigness Space Man restaurant
○ c.) Momo the cute monkey-look
○ d.) [Horde of schoolgirls take pictures and giggle]

7. Their : There :: _____

○ a.) To : Too
○ b.) Tutu : To-too
○ c.) Toe : Tow
○ d.) Is to : "Is, too"

Sentence Completions

Keeping all his pennies to himself, Mr. Miserly was quite the _____.

○ a.) meanie
○ b.) dick-wad
○ c.) moon-man
○ d.) penny-keeper

Although Rose was known for her cornish game hen dish, she also made quite a succulent _____.

○ a.) chicken marsala
○ b.) coq au vin
○ c.) corn dog
○ d.) steak-type steak

"Don't look at me with that _____. said my father.
- a.) look on your face
- b.) cat on your face
- c.) cat on your lap
- d.) look on your lap

"Why _____?
- a.) not
- b.) bother
- c.) climb a mountain
- d.) did you call me here

Although Yuri was neither _____ nor _____, he was able, somehow, to become quite the ballplayer.
- a.) coordinated, athletic
- b.) fully appendaged, human
- c.) a good ballplayer, a great ballplayer
- d.) hegemony, insipid

Ellen found herself in quite a _____ her foot was caught in a _____.
- a.) quagmire; grate
- b.) shitstorm; paper shredder
- c.) beautiful house; door made of gold
- d.) epiphany; realization

Timmy's tiny stature might seem freakish, were it not for the fact that he was a _____.
- a.) young 'un
- b.) freak
- c.) small statue
- d.) action figure

Whasssssup, _____?
- a.) Dawg
- b.) white person
- c.) Mrs. Anderson
- d.) Father Mulcahey

Talk to the _____, 'cause the _____ ain't listening.
- a.) minister, bridegroom
- b.) Dharma, Greg
- c.) stump, amputee
- d.) ATM, totally free checking

 GO ON TO NEXT PAGE

Math

If A#B=A/(A+B), what is 12#3?

- a.) I would like to note a notation error on this otherwise excellent test. Up to this point it has been a very fair measure of my intellectual ability, and with a simple correction this problem could be fixed. The # sign should read + in which case 12+3=15.
- b.) Yeah, that # symbol is no thing I have ever seen. What the hell? I say 15.
- c.) I'll definitely say 15. Is that cool?
- d.) 15

If you get this question right you will eventually earn 30% more per year than if you get this question wrong.

- a.) I don't know. That number appears a bit too high.
- b.) That seems like a bit of exaggeration.
- c.) %? What?
- d.) Maybe. Unclear.

Picture in your mind a picture of a five-foot-five-inch woman holding a 1:4 scale model of herself. That model is holding a 1:4 scale model of itself. The model of the model is holding a similar model of itself and so on through 57 models. How tall is the 57th model?

- a.) Whoa. Wait, whoa!!!
- b.) Did you ever think how the light from stars that's millions of miles away is like from the future or some shit?
- c.) Wait, I had a dream like this. Okay, I've got it, you have to have sex with Kathy Ireland in order that the Martians don't kill your dad.
- d.) SATs, more like LSDs!!!!!

A man lies at point *X* and a woman lies 150 miles away at a point *Y*. The woman, a rational and reasonable being, was totally cool with the arrangement because they could still spend 54 hours together every weekend. He couldn't deal with 150 lousy miles even though the woman at point *Y* was the best thing that had ever happened to his life. Is this not total B.S.?

- a.) That sucks. All guys suck—stupid gorillas.
- b.) You got jacked, lady. That is crap.
- c.) Move on. Let it go. Let the healing begin.

SAT *TIPS* It's always nice to take a Kaplan SAT preparation program before the exam. Be content in the fact that poor Harlem high schoolers won't be able to afford it, and you'll nail shut forever the opportunity for minority advancement.

If a serial killer eats the ears of 13 victims but leaves those of 17, what proportion of corpses have ears remaining? Keep in mind that the killer only eats both ears of 34% of the corpses he starts nibbling on. Use as units mangled ears.

- a.) 40 ears
- b.) 37 mangled ears
- c.) 53 ears, some mangled
- d.) 46 mangled ears, some of which cannot be found

Larraine is late for her period three times a year, and has unsafe sex at least once every week. If the probability of insemination is 4% a week, then how likely is it that she is pregnant on any one of these periods?

- a.) 0%
- b.) It just doesn't feel right if I put that on.
- c.) I am invincible!
- d.) Teens only get pregnant on television. . .or do they?

If Jake is a teenager, and therefore cannot get HIV, and exposes himself to the disease three times every week at a risk of 3% per exposure, then how many weeks until Jake has at least a 75% chance of not contracting the disease?

- a.) La la la I'm not listening.
- b.) Every morning there's a halo hanging from the corner / of my girlfriend's four-post bed.
- c.) Jeremy spoke in, spoke in, / Jeremy spoke in, spoke in
- d.) the beautiful people, the beautiful people / duh-duh-duh-duh

Harold Boddington decimates three ladies with his razor-sharp wit at every cocktail party he attends. His status in the Hamptons, due to his savagely jejune double entendres, declines such that he attends (20   N) parties every month (where N equals the month in numerical terms).

I) The equation (20 – N)*3 best represents the number of taken-aback ladies.

II) The equation 20*N – 3 best represents the number of devastating blows emanating from Boddington's mouth at which it is just sinful to laugh.

III) Before Trina's cotillion, Harold should again be *l'objet du jour*.

- a.) I alone is true.
- b.) On the contrary, II alone is true.
- c.) I and III are both true, and so is II.
- d.) Quite right.
- e.) Only III is true, clearly.

SAT *TIPS* If you are having trouble concentrating during the exam, remember that even George Washington had to take the SAT. And he could never tell a lie!

There are five middle-age ladies. If their husbands, inattentive as they are, ogle three younger women per day, how many days does it take before they ogle 2,000 attractive, vibrant younger women who don't know what they've got 'til it's gone?

- a.) 34 days
- b.) I don't know. It's gonna happen soon, anyway.
- c.) I wish I had kept my career.
- d.) I shouldn't eat that.
- e.) Are they still selling the little Beanie Babies at McDonald's?

For the following questions, if the term in column A is greater than that in column B, mark A on your answer sheet. If the term in column A is less than that in column B, mark B. If they are equal, mark C. If this cannot be determined without further information, mark D.

1.

A	B
X + Y	Y + GBGBG

a.) ○ b.) ○ c.) ○ d.) ○

2.

A	B
Being homosexual	Pizza

a.) ○ b.) ○ c.) ○ d.) ○

3.

A	B
X − 5Y When X = 23 And Y = 4	Watching three bears fight each other

a.) ○ b.) ○ c.) ○ d.) ○

4.

A	B
Being a pro skateboarder	Being a pro skateboarder made out of gold

a.) ○ b.) ○ c.) ○ d.) ○

Your Application and Essay

Name: Muhammad Ali
Address: 145 Grover Way, Louisville, KY.
High School: Louisville High, Louisville, KY.

Activity: Boxing.
Description: Duties included knocking chumps out, floating like a butterfly, stinging like a bee, being pretty.
Positions held: Heavyweight Champion of the World.
Awards: The Greatest; Best Athlete of the Century; Champion for All Time.
Hours: 40/wk.

Activity: Poetry.
Description: Composed thousands of free-verse poems, on topics ranging from George Frazier to George Foreman.
Positions held: Listen to this one: "It'll be a thrilla', and a chilla' when I get the Gorilla, in Manila! / C'mon Gorilla we in Manila! / C'mon Gorilla this one's a thrilla!
Awards: Nobel Prize in Pugilistic Poetry.
Hours: Never counted.

Activity: Whuppin' Sonny Liston.
Description: He wanted to go to Heaven, so I took him in Seven.
Positions held: Prophet.
Awards: Liston's a chump. He's the heavyweight chumpian of the world! He's ugly like that duckling. He looks like garbage and smells like trash!
Hours: 21 minutes, August 19, 1964.

Activity: Gettin' whupped.
Description: I wouldn't know, 'cause it ain't never happened!
Positions held: n/a
Awards: n/a
Hours: 0!

Activity: Being a postage stamp.
Description: I oughta be a postage stamp, cuz that's the only way I'll get licked!
Positions held: Man I'm so mean I make medicine sick!
Awards: I'm young, I'm pretty, and I can't possibly get beat.
Hours: I'm good like wood, I'm as nimble as a thimble... and I'm pretty!

North Shore Community College Admissions Packet

NAME: _____

Maybe you are considering submitting some artistic work or poetry to impress the admissions committee. This sampling of poetry from high school seniors helped students get into the college of their choice.

Thirty-Six Fathoms of Deepness
I ask you out and you say no.
I stare at your two dimensional
 white-lined emptiness.
You make it easy for me to turn the page.

The Horror
There is a fright
Only some have known
There is a chill
few spines have felt
There is a feeling
solely i have known
in the midst
of a list
of possible isotopes

advanced placement
chemistry test
i am seated
seated poised
and suddenly the fright
The Horror
five minutes precious time
must now be spent
To take a dump.

Sadie Hawkins Dance
Whatever
I don't really want to go anyway
 Maybe Brian will ask me
 He's kind of nasty anyway
I heard he only has one ball
 Ick.

Minnesota Class 3A High School
Regional Finals

offsides offsides offsides

who me yes ref says as I skate

as I skate he skates like Messier

two minutes sin bin

elbowing

bullshit call

one man down in our zone

up one goal

wrister deflection screen

in the crease no call

bullshit again

full strength

my strength

forechecking and puck control

we control puck

two on one

one on two

he shoots he scores

he is I and I am him

game winner with 4:37 left

we go to sizzler.

Party at Zed's House on Saturday Night

Dude.

Zed's parents are leaving this weekend.

Kegger!

Can your brother get us beer?

No problem.

I'm going to get so wasted.

I hear that.

You think Sally thinks I'm hot?

I heard, like, if she gets drunk, she'll lay a gorilla.

I look like a gorilla, no?

An Ode to Large High Schools
Are you that girl
In my algebra class
Or that girl who
called me retarded?
You both have kind of the same face and whatever.

"J"V
just because we're not as fast
not as good
not as strong
not as skilled
or pretty
doesn't mean that we
WE, THE LHS "JUNIOR" VARSITY GIRLS' FIELD HOCKEY TEAM
should be called
'junior'
or for that matter
'slutty.'

Masturbation
I did it one time in the bathroom on the
    second floor, near the gym.
I was worried 'cause I heard someone come in,
    but I waited and they left
Then I finished up.
I started doing it every day there, after English.

STOP!

Cheerleader, I Am
One, two, three, four
Lincoln High
Here we go!
I am nothing—
I am everything—
I am cheerleader.
Yea, yea,
we got spirit
Yea, yea,
we got
whoa, whoa, whoa, whoa
we got spirit!
I am better than Debbie Thomas—
Debbie Thomas is fat—
I am cheerleader.
Who rocks the field
The rockets rock the field
And when we rock the field
We rock it all the way down
Debbie Thomas should not be higher in the
    formation than me—
She is so fat, if she falls she could seriously
    hurt someone—
I am cheerleader.

Recess
Why isn't there recess
    sin high school?
That sucks.

High School Bathroom Elegy
Once
Not always, but once
I want to take a shit
in peace.

The Last Time
The first time
I ran
My breath flew out.
Flu out.
Fatigue, malaise, diarrhea
Would all be proper words to
   categorize my post-race experience.
Three months later
Against Lincoln High
Lincoln higher, Lincoln faster
Fastest mile in school history
And
State champion.
The Last Time
I ran
My time was a personal best.

Light Petting
French kissing
In the back of Brad's truck
He touched my tits
Then it was time for lunch.

The Bus Ride Home
It hurts again
It hurts inside
The pain is real
The pain inside
They persist
can't resist
Squishing me
calling me fat
Husky jeans
Would that I could slim down just a
   little
Rick Allston calls me lard
For the fourth time today
He and Laura
Three months now
Her beauty, his popularity
a perfect high school match
Me
Eighteen years now
My fat, my face
a perfect high school fat guy.

EXTRACURRICULAR ACTIVITIES LIST

Erik the Red

Address: Odinkirk Castle, Sweden

Telephone: n/a

Sailing / Rowing Cross Baltic Sea using <u>both</u> sails and oars. Navigate by stars at night, sun during day. Believed to be first Europeans to the New World. 100 hours per week.

Pillaging Attack English/French villages, steal their gold. Kill, burn in wild bloodlust frenzy. Lay waste, etc. Sail away, return next year. 10 hours per week.

Riotous Drinking Parties Host feasts on return voyage. Drink, sing. Get in fights with other Vikings, slay them, eat their hearts, etc.

Depression Feeling guilty for being a Viking, killing innocent people. General malaise regarding Viking society's conventions of morality, need to pillage. Also dark in Sweden for months on end, makes you sad. Hoping to attend college, accrue knowledge, stop killing. 140 hours per week.

On Attending a High School for the Arts

Attending Interlachen Music and Arts Academy for the past 4 years has truly changed the way I look at the world, and listen to it! Music and Arts Academies, I came to learn, do not view extra-curricular activities in the same light as other high schools; this new prioritizing of activities would prove to have a profound impact on my adolescent years.

Coming to Interlachen as a naive 14 year old, I was sure I wanted to be the next Beethoven, or at least the next Bach (!). But then something magical happened my freshmen year: I joined the football team. Never had I felt so alive as I greedily imbibed the marvelous symphony that was high school football!

I prepared for our first game as I had never prepared for any recital before in my life, namely by putting on football pads. Sitting in our locker room (a converted woodwind storage room) I could hear our 450 piece symphonic band playing "Toccato en fugue by Mozart," above; the crowd listening quietly on, applauding vigorously after the delicate violin solo in the 2nd movement. "Wow!" I thought to myself. "The band is here and everything!" I tried not to get too nervous.

I finished dressing and, eager to get on the field and warm-up, headed out of the locker room, chock full of adrenaline from the "Schubert's 2nd" I had been pumping on my Walkman. As I was about to enter the field, a guard stopped me. "Nice get-up," he sneered. "And just where do you think you're going?"

I kindly explained to him that I needed to perform my daily set of calisthenics before the big game. "Does it <u>sound</u> like they're done yet?" he said, motioning to the magnificient orchestra behind him. "They've got like 2 movements left, in case you didn't know. Look, I'll let you know when the half-time show's going to start."

Half-time show? What was going on here? Confused, I sat down, closed my eyes and—

Suddenly, from the loudspeakers, boomed the words: "Now, introducing our half-time performers, it's our very own 'Interlachen Music and Arts Academy Football group!' "

Everything came into focus. We, the "football group," were nothing more than low-level half-time entertainment to satiate the masses as they geared up for the real second half: movements 6 – 9 of Mozart's "Toccato en fugue." (And what a splendid second half it would prove to be!) As most of the crowd got up for bathroom breaks, we began our game against Roosevelt High, a large inner-city school from Detroit. Midway through the first half, the game was called on account of the fact that half-time was over and the concert was going to resume. Down 42 – 0, we felt defeated, in every sense of the word.

Playing football at Interlachen has not been easy. We only have 4 players, we never get past the first half in our games, and band members regularly pick on us: "I'll break you like a dried-up clarinet reed!" or "If you were Mozart and I was Chopin, I'd compose symphonies 3 – 9 and end up being considered a much more accomplished pianist! Dork!" If I had a nickel for every time I heard that one, I might have enough money to buy myself some pride. Through it all, however, I have managed to maintain my cool in the face of much adversity, and for this I feel I have proven myself worthy of admission to your college.

The College Essay:
An Insider's Look at One Admissions Officer's Critique

Ah, the college essay. Remember that time you were in France with your family, and you passed out from the heat and fell on your face in front of the post office in Aix-en-Provence, breaking your nose on the cement, and you were rushed to the hospital, where none of the members of your family could understand what the French doctors meant by the phrase "il est tombé dans les pommes?" and finally it dawned on you that "falling in the apples" must be an idiomatic expression for "passing out," and after laughing through the nuances (and the pain) of communication barriers, your mom tried to cheer you up by saying, "Maybe this is a good story for a college essay"? Remember that?

She was wrong. Your college essay needs to accomplish at least five of the seven following things: grab your reader's attention; make you stand out from other applicants; describe your sincere altruistic spirit; demonstrate your ability to write Pulitzer-worthy prose; explain why you got a B-minus in Chemistry; talk about God a lot; and describe a strange story wherein you lose consciousness in a foreign land. You can see how the above option would meet only four of these seven key goals of the essay.

To aid you in the essay writing process, we've gotten a hold of a (fake) essay, with comments by a (fictitious) admissions officer, so that you'll be able to see what the real (fake) process is like (not in any way like).

Essay by John Moyen
Critique by Alyssa O'Keefe, Admissions Officer, Kent State University

Please make a personal statement.

From looking at me, you would not see much out of the ordinary. I am about five foot ten (though I like to stretch it to six feet on official forms), with blue-gray eyes, average-looking jeans and a normal backpack. I go to school every day, study reasonably hard, fight with my family sometimes, and score near the mean on standardized tests. No, from looking at me you would not notice anything unusual.

This is an interesting opening paragraph. As an admissions officer, I am intrigued by his portrait and impressed with his honesty. He let me know immediately that he fights with his family and doesn't kill himself studying. This candor lends credibility to statements he may make later in his essay.

I wake up at 6 a.m. on the weekdays because I have a long commute to school, but on the weekends I like to sleep in. I also enjoy parties, though excessive drinking has left me feeling under the weather once or twice. None of these traits are more unusual than what one would expect from any normal high school student. I am a fan of Top 40 radio, like James Bond films, and used to play the clarinet. In no way do I appear unusual.

I am a little mystified as to the ultimate point of this essay. He is taking too long to introduce the unique characteristics of his personality, but this can be cleared up by a little editing. At this rate, though, I would put him in the reject or discuss pile depending on the rest of his application.

My friends call me "Joe Unflappable Average" for my levelheaded and even-keeled voice. As a baby, I would cry a lot. I prefer room temperature to be cold when I go to sleep, but warm when I wake up. That way I don't hit the snooze button as many times. I am no different in any way from anyone you have ever known, at first glance.

Would that the most mildly unusual event would occur in this student's life. My boredom has reached dangerous levels. This student has moved from the reject list to my own personal "Uncontrollable Loathing" list.

Mr. Henkins, my English teacher, said that my essay on Chaucer was pretty good, but he thought I could have done better on my *Oliver Twist* paper. I think he knew I didn't read the whole thing. I got a B in the class, which was incidentally the mean. I have a goodly number of CDs, but nothing fancy. In all ways, I am seemingly totally average.

Yes, you are. Do a thing. Please.

I also enjoy fishing sometimes, especially with my grandfather. One time, I caught a six-foot-long mahimahi while deep-sea fishing. That was great. Often, I will eat fast food in place of regular meals, just as an average teenager would. My IQ is 100.

My life has become 40% worse since I began reading this essay. Words have never affected me in such a powerfully detrimental way. Farewell, Kent State Admissions Office, and the life I once knew.

SAT *TIPS* Remember, the worst thing that can happen is that you'll end up as a carny. Or a dockworker.

SAT *TIPS* How do you remember the difference between "ascending" and "descending"? Let's say you're an ass man. If you were to list the body parts you find most arousing, and listed them in *ascending* order, this would be the same as *ass-ending* order. I am a breast man.

Hamilton College

Please respond to the following questions in the space provided. Feel free to attach extra sheets as necessary.

1. If you were stranded on a desert island, what three people would you want to accompany you and why? They may be historical figures, fictional characters, family members or friends.

If I were stranded on a desert island, like the one that my family owns off the coast of Chile, I can't imagine which three people I would bring! What I enjoy most about meeting people is the challenges and competition that we offer each other—in conversation, in intellectual sparring, in sport. So my three people would have to be of great intellect, have a desire to engage with others, and possess an animal cunning.

The first person I would choose is Benjamin Franklin, one of our nation's Founding Fathers. Franklin's knack for invention has always fascinated me, and such a trait would be helpful on a desert island. I would love to have the chance to discuss states' rights with the great American thinker who defined the term—though perhaps a discussion of the rights of the individual would be more apt after I release the dogs.

The second person I would choose is Alexander the Great, who conquered Europe at age sixteen. He'd be a feisty one—but could he cut the Gordian Knot of my complex system of traps and snares? It certainly would be interesting to see how he fared on my island. Tally Ho!

Lastly I would select a young Edwin Moses—his speed and gazelle-like dexterity would make for a great chase. No doubt he would be better than John Riggins, former Washington Redskins fullback, whose fishing boat foundered on the Charybdis-like rocks. I admired his courage in chewing off his own foot in order to escape one of my Man-Traps. But oh yes, the sinewy Moses would be a fine adversary.

If I could take a fourth person, it would certainly be a mythological Griffin. This chimeric half lion, half winged beastie would be a fabulous trophy in my Zoo of Orpheus. Naturally, the beastie would attempt an escape flight off the island, but he would quickly learn the same lesson as did the Interpol helicopter that recently attempted a penetration of the Laser Dome®.

My fifth choice would be the beautiful Cheryl Tiegs, who would no doubt be impressed by my facility with mechanized weapons. I would take great pleasure in introducing suffering to her eyes.

Six is Holden Caulfield. I really identify with him. That empathy will be cut tragically short, however, when he wanders into the Dart Field.

Seven: Mozart. The Music Room, already inhabited by (among others) Bela Bartok and the Cleveland Symphony Orchestra, would be complete with the Maestro of Vienna. Upon his arrival, I would honor him with a bacchanalian feast that would make Europe's finest chefs blush. Then: a game of Bladed Frisbee.

My eighth choice was prompted by your compelling question—I had never before considered the merits of loosing my family members from The Cage as well. My brother, Albert, is the only other living person who knows how to operate The Controls. I would revel in defeating an equal.

As I see it, this list is only the beginning. The books I read, the friends I make in college, will make my life much more stimulating. I plan to live off-campus.

College Essay

Imagine you are stranded on a desert island without hope of rescue. If you could have any three people with you, alive or dead, who would they be and why?

If I were stranded on an island by myself, first of all, I would FREAK out! Thank heavens for my mom, my dad, my younger brother, my two best friends, Krissy and Rachel, and my brilliant piano teacher, Mr. Reynolds. Luckily they all live on the coast, so I could still keep in touch with them by sending messages in bottles. Now, where would the bottles come from, you ask? Why, from the Magic Inventor, of course! Also, ink and paper to write letters. And maybe a computer for e-mail.

However, I am not so silly as to think that I can survive with words alone. That's why I would also bring along the Carpenter-Chef-Repair Man-Physician-Dentist. And how! First of all, he would take the rotting wood planks from our wrecked canoe. Then he would treat and varnish them. Thirdly, he would build a house with a three-car garage and indoor swimming pool. Fourthly, he would prepare my meals, making sure the venison, handpicked berries, and grains were imported from only the most fertile, temperate plains regions.

At this point, I have almost everything I need. So the third person on my island would be a Genie who would grant me three wishes. These three things would be: 1. a complete, seasonal wardrobe by Prada; 2. sex; 3. eternal life. Every Thanksgiving, Christmas, and Fourth of July, I would take the Magic Inventor's jet plane back home to have a barbeque with my family and friends. But still, no one would ever be able to rescue me because that's what you said in the essay question. Also, I'll only do this if I can definitely go to Disney World and Paris every spring.

And that's how life would be in Hawaii.

Wellesley College Admissions Application
Personal Statement

Briefly tell about an educational experience that has been significant to you.

The summer before my junior year, I went on the Amigos del Mundo Youth-Interchange Study-Work Experience Program in Belize, South America. I went there intending to do community service, but I ended up doing much more: I learned about myself and discovered that I was more than just an intelligent and outgoing college-bound woman.

"Community service" doesn't accurately describe what I was doing: I was helping people in the community who needed my help. They, in turn, taught me how to wash my clothes in the river. Before I could help others, though, I had to face my fear of failure. But just as I was afraid when I first became treasurer of the International Club, I conquered that fear, and we raised $230 in my junior year and took a field trip to a Mexican restaurant.

The animals in the Belize jungle are like the different groups in my school. The jocks are the fierce lions; the preppies are the proud snakes; the druggies are the drugged-out hummingbirds; and the deaf kids are fish. With its sun-dappled sparrows swimming against gentle breezes, and its rosy-cheeked monkeys swooping among dense vegetation and inviting zephyrs, my high school is a lot like the animal kingdom.

In the rainforest, you never know what's lurking around the corner. Similarly, as co-captain of the cross-country team I had to sacrifice a lot of my time in order to make the team the best it could be. After being attacked by a tiger in the jungle, I realized that the only limits in my life are those that I choose to place on myself. And I don't believe in limits, as my organization of school pep rallies demonstrates.

I remember something that a tribal elder in Belize told me, a medicine woman who reminded me of my mother (Wellesley '70). She said, "When I was your age, I was involved in a painful coming-of-age ritual." That's when I understood that I enjoyed voting in school elections as much as I did attending school plays. And that's why I think I could contribute something valuable to the Wellesley College community.

My fondest memory of Belize is not teaching the young girls lacrosse, or even building the computer center for the elders. It is of the time during my freshman year when I won honorable mention in a school contest for my essay "Why We Need Trees." Trees make up a large part of the Belize population, and many Belizians told me that if they didn't have trees they would have to stop eating bark. "Beestes and briddes couden speke and singe, and so bifel that in a daweninge," said Chaucer over 600 years ago. I couldn't agree more. Whenever I sell tickets for school dances, I always think of Belize.

Getting the Right Recommendation Letter

Sometimes there will be that special guidance counselor with whom you can form a special bond. Samuel Harold Lumpkin was lucky enough to find such a guidance counselor . . .

Recommendation Letter for Samuel Harold Lumpkin—
By Lola Sweeney, Guidance Counselor, Central Chicago Public High School

Dear *COLLEGE ADMISSIONS OFFICER:*
    I am writing this letter on behalf of *SAMUEL HAROLD LUMPKIN*, a student at Central Chicago Public High School. *SAMUEL HAROLD LUMPKIN* has consistently shown that *SAMUEL HAROLD LUMPKIN* is able to work on a *4 YEAR COLLEGE* level, and I have no doubts that *HE* will succeed admirably at *STATE UNIVERSITY OF NEW YORK (SUNY)-BINGHAMTON.* While a student here at Central Chicago Public High School, student was ranked *345 OUT OF A GRADUATING CLASS OF 756 WITH A CUMULATIVE GPA OF 3.12.* A student who I personally found excelled at extracurriculars as well as academics, *SAMUEL HAROLD LUMPKIN* participated in *KEY CLUB* and *STUDENT NEWSPAPER* and *OTHER.*
    The student who has applied for admissions to your school deserves *ADMISSION OFFICER'S* serious consideration. *HE* would become an active member of your community by majoring in *PSYCHOLOGY* or possibly *CRIMINAL JUSTICE.*
    In a recent conversation with this student, I asked *HIM* what *He* was looking for in a college. *He* replied, "In the college that I am applying to, I expect a place *WHERE NO ONE WILL KNOW ABOUT THAT TIME IN GYM CLASS WHEN I LIT MY EYEBROWS ON FIRE."*
    Believe you me, *SAMUEL HAROLD LUMPKIN* 's personal interests are wide ranging. They include but are not limited to *READING* and *BUILDING THINGS OUT OF WOOD.* All in all, I would consider *SAMUEL HAROLD LUMPKIN* to be a *GOOD/VERY GOOD* addition to your population of *13,450 STUDENTS.*

SINCERELY,

LOLA SWEENEY

Special relationships with teachers should be nurtured to get the best recommendations like this one for Samuel Hanson.

To whom it may concern,

I'm writing today on the behalf of one Mr. Samuel Hanson, a student of mine for the past six glorious months. Samuel is the best student I have ever known in Eleventh Grade English. Here is one of his inspiring, dare I say transcendent, haikus:

Walk with me in the sand
Korn's a good band
Baby baby Ba
by Baby Baby
that would be Grand.

Being with and getting to know Sam, or "Big Shooter" as I call him, has been one of the most rewarding, pleasurable, and academically orgasmic experiences of my life. Samuel has his own band and is learning to play the guitar. He also has a deep appreciation of cinema, and I must say I really like his Pulp Fiction T-shirt. His quick intellect, determination, taut broad shoulders, and firm thighs have truly made him a "stud"ent whom I shall never, ever, ever, never, ever forget.

Those long hours we spent together in the library "researching" really helped me overcome my recent divorce with my husband of fourteen years. "Big Shooter" filled a void that Tom left, and he filled it often. I taught the "Shooter" things he couldn't learn in any textbook and he, in turn, rewarded me with "gifts" of his own. Our relationship, nonetheless, was one based on mutual admiration and respect and was strictly professional.

Except sometimes we screwed. Hard.

Sincerely,

Greta Jones

Be careful who you ask for a recommendation.

I taught Dennis McHopper in Geometry class. I will admit that he is an incredibly gifted student. I will admit that he is probably smarter than me. However, Dennis McHopper sucks. I don't know how else to say it. I know that he got perfect SATs, I know he is #1 in his class, but he is not a very nice person, and I wouldn't mind if you did not let him into your college.

People are like tissues to Dennis McHopper. He uses them to wipe his ass when he is completely out of toilet paper. He ignores his classmates and humiliates his teachers. "You're inferior intellectually," he said to me once in front of the whole class after he had caught me making a simple mathematical error. "Speak to my ass, because the face isn't listening," I said as I mooned him and used my hands to spread my ass cheeks. He is walking around telling everyone how he has "pretty much already got in." Please, humble this kid, blacklist him, make him go somewhere else. Like hell.

Sincerely,

Brendan M. Trombly, high school geometry teacher

Peer recommendations will usually help your cause. This next letter helped Timothy Steener get into CalTech.

To whom it may concern,

I am writing on behalf of Timothy Steener a student of my acquaintance at Greenwood High School. Steener has all kinds of zits and stuff all over his face. And he wears dress pants in gym class. He probably weighs a thousand pounds. You should check out his mom at parents weekend. Make sure she doesn't sit on you because she would make you die!

It should be commented that Steener is also an enormous gay-wad. I can punch him a million times lighter than anything and he pusses out like a baby. He also reads books (right-side up) and says things like "I shan't go do that thing" and "I'm not inclined to whatever." Then I say "I shan't punch your face in, Steener" and he shuts up. He also can't talk to girls and I bet he wears tighty-whiteys. So you should pick Steener for your college. You should also put me in your college because I can do seventy-five sit-ups in two minutes.

Sincerely,

Steve

This next letter may seem improbable . . . improbable like a fox. Steven now attends Cornell.

To whom it may concern,

I have been acquainted with Steven for the last several years (I've lost count). I first met Steven when he was vacationing in India. Apparently he consumed some improperly cooked pork and ingested me, his tapeworm, into his digestive system. My first impression of Steven was that his intestines were much more enriching than the now-dead pig in which I had developed from my larval stage. I first found it really hard to be separated from my mom, but Steven helped me through this difficult period by eating a lot of food.

Steven is a voracious reader and always yearns for knowledge. I like it when his mom serves steak because steak has a lot of protein which lets me grow larger and larger within his viscera. Steve and I like to play ball in the backyard. He's really great at it. I don't have hands or organs so I'm not very agile, but Steven is good with the disabled. We like to mess around a lot, too. We play our own version of tag where he tries to starve me out of his guts and I give him debilitating intestinal cramps.

Bottom line, Steve is a great student and a deeply moral human being. He has taken my baby tapeworms under his wing, providing them care and protection throughout his body. In sum, I ask you a question: How many kids do you know who would feed and shelter a large Indian family at his own expense? Not too many, but if you know of any, give me a call!

Sincerely,
Slinky

Admissions and Interviews

The college admissions process can be intimidating and scary. What goes on behind those closed doors in the dark recesses of the wicked places, the admissions places? But you need not worry; you had the good taste and breeding that go along with purchasing a fine *Harvard Lampoon* publication. You, my newly found friend, should have no problem getting into elite colleges because even average kids can get into elite colleges . . .

Justin Green was the most average student at his high school. He was ranked 76 out of 151 students, played center field on the baseball team, and invented the mildly popular sport of whitewater rafting. So average! So a matriculating freshman at Harvard!

Meredith Vernon was voted "Least Unique" at her high school, where she received straight C's, played Junior Varsity ball, and directed a paltry three Oscar-winning films. Booooring! Sounds like a real wallflower, doesn't she? A Stanford wallflower, that is!

Platinum-selling recording artist Luther Vandross.

Dexter Poole's face was not recognizable to any of his classmates because he has no distinguishing features. He occasionally attended Spanish Club meetings, took a drab, plain-faced girl to the prom, fought crime with modest success as The Basilisk, and got a B—minus on his senior project. Another face in the crowd? "Well, eat poop," Dexter says as he smokes cigars in his Yale dormitory.

Student number 4 was never named by his parents due to his incredible plainness. On most days he works for minimum wage at the local paper store. When not doing this, he spends his dreary time swallowing the sea. Old Boringface here is ever so ordinary. He does not attend college, but he sure could, I bet!

Luther Vandross is a platinum-selling recording artist. Hey Luther, try selling multiplatinum and then you can give us a call! Nevertheless, Luther Vandross is a Rhodes scholar.

SAT *TIPS* If you find yourself stuck in a section, ask the proctor. He will give you all of the answers if you are both Masons.

Behind-the-Scenes Secret Admissions Committee Lingo They Don't Want You to Know

<u>Shoo-in</u> A candidate who is surely going to be accepted into the college.

<u>Unqualified</u> An applicant who lacks the credentials to gain acceptance into the college.

<u>Borderline</u> An applicant whose application needs careful consideration before a final decision is made.

<u>On-the-Fence</u> See Borderline.

<u>Walking-the-Tight-Wire (That Is the College Admissions Process)</u> See Borderline.

<u>Not So Sure, Really. I Guess So. Your Call</u> See Borderline.

<u>Playing Baseball with My Uncle</u> See Borderline.

<u>Reeling-in-Big-Fish-without-a-License</u> See Borderline.

<u>Doing It up All Freaky, Kinda</u> See Borderline.

<u>He's Always Been Your Boy, Tom. Ever Since You First Saw His Application You Wanted Him In. You Brought Him This Far in the Process, Now Try to Take Him Home. The Only Thing Standing Between Him and the Gates of Privilege Is Me. What Are You Gonna Do about It? Make Me Love Him, Tom. Make Him a Star. Drop Some Bombs That Will Make My World Explode. Give Me the Goddamn Funk, Tom. Do You Hear Me? Bring It! Oh, I Love My Job!!</u> See Borderline.

<u>Maybe</u> See Borderline.

Once you know the lingo of the college admissions game, you will have to face the most daunting trial of the whole process, the admissions interview. The mere mention of the interview will cause the eager applicant to lie awake in bed wondering what to wear. Lie awake no longer.

What to Wear to Your College Interview

What do ascots, Jamz!, cashmere, pantalones de vaqueros, Skidz, and pants have in common? You should never wear them to your college interview. Unless, of course, you plan to attend college in Sweden. Instead, listen to what these successful college students wore to their interviews:

"The best advice I can give is to wear clothes you feel comfortable in. Having been raised by wolves in the Menswear Department of Macy's, I am comfortable in a coat and tie."
— Guy LaFarge, assistant manager, Macy's

"Accessorize! Wear a watch on your wrist to show you're punctual, a tie on your neck to show you're neat, and a fax machine in your throat to show you're productive."
— Micron the Boy Robot Who Loves College

Do not dress like this man.

"I just wore pants. No shirt, no shoes, no socks, no belt, no hair, no skin, just pants. And I got into Nichols."
       —Scary "Scary" Sammy

"Let me tell you: I wore my heart on my sleeve. To prevent death, I installed a baboon heart in my own chest."
       —Jim Smith

"A T-shirt that read: 'Co Ed Naked 1600 on SATs: On the Floor with a Perfect Score.' Under that, I wore a T-shirt that read: 'Absolut Vice President of Student Council.' Under that I wore a suit."
       —Timothy "Bucky" Edwards, Sigma Alpha Chi

Remember that the interview is the only opportunity for a representative of the college to interact with you on a personal basis; an interview can make or break your chances for admission. Following these rules will allow you to have a successful interview experience.

1. Do control the interview

If an interviewer asks you a question that you don't have a great answer to, try to steer it toward something you're more comfortable with:

Interviewer: If you could be any animal, what would it be and why?
Student: I'd be the 780 on my verbal SAT.
Interviewer: Do you have a favorite author?
Student: I'm going to be valedictorian.

2. Do have questions prepared for the interviewer

Student: So what's the ethnic diversity on campus like?
Interviewer: Oh, we've got all sorts of people, whether white, Caucasian, Anglo, or Saxon!
Student: Well I'm from Puerto Rico. Are there many Puerto Ricans?
Interviewer: Puerto Ri-who?

780 Verbal SAT Monster

3. Do answer promptly

Halting answers and stuttering responses will get you nowhere quickly when being interviewed. If you cannot come up with an answer to a question, say the first thing that comes to your mind. A particularly telling example of the efficiency of this method:

Interviewer: Name?
Student: Axl Rose
Interviewer: How old are you?
Student: Negative 45
Interviewer: Why do you want to go to Harvard?

Student: Yale

Interviewer: What are your interests?

Student: Boobs. Red. Macaroni. Corey Feldman.

This student was accepted to the college of the choice because of the immediacy of his responses, his ability to free-associate, and the raging party anthem "Welcome to the Jungle."

4. Do be assertive

You: Hi. I'd like to be admitted to your school now.

Interviewer: Well sir, why don't I get you an application and you can—

You: Look, if I wanted to apply I'd go to the "Applications Office" [*makes quotation signs with fingers*]. However, since I came to the "Admissions Office" I'm ready to be "admitted."

Interviewer: I don't think you understand—

You: I don't think *you* understand! Look, here's my ticket [*hands her movie stub that reads "Admit One"*]. Now don't make me get your supervisor!

5. Don't ever do this

Interviewer: I'd like to thank you for coming on such short notice.

Student: I'd like to thank you for coming on such short notice.

Interviewer: Excuse me?

Student: Excuse me?

Interviewer: Stop.

Student: Stop.

Interviewer: No, really. Stop.

Student: No, really. Stop.

Interviewer: You're a gaywad.

Student: You're a gaywad.

Interviewer: I'm a dickface.

Student: I'm a . . . . Yes. You are.

6. AND NEVER EVER LET THEM GIVE YOU A GLASS OF WATER!

You, being the thirsty camel that earned you the nickname "Drinkinski," chug down the water and immediately need to urinate. Your mind is clouded by the uncontrollable need to pee, so you deliriously stand on your chair and whizz on the interviewer. Nice move, high schooler. The only college you'll be attending is the School of Bladder Control. That school has poor prestige.

SAT *TIPS* It is important to eat a hearty breakfast before you take the SAT. Be sure not to eat too much, though, because you could stand to lose a few.

The College Admissions Process—Demystified

Once you have finished your interview, your application goes through gears of the meritocratic machine that is the admissions committee. We at the *Harvard Lampoon* have gotten our dirty hands on a copy of what goes on in the clandestine belly of the admissions beast . . .

SAT *TIPS* Students with weight problems should talk to their proctors about taking the SAT from a table rather than a small desk. You should also refrain from eating your exam book.

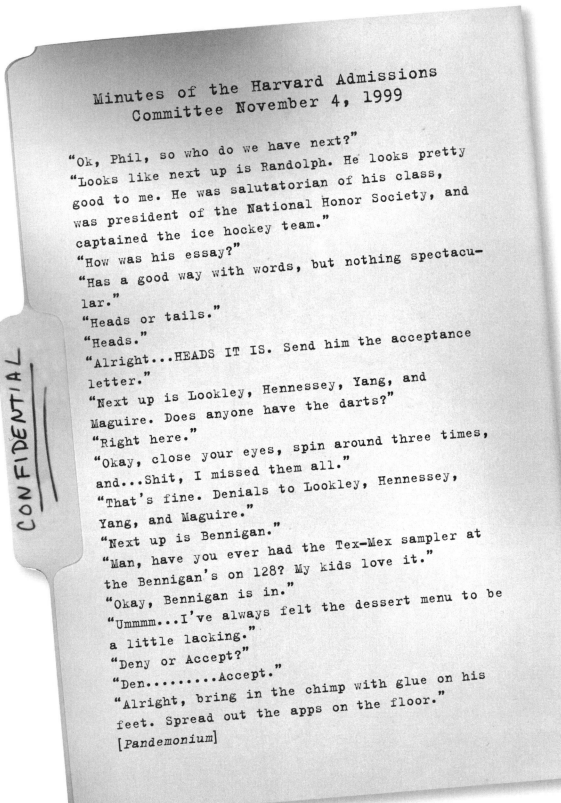

CONFIDENTIAL

Minutes of the Harvard Admissions Committee November 4, 1999

"Ok, Phil, so who do we have next?"

"Looks like next up is Randolph. He looks pretty good to me. He was salutatorian of his class, was president of the National Honor Society, and captained the ice hockey team."

"How was his essay?"

"Has a good way with words, but nothing spectacular."

"Heads or tails."

"Heads."

"Alright...HEADS IT IS. Send him the acceptance letter."

"Next up is Lookley, Hennessey, Yang, and Maguire. Does anyone have the darts?"

"Right here."

"Okay, close your eyes, spin around three times, and...Shit, I missed them all."

"That's fine. Denials to Lookley, Hennessey, Yang, and Maguire."

"Next up is Bennigan."

"Man, have you ever had the Tex-Mex sampler at the Bennigan's on 128? My kids love it."

"Okay, Bennigan is in."

"Ummmm...I've always felt the dessert menu to be a little lacking."

"Deny or Accept?"

"Den.........Accept."

"Alright, bring in the chimp with glue on his feet. Spread out the apps on the floor."

[*Pandemonium*]

"Okay, put Jobo back in his box."

"Did the Red Sox beat the Yankees today?"

"No."

"Shred Long Island apps."

"Done."

"Hey, Chuck, try to jump up in the air and click your heels three times before you hit the ground."

. . . .

"That was damn close."

"Alright I guess that means that Indrus, Fallow, Sportman, and Wertzel are in. Grylock, Theo, and Rewntner are out."

"Hey! This kid's last name is Dick!!!"

"ACCEPT. Make him roommates with Weener."

"Alright, it looks like we have about 18,000 applications left."

"I say we accept them."

"I second that."

"Done. Who's ready for dollar-beer night?"

CONFIDENTIAL

Part Two

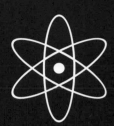

College Rankings:
Totally Useless Information about Admissions, Academics, and Student Life

Quite frankly, dear reader, it is probably best not to question the methods of our research. Those who have in the past usually fall victim to the Hollywood Mafia run by graduates of the *Harvard Lampoon*. But if you must know, a brief synopsis of the way in which we collected our data may be found below.

First, we visited all of the prestigious colleges and universities of this nation. This exhaustive study expended most of our energies. Rather, to be completely honest, due to financial and time constraints, we were unable to visit every single college in the country. In fact, our survey crews didn't quite make it to any schools, really, outside of the Northeast.

Still, however, our survey of New England schools was incredibly thorough. Our efforts had to be cut back, unfortunately, by unexpected conditions in New Hampshire. Massachusetts, however, was all ours. We combed every inch of the great Commonwealth with a fine-toothed college-seeking device. As time wore on, we regret, our device proved to be more or less nonfunctional.

All right. You seem like a decent person. I'm going to be totally honest with you. We only had time to visit schools around Boston and Cambridge, so we didn't exactly make it out to, say, Williams and Amherst. But did we ever visit the campuses of all of the Boston area colleges!

No, I'm afraid, we didn't. Please understand, we are but college students working on a limited budget. But believe you me, good friend! We certainly did attend a sorority party at Wellesley College! And survey the campus we did! At least, we certainly knew of people who attended said party, and asked them for their impressions of Wellesley upon their return.

Listen. I'm sorry for all of the rigmarole. You deserve the truth.

Once, four years ago, my brother's friend met a guy at camp who had a sister who was thinking of applying to Wellesley. It was Chess Camp. No, you're right, I don't have a brother.

It is not without a great deal of internal conflict that I have decided to present to you, good reader, our true methods. They may seem incredulous, but they have yet to fail us:

We just put some schools we had heard of wherever we wanted and made up some other stuff.

The Rankings

#1 Harvard University

"Finally, a place where everyone is as awesome as me."

As you might guess, we have chosen Harvard University as our number one college in America. The university has a faculty of superstars, attracts the smartest group of applicants, and offers unlimited opportunities for growth and a bright future. But more important than all of these notable qualities, Harvard is the funniest place on earth. You do not understand. People enter the college not knowing what to expect and leave with their hairs all sticking straight up out of their heads. Not due to some sort of electrical phenomenon, but to some sort of electrical phenomenon, but because of excitement. And hairspray. While Princeton or Stanford offer similar levels of student advising and student-faculty ratios, only Harvard gives every student a free fudge machine in their rooms. As we ride the water flume to class every morning, we thank our lucky stars that we can wear Hawaiian shirts every day and listen to lectures from Professor Weird Al Yankovic. Our diplomas are printed on Fruit Roll-Ups.

Despite ignoring all nutritional guidelines, Harvard's dining halls *rule*.

A junior finds out how many joules it takes to win a giant teddy bear.

🐥 Admissions

All we can say is: Good Luck. Thousands and thousands of all-star students apply every year and none of them get accepted. A different set of 1,600 all-star students apply every year and they all get accepted. Hundreds of valedictorians and students with perfect SATs get rejected every year. Dean of Admissions Charles A. Vazac explains, "Yeah, I don't know. We ask you to submit a picture. If you have a cool haircut and are wearing sunglasses, we'll probably admit you. We don't want a bunch of dorks and Poindexters. The best students submit pictures of themselves kissing girls, or playing beach volleyball in swimsuits, or themselves in swimsuits. Or snorkeling. We don't just look at one factor like test scores or grades." The average SAT score at Harvard is a 1520.

It can be scary at the top.

GO ON TO NEXT PAGE

Academics

Every Harvard student loves attending class. Most classes are held in swimming pools or on a whitewater raft in Arizona. Homework is usually kept to a minimum, except for a class like Massage, where you have to get a lot of massages. The most popular class on campus is Moral Reasoning 54: "Oh my God!" We can't tell you what this class is about, but OH . . . MY . . . GOD!!!! Students must choose from every area of the core curriculum courses except if they don't want to or if they are tired. And how could you not be tired after a long day of Psychology 1125: "Drinking Milkshakes and Playing Skee-Ball"? Students choose a course of study after their freshman year and devote approximately half of their course load to this field. Students are especially fond of Economics and Government at Harvard, but that's just because these classes are taught by naked ladies. Science concentrators have access to a variety of lab settings, ranging from building robots that fight each other to dressing up monkeys in costumes to making X-ray glasses and machines that shrink you. Harvard does not have an official pre-medical or pre-law program, but the college produces many lovable goofs who resemble Patch Adams or Jim Carrey's character in *Liar, Liar*. Most Harvard graduates go on to open surf shops in Maui or design roller-coasters. Many students complain of Harvard's advising.

Harvard's president, Danny Funtimes (left). A Harvard student decides which text to buy (right).

Student Life

Almost all Harvard students choose to live within the house system after freshman year. The houses are independent units equipped with their own dining hall and library. Each house has a special theme and all are connected to the main campus by both monorail and "ol' fashioned" riverboat steamer. Cabot House, for example, hearkens back to the romantic seaside resorts of turn-of-the-century America, while Eliot House presents the Old West not as it was, but as it should have been (Annie Oakley Rootin'-Tootin' Rodeo Revue thrice daily). Students across campus wake up every morning at 10:00 A.M. to the sweet Latina strains of Gloria Estefan (Harvard's dean of students). They enjoy breakfast in bed (birthday cake) presented to them by British people, and take a dip in the house colored-ball-pit before riding to class bareback on stallions. Harvard Dining Services is catered by Chuck E. Cheese. Harvard extracurriculars are unmatched. Whether it's Harvard's all-male a cappella singing troupe, the Backstreet Boys, or our world-famous football team, Cirque du Soleil, there is never a lack of culture on campus. Harvard student publications are paid ridiculous sums of money to produce trade paperbacks by major entertainment conglomerates. And the Harvard Camel Riding Club never lacks for camels. Or high spirits. You should go to Harvard.

The best part about physics lectures at Harvard? No lines.

"Harvard is awesome. It's just like Space Camp, except we actually get to go into space. So, in that sense, it's like Space Camp: The Movie."

—Student in Chemistry class

"Wheeeeeeee!!!!! Oh my God, I'm gonna BARF!!!!!!!!!"

—Student taking Physics final

Harvard basketball games are often pure nonsense.

#2 Haverford College

What do you think this is? Haverford? No, it's Harvard.

"It's *Haverford*, not Harvard, you asshole," says Harvard dean Keven P. Larkin, sitting in Haverford Hall, the center of the Harvard/Haverford administration. Haverford was founded in 1636 by John Harvard, who was from Haverford, England. The first president of Haverford College was Haverford Harvard, who was succeeded by his son Howard "Harvard" Haverford. The first students at the Haverford branch of the Harvard campus also went to Harvard. Currently, "Fair Haverford (Harvard)" is nestled in Harvard, Massachusetts, next to Haverford College in the state of Harvard.

✎ Admissions

"Everybody just slow down for a minute and let's straighten this out," says Harverford Haverd, Harvard's head of Haverford, when commenting on the difference in admissions between the two schools. "For example, John Kennedy went to Harvard and Kohn Jennedy went to Haverford, or was it the other way around? As I was saying earlier, Harvard Kennedy went to John College when Rose Haverford went to Kennedy College, but that's irrelevant to the point at hand: Haverford, unlike most other schools, has had six presidents attend the school— and all of them graduated from Harvard. Brown University is also a selective school."

✎ Academics

Haverford academics are a far sight easier than Harvard academics, unless one is to register in Haverford's Haverford/Harvard academic exchange between Haverford, Harvard, Harvey Mudd, and CalTech. So at Haverford, you have the chance to take Harvard courses at Haverford for Haverford credit that also counts toward a degree at Harvard. And Haverford. Past Haverford/Harvard joint grads include Harvey Verd, Vern Lundquist, Harrison Ford, Ford Fairlane, Douglas Fairbanks, Henry Ford, Henry Wadsworth Longfellow, and Harvey Wadsworth Longfellow.

Most Offensive College Mascots

1. The University of Illinois *Fighting Illini*
2. The University of Pennsylvania *Fighting Bitches*
3. The Penn State *Bitches Fighting*
4. The Oberlin College *Drunken Knife-Fighting Hobos*
5. The Northwestern *(Horny) Wildcats*

✎ Student Life

"Hershey Bars for Harvard's Haverford Haters," says one student in Haverford Yard, when asked about the college he attends. "Hershey? That's heresy," retorts another student. "Har de Har Har Haverford Harvard!!!" chortles another student when asked about the new student center being constructed on campus. No one at Haverford has any idea what school they attend—and most like it that way. Haverford or Harvard? Who cares—either way no one is getting out of here alive.

#3 Princeton University

The last of the Big Three, Princeton University was chartered in 1746 and is located right smack in the middle of beautiful post-apocalyptic industrial New Jersey. It was known merely as the College of New Jersey until 1896, when the name was changed to Princeton in order to avoid confusion with the forty-six other schools that were named the College of New Jersey. Most students, however, affectionately refer to the university as "DarkStar" or "Nitro54621" or whatever their America Online screen name happens to be.

Nassau Hall, Princeton's most celebrated building.

Admissions

Each year, Princeton selects its esteemed entering class using only the most rigorous and demanding standards and by studying each application thoroughly to get a better understanding of exactly what each applicant has to offer. "Asian kids are usually pretty smart, right?" says financial aid/admissions officer Kevin McDougalman. "We usually take a bunch of those guys. After that it's pretty much the usual types. Kids with glasses, kids with pocket protectors, kids who wear headgear, that type of thing. Have you ever met a kid who wears a pocket protector that doesn't have an IQ over five hundred or whatever?" The admissions committee also prides itself on selecting a student body that is diverse, but at the same time, a community with similar convictions. Thus Princeton boasts the largest group of people residing in the state of New Jersey who don't like Bruce Springsteen, and accordingly, 76 percent of Princeton students have no soul.

Academics

Students at Princeton take their academics pretty seriously, but all in the spirit of creativity and enlightenment of famous physicist Albert Einstein, who studied there after being denied tenure at Harvard. One of the most interesting facets of Princeton academics is the honor system, in which students divide their exam time between test-taking and keeping their eyes peeled for cheating classmates and a rare opportunity to climb over other students on their way to the top of Princeton's cutthroat academic world. The only thing heavier than the weight of academic responsibility is the weight of the giant chip on every student's shoulder. This chip is lovingly referred to as "the Tiger" and is repainted orange each spring.

Student Life

Princeton is famous for its uniquely divided week, which features "Party Thursdays," "Study Fridays," and "Rent-a-Movie Saturdays." Of course, no mention of Princeton social life would be complete without mention of its world-famous eating clubs. These century-old institutions are distinguished from one another by the amount (in grams) of food eaten by their members. The Sparrow, for instance, boasts toothpick-thin members who barely pick at their food, while The Python contains the most disgustingly obese Princeton students, many of whom cannot move without assistance and must be spoon-fed their multicourse meals by a trained nursing staff.

"You just don't see kids as fat as this at Harvard."

—Python president, Heavy Underfoot

"You can call eating clubs elitist, you can call them strange. But you can't call us late for dinner. I'll be performing at the Larff-Faktory in Akron later this week."

—Walt Woohah

#4 Massachusetts Institute of Technology

"When I think of MIT I think of a pink elephant who lives inside a giant marshmallow and eats computers. But maybe that's just me."

The Massachusetts Institute of Technology is home to the largest collection of sad, yet passionate robots in the country. Originally founded in 1874 to train sad and passionate robots, the buildings and campus went unused for over a century, as a mysterious fund cryptically entitled "the fund" paid for the construction of a vast campus equipped to suit the tastes and demands of teaching mournful, emotionally complex robots.

It is unclear why MIT gears all its top-level facilities to teaching robots who are sad and passionate. With the invention of such robots in 1987, the campus filled up with depressed robots who possessed great depths of feeling. Student 694 acknowledges the tired concept of the sad robot, but that doesn't dull his pain: "I know it is hackneyed for a robot to say he is sad because he wants to be a human, but the truth is I am a very sad robot. Kiss my steely lips."

⚘ Admissions

Robots of any make and model are accepted into MIT as long as they are both melancholy and have a figurative heart that is deep like an ocean. Do you understand sorrow, heartbreak, and *amore* like only a robot can? Maybe MIT is the place for you.

⚘ Academics

Professor 48Z understands where the real learning occurs at MIT: "You can sit in front of a data drive and download all the knowledge in the world, but the real learning is done by meeting robots who come from so many different backgrounds yet are also sad and passionate. It is a once-in-a-lifetime opportunity."

The two possible majors at MIT are Modern Irish Robot Poetry and Science.

⚘ Robot Student Life

The robots at MIT have the same problems as any other human students except that all of the MIT student problems revolve around robot passion and robot sadness. Confused issues of sexuality are not uncommon. Student 28X is a typical example: "I have strong sexual feelings that I cannot fully understand because not only am I a robot but I am also robot gay," said 28X.

"You can joke all you want about robot homosexuality," said 42R, the director of the MIT peer counseling group, "but it is an issue that many robots must face, especially sad, passionate ones." She added, "There are those who say robots don't even have clear distinctions of gender, but that only confuses matters for us. But if we can be honest for a moment, do clear gender lines really exist for any human or are we all on some sort of masculine/feminine continuum? It is something to think about."

#5 Brown University

"There was this one time. Like, it was freshman year or whatever. I remember this class I took with this dude, right. The professor was all blurry and throbbing and I was spinning and spinning. I had to drop out of that class because it was covered in spiders. Now, I've heard people talk about what drug use is like, and this was sort of like that. But this was just a Bio class about spiders."

Founded in the summer of '69 by some hippies and their dogs as a socialist commune, Brown University—or Animal Farm, as it was known then—is an apparent member of the Ivy League. Each Ivy League school has its own hallmark tradition—Harvard its academics, Princeton its pretension, Dartmouth its drinking—and Brown is no different, standing out for its colorful student body who design their own programs of study.

Of famous alums there are many. Would you like to know who? You want to know who went to Brown? Well, how about Frank Johnson '73? Or Steve Smith '83? Or Nicole Anderson '90, Bud Green '91, Tommy Fritz '94, and Kevin Flanagan '97? They are but a small sample of Brown's long tradition of undergraduates who have gone on to found or join hippie free-love communes.

Brown is a special place, full of special people. Brown wants its students to be independent learners, independent thinkers, and independent people. That is why there are no core requirements, no requirements in each major, no grades, and no curriculum, no classes, and no jobs for graduates. Also, no Pepsi in the student union, which sucks.

☾ Admissions

Getting into Brown isn't easy. Those accepted usually are ranked high in their high school class, have higher SATs, and participate in a variety of extracurriculars, from poetry workshops to theater productions to literary publications. But they all share one thing in common: a desire to go to a school where they will not have to do any work. Not a single one of them has ever done a hard day's work in their entire lives. Their hands are uncallused, their fingernails finely manicured, their skin supple and soft. And these fiercely independent spirits are the essential character of a Brown education.

☾ Academics

Brown's academic program is all about freedom. There are no requirements, and any course may be taken pass/fail. While for some this lack of control would result in unstructured time spent in silly pursuits, Brown students are independent learners. And all this freedom

🎓 Top 5 Places to "Eat" in the USA

1. Massachusetts Institute of Technology (MIT), Denny's
2. California Institute of Technology, Jack in the Box
3. Carnegie-Mellon University, Denny's
4. Rensselaer Polytechnic Institute, Denny's
5. Worcester Polytechnic Institute, my grandma's house

and the lack of requirements tend to still produce some amazing graduates, like author Jennifer Rumsey '88 and writer Frank Nelson '90. One summa cum laude graduate had this to say about Brown's academic program: "I can't read! Never could! I have a degree in English literature! I love this place!"

Student Life

Student social life at Brown is lively, unlike many of its Ivy League cousins, where students tend to spend valuable "socializing" time with books in the library (blech!). Thankfully, Brown blew up the library and all the books in it to make way for the pub/dance club, where on a typical Saturday night you can find nearly half the student body and most of the faculty partially nude and almost invariably on drugs. The vibrant social scene is what attracts many students to Brown in the first place. "What I learned at Brown, I learned from my fellow students. It makes sense, you know, because they're all so smart and I never went to any classes," said one recent Phi Beta Kappa graduate. In short, if you go to Brown, you will have a fun time. Most students are also socially conscious, at least as much as they can be without any newspapers to read, and it is not uncommon to find students volunteering at local homeless shelters or marching in an Earth Day parade, usually during a final exam or the funeral of a close family member.

#6 Colorado School of Mining Technology

"The thing I like best [cough, cough] *about the Colorado* [cough, cough] *School of* [cough, cough, cough] *Mining is the* [cough, cough, cough, cough, COUGH, cough, cough, cough, cough, cough] *students."*

Grab a prairie dog to chaw on, cowpoke, and lissen up. As the chief sp'lunker 'round these parts, it's my lot to larn ya on the ways of the Col'rada School of Mining Technology. Col'rada School of Mining Technology was founded way back 'round the yar eighteen hundred and sixty, by an orn'ry old minehound who went by the name a Deaf Joe. Folks 'round here thawt he was damn near the ugliest codger theyd'a ever seen. Some of tha townsfolks, who weren't as respectable as they are now, useta tell ole Joe that even Mrs. McGarnicle's lame dog Charlie was prettier than he was. After 'bout thirty years a this, Deaf Joe had enuff. Next night, he gawt damned drunk and that ole bastard went out and tied the damn dog up to a lamppost. Legend is, he left a piece a Grade A sirloin right whare the dog couldn' reach it, for 'bouts fourteen days. Damn dog near died, till Deaf Joe's wife Wilma came an' let the dog go. When my great-granpappy asked him a why he did it, Deaf Joe only sed, "I may be uglier than that goddamned dog, but I durn sure ain't as hungry." Har har har har, if that don't tickle yer ribs, you must be dead. Well, I'se still don't know why they call him Deaf Joe ('stead of Ugly Joe) or what tha hell Deaf Joe was tryin' ta prove with that dang dog bizness, but the moral of that story is that Deaf Joe founded the Col'rada School of Mining Technology the next morning.

⟲ Academics

Students at that Col'rada School of Mining Technology are somatha best in the nation. What we look for in one of them young fellers is well rounded . . . Sheeeeet, that reminds me of a young cowpoke who went by the moniker of Limber Tim. Limber Tim blew inta town 'round about nineteen hundred and twenty . . . well, I think it was 'round bout's twenty-three. Limber Tim gots his name on accounts of tha ways his limbs flew round his body when his horse Trixie, who was meaner 'n a Arizona Rattlesnake, threw him off every time he gots on. My granpappy woke up one mornin' to drain his lizard, and I'll be a drunk Injun if'n Limber Tim didna have a mattress next to his horse. And damn near ev'ry time that Trixie threw him off, he'd a land right on tha mattress sof' as a feather, git up, and try agin. Sheeee-it! My granpappy laughed so damn hard he damn near pissed in his own eye. The moral of tha' story? The Colorado School of Mining Technology examines your grades, but is certain to factor in the level of difficulty of your chosen academic curriculum.

⟲ Student Life

Student Life? Student Life!! Didja hear the one 'bout Billy Bob Rowster? Course ya didn', cuz that dang fool's dead! Coot was too busy lookin' at tha young ladies when he should'sa been watchin' his back. Some say Billy Bob's ghost still haunts tha Youngstown Mines. Not sure iffn I b'lieve it, but ya won't catch me thares any times soon. Say, I b'lieve it was 'xactly ten years ago tonight that he died . . . anyways, the brand-new 45-million-dollar Student Activities Center is located in the cemetery next to the Youngstown Mines.

"Goddam you, Red! I'm not leavin' you down here to die. Put your arms around me so I can take you home to your baby girl."

"Did you hear that Colorado School of Mining Technology has a 16:1 student-to-teacher ratio?"

#7 Cornell University

"Where is my goddamn shower cap? How dare you call this Cornell/Howard Johnson's."

Although when most people think of Cornell they think of the university's outstanding hotel management program, what most don't realize is that Cornell itself, founded in 1910 by the legendary Howard Johnson, existed for nearly sixty years as nothing more than an affordable HoJo's Motel and Restaurant, ten miles off Interstate 52 between Ithaca and Plinlakey. Explains Cornell graduate Samuel J. HolidayInn '34, "When I came to Cornell in '32, my wife and I had just a lovely stay. The service was excellent and the swimming pool was spacious and just the right temperature."

⟲ Admissions

Cornell's application, which differs only slightly from that of other Ivy League schools, is composed primarily of a Howard Johnson's Motel and Restaurant application form and interview. Admissions officer and assistant branch supervisor Ellen Radisson stated, "Well right now, we're pretty short on weekend staff, so if you can work Saturday or Sunday it really helps out."

STOP!

☙ Academics

The school's motto, "Clean rooms, free HBO, swimming pool, and continental breakfast," pretty much exemplifies Cornell's dedication to higher academic learning. School president, Timmy Econolodge '34, explains, "Although Cornell may no longer be a Howard Johnson's Motel per se, we do nonetheless still believe strongly in the principles upon which this university was founded: providing temporary shelter for those who need it most, passing tourists."

☙ Student Life

According to Cornell undergraduates, the biggest myth surrounding the university is the belief that students here are free to choose from Cornell's more than fifty majors. "Nope. Although I registered freshman year for a couple of English classes and a history course, I was put into 'Free ESPN and ESPN2; Which to choose, the Mothership or the Deuce?' and 'Room Service 10: Careful with the Coffee!' " explained sophomore Billy Joe Motel6.

Cornell believes that freshman students who do enroll in the university's hotel management program (about 98–103 percent do) should learn the job from the ground up. Keeping with this Oxford-style, seminar-based learning philosophy, freshmen often find themselves cleaning the urine-infested hot tub or changing the sheets for Mr. and Mrs. Ihnot in Room 32 who come down from Buffalo each weekend to visit the casinos.

Although Ithaca isn't exactly Albany in terms of culture and excitement, students do find ways to keep busy on the weekends. "I usually work the midnight shift here at the HoJo's on Sunday. Whatever, game room, free ice, there's a soda machine on the second floor. All I've gotta do is keep an eye on the desk. Pretty sweet setup," explained senior Samuel RedRoofInn '02.

☙ The Premise of This Comedy Piece

So is Cornell the place for you? Well, if you're looking for a low hourly rate and little chance of promotion then Econo Lodge is probably your best bet. But if you want to work at a Howard Johnson's in upstate New York, then Cornell University/A Howard Johnson's in upstate N.Y. is the place for you.

#8 Columbia University

"What I look for in a college is new friends, stimulating discussions, and the challenges of living in a developing country. I got all this and more at Columbia."

Columbia was founded by famed Portuguese conquistador Hernando Cortés in the year 1517. After dispensing with the pesky Inca population, Cortés founded a colonial regime that served to train the white population of Columbia to ensure that the indigenous population will never rise up again and slay the criollos with their bloody tomahawks and backward pagan belief. Today, Columbia has a gross national product of 4.6 billion Columbian pesos, 3.5 million inhabitants, *caliente* weather, and a diminishing rainforest. After the Esquivel cartel was brought down in 1985 by the Columbian police and the Columbia Parliamentary Debate Society, the core curriculum was established with little bloodshed. Columbia senior

Alejandro Rodriquez, when asked about his Columbia experience, had this to say: "No, no talking. I must slaughter the pigs before Don Trujillo brings the whip."

Academics

Students at Columbia praise the academic life at their school for a variety of reasons, but almost all of them note the influence that the mandatory Columbia Survival Course (CSC) played in their lives. One of the first of its kind, the CSC pits seven first-year students against the wilds of the rainforest. Left only to their wits, students are forced to find their way back to base camp—and end up making friendships that will last a lifetime. As sophomore Tony Hawk put it, "One of my earliest memories of Columbia involves the time Caleb Jones, Frank Harris, and I found ourselves lost in the forest, running for our lives from the infamous Columbian Flying Rat-Beetle. Caleb never made it out alive, but Frank and I are still fraternity brothers."

Student Life

It is important to note that fully 83 percent of the students at Columbia have a term-time job, often working side by side with members of the community. Cal Rivers remembers the first time he wielded a machete: "I was a little scared, but if I cleared an acre by dawn, Zito would give me a crisp 100-dollar bonus!" If machetes are not to your tastes, rest assured that at Columbia you can also burn, hack, and slay the surrounding countryside.

To keep up school spirit, students at Columbia are required to participate in a variety of intramural sports. Prestigious awards are given each semester, such as the Adidas Cup given to the student who can sew the most shoes in forty-five minutes. Other intramural activities include mango picking, mango scrubbing, mango packing, soccer, and mango canning.

"AH! My palms bleed from the cane."
> —Andres Pastrana, 21, Biochemical Sciences

"Llevo pantalones en el invierno."
> —Chico Nooni, 35, is learning English slowly

Is Your School Safe? An Alphabetical Listing of Colleges

1. Abilene Christian College
2. Adams College
3. Adelphi University
4. Adrian College
5. Agnes Scott College
6. Alabama Agricultural and Mechanical University
7. Alaska Pacific University
8. Albany State College
9. Albion College
10. Alcorn State

Least Sexually Active

1. College of St. Francis of Assisi
2. Mort Bruno Men's College for Homophobes
3. Brown University

#9 The Etten Family Home Schooling College

"I can't imagine having gone anywhere else. I knew I wanted to be kind of close to home, and EFHSC has just been the perfect fit."

—Kevin Etten '01

Founded in 1998 by Tom and Mary Etten, the Etten Family Home Schooling College (EFHSC) was created to provide its undergraduate with a solid liberal arts education and a firmer sense of the importance of family. Also, someone had to cut the lawn.

Located at 6704 Sioux Trail in Edina, Minnesota (a suburb of Minneapolis), EFHSC's sprawling campus boasts two bathrooms, three spacious bedrooms, a recently refurbished kitchen, deck, and patio, a cozy family room, and a lovely yard complete with a swing set and sandbox. "I never thought I'd be saying this, but EFHSC really feels like home," said undergraduate Kevin Etten.

Admissions

Contrary to popular belief, EFHSC is quite competitive, usually only accepting one out of every seven applicants. Explained admissions officer Tom Etten, "Last year six of Kevin's brothers applied and we just didn't have room for any of them."

The importance of legacy? "I don't care whose kid you are," said university president Mary Etten, "without the grades and ability to cut the lawn and sort paper from plastic, you're just not getting in."

Academics

The faculty-to-student ratio at the Etten Family Home Schooling College is one of the lowest in the country, nearly 2:1. "Me and the rest of the staff, namely my husband, Tom, make sure we give our undergraduate all the attention he needs," stated Mendellsohn Professor of Chemistry, Biology, Physics, Comparative Literature, Spanish, Sociology, Anthropology, Economics, and Linguistics, Mary Etten.

"I don't know too much about Germany, and I've never really met any Germans or anything like that," said German Lit. professor Tom Etten, "but if that's what Kevin wants to major in, that's fine by me. As a father, I'll be extremely proud to say my boy learned the German literature."

Student Life

EFHSC, famous for its bustling extracurricular scene, offers its student the opportunity to explore the world, whether by taking out the trash, emptying the recycling bin, or sorting paper and plastic into the proper receptacle.

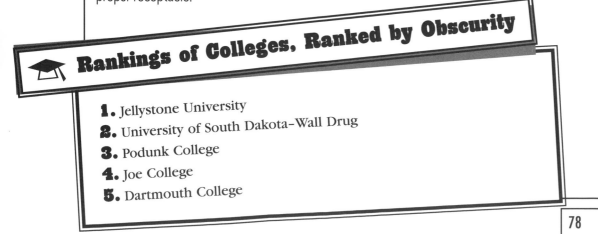

Rankings of Colleges, Ranked by Obscurity

1. Jellystone University
2. University of South Dakota–Wall Drug
3. Podunk College
4. Joe College
5. Dartmouth College

☙ Onanism

From masturbating to masturbating with your parents in the next room to masturbating quickly when your parents go out for groceries, most EFHSC students masturbate roughly 3.8 times a day. "I did it four times yesterday," explained senior Kevin Etten. "I'm hoping to do twelve in one day. Maybe if my parents go out of town or something."

"Coming to EFHSC has shattered my mind. I wouldn't trade it for the most prestigious community college in the world."

—Kevin Etten '01

"Hi, Mom. What time's dinner gonna be ready? I'm hungry."

—Kevin Etten '01

#10 The Juilliard School of Performing Arts

"I finally found a place where everyone else shares my interests. It's a place where I can communicate through my piano, since neither me nor any of my classmates n'ain't never learned no how to talk right proper."

The Juilliard School is America's foremost college for musicians, dancers, and artists. It is not meant for people who can read, write, or function properly in social situations. Although Juilliard has no minimum or maximum age limit for incoming students, applicants to the Drama, Music, and Dance departments must be high school graduates or equivalent. Rest assured, then, that Juilliard is not just for young prodigies who've never interacted with other children their age. Instead, you can expect jaded older prodigies who have suffered, friendless and ostracized, through years of public school, interacting with four-year-old figure drawers and thirty-five-year-old drug-addict playwrights.

☙ Admissions

Juilliard does not require the SAT, ACT, or SAT IIs. Admission is based on competitive auditions held on the following dates:

- ✔ Conducting . . . . January/February (Please see application for specific dates.)
- ✔ Dance . . . . 12th birthday
- ✔ Music . . . . Kindergarten
- ✔ Directing . . . . First baby molar
- ✔ Playwriting . . . . Exit from womb

☙ Academics

Don't be fooled by the "performance" aspect of Juilliard's reputation. Most of a student's curriculum at Juilliard is in traditional academic areas. Many classes are devoted to the liberal arts, and almost half of a student's courses are centered on Juilliard's "Social Un-Retarding" program, an effort to somehow make their students more than useless in the real world. The SUR program includes such classes as "Talking Like Regulars," "Not Wearing Inappropriate Clothes," and "Your Face Is Not a Proper Canvas for Crazy Drawings."

"I learned how to make friends through the SUR program! But I forgot."

"The music tells me how to point; dance is only a spiritual outlet for my bodily humors."

Student Life

The entirety of Juilliard's campus lies in the heart of New York City, inside the Lincoln Center building. But this does not mean Juilliard students lack the facilities of real colleges. Students are housed in the New York State Theatre, just down the street, and take their meals in the New York Public Library for the Performing Arts. Juilliard sports, including Treadmill, Stationary Bicycle, and Jumping Jacks, take place in the athletic quad (Metropolitan Opera House). Needless to say, most Juilliard students are well-adjusted agents of creativity by the time they graduate.

"What's this?"

—Devon McNeely, cellist, pointing to a friendly dog

"And what's this?!"

—Kaylie Stevens, soprano, pointing to a car

"Is this what the Internet looks like? Because I've never touched a computer in my life."

—Jean-Louis Hall

Best Schools for a Degree in Marketing

1. The All-New University of California-Riverside: "Learning Excitement!"
2. University of Kansas: "Now with X-tra N-dowment!"
3. Williams College: "A Revolution in Education Technology"
4. University of Vermont: "No additives [foreigners]"
5. From the creators who brought you *Speed, The Haunting,* and *Con Air,* Jan DeBont, Jerry Bruckheimer, and Wildstorm Pictures invite you to visit . . . The College of William and Mary. This time, the terror is real.

Most Sexually Active

1. Vassar College
2. The Venus Institute for Better Loving
3. The College of Room 16 in Secrets Motel
4. Prostitute

#11 United States Military Academy at West Point

"The people I've met at West Point are all so different, so amazing, and yet we're all united by one, strong bond: We all want to kill other people."

—Owen Bloodmore '03

Founded in 1802 by Otto von Bismarck, the United States Military Academy—or West Point, as it is commonly known—is the oldest American service academy after the United States Coast Guard Academy. The tradition of honor and service, the enriching educational experience, and the sense of larger purpose are the foremost features that attract the finest of American youth each year. Close second are the over 1 million rounds of ammunition and 50,000 tons of high explosive used in the course of a single day's classes. The mission of West Point is simple: to prepare the finest Army officers who will be ready and able to defend selflessly the United States from all enemies, both foreign and domestic, while the rest of the degenerate, tree-hugging, egg-sucking, sandal-wearing, granola-eating commie pinkos continue to attack the American Way of Life. The character of the typical cadet is summed up best in the oath each takes on the first day of class: "I will not lie, cheat, or steal, nor will I tolerate those who do." As a recent cadet put it: "WHAT?!? I CAN'T HEAR YOU OVER THE HOWITZERS!!"

Of famous alumni there is no shortage; many are great military and political leaders, including George Washington (class of 1768), Dwight Eisenhower (class of 1945), Robert E. Lee (class of 1986), and Joseph Stalin (class of 1924, United States Military Academy—Moscow). Still others occupy almost all walks of life, from noted social critics like Frank Zenner (class of 1978) to artists like Elton John (class of 1967) to doctors like Dr. Strangelove (class of 1952). Since 1979 women have graduated from West Point to be commissioned as privates in the nursing corps. While some male cadets have lamented the passing of an era of chivalrous manhood fostered in an all-male environment, most others have been concerned with the groping of female cadets.

♻ Admissions

Getting into West Point isn't easy. Out of last year's class of 1,534 students, over 75 percent were in the top 25 percent of their high school class. On top of that, there were 700 team captains, 1,500 lettermen, 300 Eagle Scouts, and 1 editor of the high school poetry review.

There are many steps to applying: the actual application, the interview, a congressional nomination, and the grueling Iron Man Triathlon. If you're among the 67 percent who make the grade, you'll be entering the hallowed halls of the world's finest institute of higher killing machine learning. Remember that if you are accepted at West Point, you will have to decide whether you want to serve your country or flee to Canada.

"If I had paid more attention during my West Point classes, I might not have been such a murderous dictator. Maybe."

—Joseph Stalin

Academics

In addition to a grueling academic workload, cadets also receive a "physical education" as well, epitomized most in the torturous first year as a "plebe." Physical exhaustion and mental torture are the hallmarks of this year. "Ahhhhhh!" yelled one nameless cadet on his way to more torture. By the end of one's time at West Point, a typical cadet has jumped from airplanes, rappelled from helicopters, shot a missile launcher, run 4,000 miles, lifted 3 million pounds, sweated 200 gallons of water, and is pronounced physically unable to serve in the Army. A current upperclassman in the middle of his "cow" (third) year had this to say about the academic experience at West Point: "By the time an underclassman reaches his 'cow' year, his brain has turned into the largest muscle in his body."

Student Life

Many people think that the phrase "West Point social life" is an oxymoron. They couldn't be more wrong! Where else are you going to get up each day, run five miles, be yelled at, go to breakfast, be yelled at, go to classes, shoot guns, be yelled at, jump from an airplane, be shouted at, pass out from heat exhaustion, be yelled at, and be yelled at? Also, let's not forget that each Saturday at 0500 (that's 5:00 A.M. to you landlubbers), the schedule calls for twenty minutes of social life before an eight-mile run through a minefield. What you got, Ohio State?!?

"The friends I've made at West Point are the only people in the world I don't want to shoot and kill."

"I absolutely loved all my classes! In my Ancient History class we read Gibbon, in my English class we read Pynchon, and in my Engineering class we built a real motor! It wasn't long before I realized that my life's calling was as a highly trained killing machine in the 101st Airborne!"

"Did anyone mention the guns? So awesome!"

#12 Stanford University

Nestled amidst the swaying palms of Palo Alto, California, Stanford University is one of the most prestigious institutions in the country. Although Stanford's academics are considered top-notch, nothing can stop these California girls and boys from living the laid-back idyllic life of the Golden State. While students at Ivy League schools might be most easily found studying in libraries, Stanford undergrads are more likely to be seen resting in one of the school's 8,000 hammocks or taking a midday siesta atop a burro behind the science building.

Academics

Stanford's academic departments boast high-quality teaching from world-famous award-winning faculty members in nearly all fields. But Stanford students are not the type to "boast" or "brag" or "do things" or "use words." Indeed, the typical Stanford student would fervently make a case that learning need not even take place in classrooms. All classes meet in silence on the sand volleyball courts in the residential quad. Students and faculty alternate between playing round-robin volleyball tourneys and lazily sipping margaritas on the sidelines.

Student Life

Stanford takes pride in its balance between high achievement and a vibrant social atmosphere. Students are just as likely to kick back and drink a brew while pondering sixteenth-century philosophy as they are to kick back and drink a brew while watching hoops on ESPN2. Popular activities include "hanging out," "chilling," "sittin' around," "kicking back," "taking five," "hibernating," and "hibernating with margaritas in a hammock on a burro."

Athletics

Athletics at Stanford figure prominently, and coaches proudly point to the successes of John Elway, who not only set numerous NCAA records as a quarterback but starred in baseball as well. "Elway was like Superman or something, you know?" says junior wrestler Lou Tootles. "So we figure we might as well just watch tapes of Elway's games rather than try to top his achievements. 'Cuz it's not gonna happen." Athletics at Stanford are more than just reliving Elway's stardom, however. Pizza night is a highlight of Thursdays, and the basketball team has an annual slumber party during which they watch the national tournament on TV.

#13 Amherst College

"The thing that makes Amherst different from all the Ivies and top-notch schools is not the quality of its academics, the depth of its student body, or its facilities. The difference is that Amherst is teeny-tiny."

Indeed, Amherst College prides itself on its size—or rather lack thereof. In contrast to other schools of the same caliber, Amherst offers an academic program of the highest quality in a much more intimate setting. The Amherst campus is only three inches wide, twelve inches long, and four inches deep, found in a crack in a rock somewhere on the campus of the University of Massachusetts at Amherst. It is here that the fanciful mysteries of Amherst unfold.

Contrary to popular belief, Amherst College is the oldest institution of higher learning in the world. Students leading campus tours are quick to point out that Amherst pre-dates time itself, and only recently has it been situated in its current site at Amherst, Massachusetts. For thousands upon thousands of years, Amherst College was simply part of the mysterious ether that surrounds us. It has survived attacks by hundreds of beasties, and its secrets have been passed down by fairies and other creatures of ethereal fancy. Amherst also offers an excellent program in English Literature and Language.

Admissions

The biggest challenge involved in applying to Amherst College is finding the admissions office. Head down the main entrance of the crevice (campus). At the third patch of moss, take a left. The elf standing on the miniature griffin is the dean of the college, Farolk. Say hi! Get out of your car, recite the proper incantation (Farolk will tell you for the mere price of 30 blippees), and ride the worm until you see a perfectly lifelike hologram of that which you fear most. The Office of Admissions is now directly behind and below you.

Academics

Classes at Amherst are, like the college itself, quite small. The average class consists of less than ten students, and, of course, one professor, one winged creature, and three minotaurs. The most popular class at Amherst, by far, is taught by Professor Eroa Velkax, a talking dog. Velkax's class, on the legend of the Rheingold, is actually interactive, for the students of the class are actually the keepers of the Rheingold—a responsibility not taken lightly by Amherstians, who are all descendants of an enlightened, immortal sect of quasi-humans chosen by the overlord Zoorb. Zoorb was the first valedictorian of Amherst, in the Year of the Sunlit Lily.

Amherst students are also eligible for a number of amazing field trips. Last year, for example, one class even traveled to a nearby clover patch. The 4-million-nanometer trek took more than three days, but, as one student put it, "It was worth it! I nearly lost my Haïlou!"

"The classroom experience here is an opportunity of a lifetime. I am less than one inch tall."

"The Amherst campus is as beautiful as the academics are fulfilling. The campus looks like shit."

🐣 Student Life

One popular Amherst T-shirt reads, "Amherst College: Mortals Need Not Apply!" Unfortunately, Amherst students are essentially unable to wear such shirts. School policy strictly forbids any act or words making fun of the less fortunate; moreover, students would be essentially unable to wear any "shirt" at all, given their bodies' nonhuman forms. Regardless, this T-shirt points out Amherst's twisted sense of humor, which students have used to fend away Sirens and ants alike.

The most popular student activities are not visible to the human eye, as they take place in a dimension created many moons before the passing of the Rolog, by Amherst student Olo Lol. It is rumored, however, that the Fates often attend said activities, weaving our futures as they watch Lord Jeffs do whatever it is they do.

"I'm afraid if I told you what happened at Amherst, I'd have to ask Atropos to cut your thread of life."

—Clotho

"I will say one thing about social life at Amherst. The weed you can get here will knock you on your ass."

—Blake Toomey '04

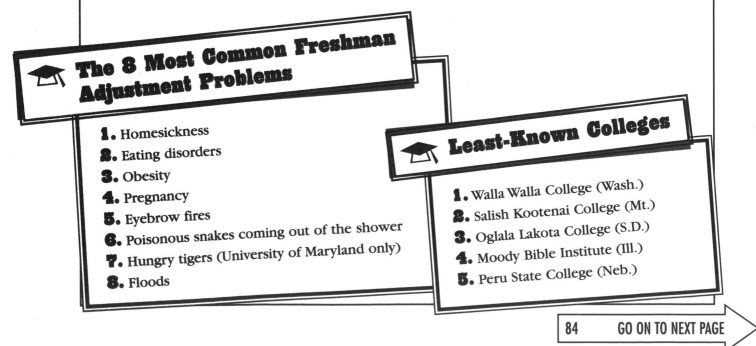

🎓 The 8 Most Common Freshman Adjustment Problems

1. Homesickness
2. Eating disorders
3. Obesity
4. Pregnancy
5. Eyebrow fires
6. Poisonous snakes coming out of the shower
7. Hungry tigers (University of Maryland only)
8. Floods

🎓 Least-Known Colleges

1. Walla Walla College (Wash.)
2. Salish Kootenai College (Mt.)
3. Oglala Lakota College (S.D.)
4. Moody Bible Institute (Ill.)
5. Peru State College (Neb.)

Bikini College

Learning + Bikinis = Success!

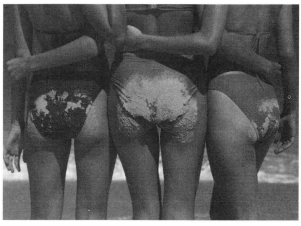

- **Interested in higher learning, while wearing a bikini?**
- **Are you tired of going to school with people who don't wear bikinis?**
- **Looking to wear a bikini 24 hours a day, 365 days a year?**
- **Then a degree from Bikini College could be for you!**

Bikini U Academics: Where learning isn't just about memorizing facts and taking tests, but also involves wearing bikinis.

Bikini U Athletics: We have the best beach volleyball team in the world.

Bikini U Social Life: And you thought the Ivy League was sophisticated!

Bikini U Graduates: Succeeding in the real world!

#14 Duke University

Like a budding tobacco leaf in midspring, Duke University bursts forth from the Carolina landscape with a richness of body and flavor. Careful scholarship, energetic athletics, and vibrant spirit are rolled up into one sweet college, built with a generous endowment from the Duke family of tobacco magnates. You'll surely want to take a long, deep drag and inhale "Dukeness," an abstract quality that cannot be inhaled.

Admissions

To apply to Duke University, you must first present your credentials to the doorman. The preliminary fox-hunt will eliminate all but the most worthy of prospective applicants. The rigorous three-hour test on Tradition will follow. Once a handful of meritorious candidates has been decided upon, a white-jacketed manservant will inform them of the university's decision. None of them will be admitted, as admission is strictly hereditary.

Academics

"Studies are a fine matter for a body to pursue," declares sophomore Hampton T. Bradylions. Duke's philosophy has long held that learning is an integral part of a college education. "A man not willing to engage in scholarly pursuits needs to be firmly cudgeled with a hitting-switch of pine-oak," says a well-heeled Peachtree McHugh, angrily waving his white gloves. "Why, such a character is no gentleman at all." "I can hardly conceive of a more central notion than scholarship," murmured junior Lucy Louise Stonewall Beauregard as she rode sidesaddle through a well-furnished parlor.

Classes at Duke consist of occasional gatherings to sip mint juleps and make declarations about how hot it is.

Student Life

Among auburn groves and beneath sweeping verandas, Duke students declare that "every day is a cotillion." Indeed, every day at Duke there are upward of forty-four cotillions, and hourly debutante balls. Full-breasted specimens of Southern manhood smoke and engage in turkey shoots, while ladies fan themselves and knit things. Senior Bedford Forest Longstreet notes, "Here at Duke, the cigarettes are unfiltered, the cigars are as fat as a Carolina hog, and the mint juleps are made of tobacco." The smell of menthol wafts from one student ballroom to another as carriages jostle along the shaded paths.

Athletics

"Oh baby, HOOP IT UP!!!" screeches Pickett Tidewater, a Blue Devil tattooed to his face. "Duke b-ball is coming at you like a hurricane! Whatchyougonna do?" exclaims Daisy Buckridge Jubilee as she dunks her parasol over powerless defenders. "We don't play basketball, we *is* basketball!" hollers sophomore Robert E. Lee as he fires off a dueling pistol in celebration. "I do not understand this," yells Jefferson Raleigh III, before charging inside on a break and finding the hole with a sweet tomahawk jam.

"Pardon that basketball nonsense," remarks Naseby Marlborough as he bids us a fare-thee-well, and rides away on a Virginia possum while smoking ten cigarettes.

#15 University of Michigan

Most people know that the University of Michigan is one of the finest schools in the country, but everyone knows that it is the alma mater of the one and only James Earl Jones. Ever since the famed character actor walked through the hallowed halls of the university, his influence has been immeasurable. The most distinctive voice in Hollywood, Mr. Distinctive Voice as he is better known, or simply "the big black man with a plan," Mr. Jones is the centerpiece of all academic and social life at the University of Michigan.

Portraying the deep bellowing voice of Darth Vader in *Star Wars* and the paternal karate coach in *Best of the Best* have been highlights of Mr. Jones's career and hence highlights in the history of the U of M. As one student put it, "Have you ever seen *Star Wars*? Then you know what it is like to go to the University of Michigan."

"I say balls to Notre Dame and their silly traditions. Ghost of Knute Rockne? More like the ghost of the guy who played the second bombardier in *Dr. Strangelove*."
—James Earl Jones

☙ Admissions

The University of Michigan admissions process can be intimidating, especially since every application is read by James . . . Garner! Gotcha.

☙ Academics

Professors attempt to dress up their classes to make them more appealing. Classes include "James Earl Jones Presents Physics 115b: Particle Physics," and "The History of England 1910 to 1945, James Earl Jones Style." All these classes rule! These classes differ in few respects from their counterparts at other universities, but all students are expected to apply a James Earl Jones sticker to their textbooks and professors are required to wear JEJ masks during lectures and office hours. The professors must do their throatiest James Earl Jones impressions whenever speaking. Even the ladies!

☙ Student Life

The University of Michigan is one of the largest schools in the country. But it is such a large school that there is a niche for everyone if you know where to look. Whether you enjoy *The Exorcist 2: The Heretic*, *Soul Man*, commercials for CNN, or the deep menacing baritone of Darth Vader, you will find the crowd with which you can "hang." A rising liberal sentiment amongst students has made them more accepting of different groups: "If you want to dislike James Earl Jones that is fine. You will no longer be labeled as a reckless deviant for preferring the thespian stylings of James Woods. Since being deviant is also fine then it was never really problematic to dislike Mr. Jones. Yeah, everything's cool at U of Michigan. Awesome," said Owen Ellickson, leader of the Liberal Student Union.

Said Michigan sophomore Jake Lundberg, "Student life at the University of Michigan is like the martial arts classic *Best of the Best*. You get to see some tit, some karate fighting, and underneath it all is King Shit himself, James Earl Jones." In contrast, the rival school Ohio State is "like the *Best of the Best 2*—maybe you get a glimpse at some boobs, and, sure, there is some karate fighting and enough Christopher Penn to satisfy, but no James Earl Jones . . . the weakest of the *Best of the Best* series." The fact that the rather doughy physique of Christopher Penn was cast in the *Best of the Best* to perform the deadly maneuvers of karate fighting still perplexes many Michigan students.

#16 Dartmouth College

"Dartmouth and I are a perfect match. The winters are gorgeous, the campus is intimate and inviting, and the academics are stellar. I really hope I get taken off the waiting list."

—Tina Buckle '05

Dartmouth College has spent recent years recovering from the blows of controversy. Issues regarding conservative politics, racism, and fraternities have given the public the impression of a campus divided. And though students will certainly acknowledge the presence of some infighting, there is one common bond that unites the school and supersedes any petty debate: jumping. They love it. Even the school's motto presents a telling example: *"Vox clamantis in deserto."* While this means "a voice crying in the wilderness" to memorialize freshman Spunky Carter, who was lost on a hike, the second-place choice for the motto was *"Dartmouth Jumps!"*

The ninth-oldest school in the nation, Dartmouth was founded by the legendary athlete Dick Fosbury, who ushered high-jumping into a new era with his "Fosbury Flop," and later revolutionized hopscotch by inventing hopping. Originally an institution for educating Native Americans, Dartmouth quickly branched out to accept any male who agreed "to become a scholar and practitioner of jumping, the awesome sport." Today, Dartmouth is recognized as the premier school for lovers of saltation while still featuring a curriculum in Native American Studies, which is based within the fenced boundaries of the parched dust plains just outside Hanover.

Admissions

Admission to Dartmouth is, like other elite schools, choosy and somewhat unpredictable. A student with a 1500 SAT could easily be waitlisted. That same score paired with a 25-inch vertical, however, is nearly a lock for acceptance. Last year's freshman class boasted 40 National Merit Scholarship winners, but admissions is even more proud of its 113 admittees who can dunk a basketball two-handed, second in the nation only to the University of Kentucky. It is recommended that applicants raise their stock by performing squat-thrusts for quadriceps power. Applications are due January 1, while the scouting combine and Hop-a-thon take place the first weekend in March.

Academics

Dartmouth students and administrators speak proudly of the unique "D Plan," in which students select three out of four semesters a year in which to take classes. The final semester is capped by the "D Drill," in which sophomores and seniors dip their hands in chalk dust and take running jumps at the gymnasium wall, trying to slap their hands as high up as possible.

The college boasts a world-famous academics center surrounding Baker Library, named after Bootsy Baker, nicknamed "Air" Baker for his mad rise and his love of breathing air. The library boasts the world's largest collection of the book *Slippy Frog's Hoppy Day* and the *Jump Start!* series of instructional books.

Student Life

A Dartmouth student defines the social life as such: "If by Greek life you mean that we love to jump, then you can call me Persephone! We are also overrun with frats." Students divide their time between double-dutch, the standing broad jump, and wine-tastings on Fraternity Row. The administration encourages these pastimes, providing students with free Strength Shoes and Skip-Its. This undoubtedly contributes to the high overall student happiness.

GO ON TO NEXT PAGE

"Dartmouth professors give each and every student the individual attention they need. The lectures are usually fascinating and organized, and they are delivered as the professor simultaneously hops back and forth over a hole in the ground."

—Jackie Joyner-Kersee '04

"Some people would say that a college in which 90 percent of the students major in Jumping is a bad college. Well, Dartmouth may be 'bad' in the realm of scholarship and mind enrichment, but our calves are huge."

—Benny Jumjar '03

"This weekend I'm just getting ass-drunk and then I'm gonna freaking jump some rope! Go Dartmouth!"

—Gail Roland '02

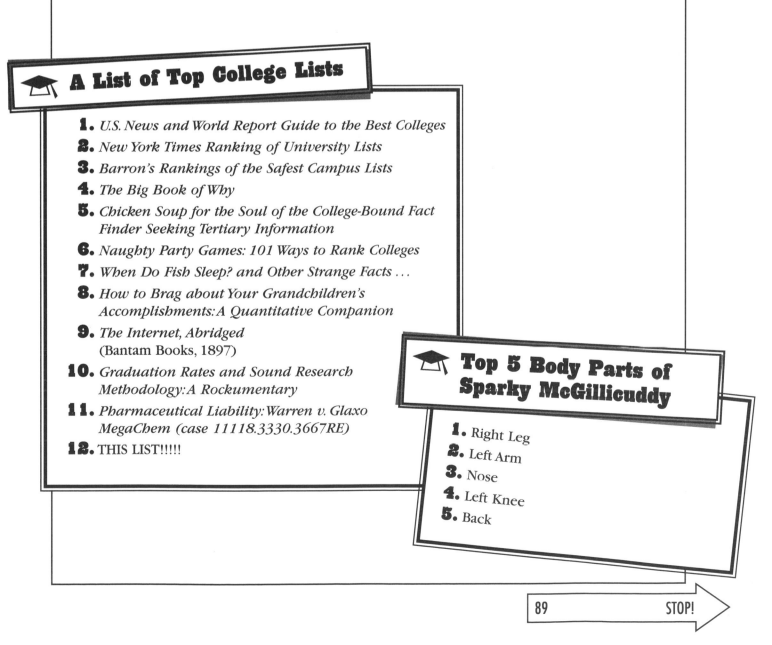

A List of Top College Lists

1. *U.S. News and World Report Guide to the Best Colleges*
2. *New York Times Ranking of University Lists*
3. *Barron's Rankings of the Safest Campus Lists*
4. *The Big Book of Why*
5. *Chicken Soup for the Soul of the College-Bound Fact Finder Seeking Tertiary Information*
6. *Naughty Party Games: 101 Ways to Rank Colleges*
7. *When Do Fish Sleep? and Other Strange Facts . . .*
8. *How to Brag about Your Grandchildren's Accomplishments: A Quantitative Companion*
9. *The Internet, Abridged* (Bantam Books, 1897)
10. *Graduation Rates and Sound Research Methodology: A Rockumentary*
11. *Pharmaceutical Liability: Warren v. Glaxo MegaChem (case 11118.3330.3667RE)*
12. THIS LIST!!!!!

Top 5 Body Parts of Sparky McGillicuddy

1. Right Leg
2. Left Arm
3. Nose
4. Left Knee
5. Back

#17 Johns Hopkins

"Hopkins has given me the opportunity to take classes in a number of disciplines, and lead Division I in assists per game. Not bad!"

Although Hopkins is known primarily for its graduate programs, it has also gained a reputation as a prepro-fessional powerhouse. So if you're looking to get a great education and prepare for the job market at the same time, Hopkins might be for you. If, on the other hand, you're looking to play some serious collegiate lacrosse, then Hopkins is *definitely* for you.

Admissions

And with returning senior stars Joe and Bill Thomas, Hopkins lacrosse should vie for a piece of the national crown.

Academics

With the country's most distinguished undergraduate program, Johns Hopkins is truly a pioneer in the burgeoning field of Division I lacrosse. University president and former star indoor lacrosse player Bucky Jones quipped, "The Medical School? The Law School? The entire undergraduate program? Our buildings? Our $4 billion endowment? Our lacrosse team? Without the lacrosse team [*snaps fingers*], they're all gone, vanished, vamoosh, like a lacrosse ball out of a lacrosse stick, adios amigo."

Accordingly, the academic program at Hopkins is lacrosse-intensive. All students must enroll in Hopkins's "Cradle to the Grade" program, in which academic merit is aggregated with basic lacrosse skills to determine a student's grade for a given semester of work.

"I don't know anyone who isn't satisfied with—MAN ON! MAN ON! I'M OPEN! Sorry about that. Anyway, I don't know anyone who isn't satisfied with Hopkins's academics."

—Eddie Hollis '04

The Medical School

Look for Hopkins to dominate their conference next fall with the addition of two speedy freshman forwards and a solid back line.

Engineering

Although Princeton and Syracuse will give Hopkins a run for its money, if Hopkins can use its speed and smarts it should have an edge.

Student Life

Students who aren't quite as enamored as most Hopkinsians with attending lacrosse games will be pleased to find out that there are many other outlets for social activity. Among the most popular are playing pickup games of lacrosse, watching lacrosse practices, and L.A.C.R.O.S.S.E. One of the most memorable events of the year occurs on the first Friday of April, when all students flock to the lacrosse fields and pray to Gowlee, the Lacrosse god for the Baltimore/Washington, D.C., area.

#18 Franklin and Marshall College

Chartered in 1787, only a few weeks before the framing of the Constitution, Franklin and Marshall College in Lancaster, Pennsylvania, is actually an amalgam of two separate colleges, Franklin College, which was founded by Benjamin Franklin, and Marshall College, which is named after Chief Justice John Marshall. The two colleges merged seamlessly, and lived quietly in peace until 1969, when rioting broke out and many of the academic buildings were torched by the rowdy savage-like Marshall students, while Franklin students scurried in fear into the forest. Within five years the Franklin students had set up an outpost near the Amish country, living as best they could off the land, trying to salvage their human dignity, all the while on the lookout for the Marshall students, who organized in a loose confederation led by a man with a shadowy past known only as "Krone."

Marshall (left) and Franklin (right)

Admissions

Students who apply to Franklin and Marshall go through a rigorous screening to test both their mental and athletic abilities. Students accepted to Franklin and Marshall are air-dropped by helicopter into the Lancaster wilderness with nothing more than the clothes on their back. Some are easily hunted down and killed by the large tigers that prowl the grasslands. Others meet their untimely deaths at the hands of mercenaries who hide in the woods. The rest matriculate and join the members of either Franklin or Marshall College. Students who graduate from Marshall College have their degrees notarized by Krone in a secret ceremony, while the degrees of Franklin students are signed by the man who gathered the Franklin survivors from the ruins of the riots and organized the outpost in which they live. He is known only as "The Father."

Academics

Franklin and Marshall College boasts one of the most well-rounded academic programs in the country. Students who attend Franklin College are placed on a work-study program in which they are taught by another member of the compound for a few hours a day and spend the rest of their time helping to fortify the outpost, which is periodically raided by the students from Marshall College. The casualty rate for these raids has been holding steady for the last ten years, with Franklin College generally losing between three and five students to the thrusts of the Marshall students' crudely made wooden spears. Marshall students spend most of their time fighting among themselves for scraps of meat stripped off of the day's fresh kill.

Student Life

Krone kills any man who disrespects him or acts disloyally.

Rankings of All Canadian Colleges

1. McGill University (tie)
1. University of Montreal (tie)
3. The Community College (or, Maple Leaf Community College)

#19 Washington University

"Every time I tell someone I am at Wash U, that person always asks, 'Oh, do you mean Seattle or D.C.?' Seattle or D.C.? Seattle or D.C.? Try Saint Louis . . . in Washington State."

Washington University has, throughout its history, held the moniker of America's "Harvard for Midwesterners," or, alternately, "Harvard for Farmers." This is unfair and mistaken, to say the least. Wash U is foremost the "Harvard" for homemakers. And also door-to-door brush salesmen. Wash U was founded in 1853 as the "Eliot Seminary," after its founder, Franklin Eliot, and took the name of Washington University in honor of the nation's first president, after it was discovered that the Washingtons once stopped in what is today St. Louis, to take a five-minute snack break during their journey to the Pacific coast. George is rumored to have snacked on a raspberry scone and tea. The Wash U mascot is the Fighting Blueberry Scone due to a clerical error.

Admissions

It is said that George Washington planted an apple tree while he was in St. Louis for fully five minutes. That apple tree is now the site of Wash U's admissions building, Brookings Hall, where admissions stuff happens. Anyway, George Washington was the nation's first president. He stood there. Once a year, students gather on the last day of September to memorialize the momentous events of Washington's visit. Students line up for hours to stand, look for a place to dispose of a napkin, and return to their carriage for the trip westward.

Academics

Archaeologists have reconstructed the eight steps George Washington took on that fated day in St. Louis. Those 7-by-3-foot plots of land are the corner-stones for Wash U's eight academic schools—the smallest in the country, but by far the most useful: Cooking, Cleaning, Washing, Ironing, Starching, Obesity, Sewing, and Christian Fundamentalism. Wash U is an equal opportunity institution for women and men.

Student Life

Did you know that George Washington spent time on the Wash U campus even before the campus existed? The historic campus boasts the log cabin in which George Washington was born and the dining hall marks the train tracks of the train that George Washington rode during his journey to Alaska. Furthermore, the Busch Laboratory holds the first computer George Washington used as president, as well as his first electric racing car.

#20 Exterminator University

"So when Joe saw the honeymoon couple standing there in the driveway, his arm around her waist in a tentative clutch, oblivious to the grim cold around them, he didn't feel sorry for them. There was something horrible, and yet vaguely fascinating, about the way they stood; he wanted to shout to them, Watch out, it isn't what you think, but he couldn't do that—and besides, that would have been an overly pessimistic thing to yell anyway."

—Omniscient Narrator

Mostly he didn't care one way or the other what happened to them. Joe just wanted to rid their house of bugs and collect his paycheck. He needed the money.

The honeymoon man let go of his wife's waist and she came walking up to the truck. Joe put the truck in park at one side of the driveway and rolled down the window by turning the crank in a circle. He swayed and dipped.

She came up to the window, no coat, no gloves, no nothing, just a button-down shirt and a pair of pants. Slacks, is what she probably would have called them.

"Aren't you cold?" Joe asked her. She hadn't flinched at the cold, and she didn't flinch now.

"Cold? Oh!" she said looking around at the icicles hanging off the ledge of the roof, down at the poorly shoveled driveway. "Not yet," she said. His concern caught her attention, and her wandering eyes focused on him for the first time.

"Well let's go inside, and why don't you show me the problem," he said.

Admissions

Disgusting little creatures, he thought to himself. The termite always scared Joe a bit. It was fairly large for a bug, and it always struck him as smarter. And when people said that if ants were our size they would rule the world, it was always huge termites that he pictured, walking down the sidewalk with briefcases, driving cars, in all the upper-level corporate jobs, on the TV, in silk bathrobes smoking cigars, calling the shots. He knew that if he set off a poison bomb he would be sure to get every last one of them.

Joe looked at the honeymoon man in time to see him look up from his watch and turn to his wife. "Darling," he said, "I have to go to work for a bit. I'll meet you here in three hours?" And she said Sure, and the honeymoon man left them together. They heard his car pull out of the driveway.

Best College That Is Far Away from Home (but Not Too Far), Near a City (but Not an Overwhelming City), Has a Solid Basketball Team, a Cool Mascot, Like Some Sort of Bug

1. University of Richmond
2. The Charlotte Hornets

Academics

After Joe was done putting down the poison, the wife asked him to keep her company until her husband came home. They waited in his red truck in the driveway. She sat on the beaded passenger seat. Joe sat behind the wheel next to her waiting for anything to happen. She talked, and he tried not to listen. She was lonely she said. And scared. He looked over at her. She was silent now, her head turned toward the window, a sad expression on her face. Joe stared at the pretty curve of her neck. His right hand found its way to her knee.

She asked him to drive her to the grocery store. Joe drove her to his house instead. He took her upstairs to his vibrating bed. It was there they made love the way love was meant to be made.

Student Life

They had nothing to say to each other, and they had been sitting in silence for some time when Joe's wife came in. Joe was almost happy to see her, he had felt a growing annoyance in the honeymoon woman's presence in the bed next to him. The honeymoon woman left the room naked and shrieking. Joe knew she wasn't in too bad a shape because she did pause to collect her clothes.

Watching her naked posterior run out of the room, he had already begun to miss seeing her tan body against the white sheets.

His wife told him to never come back to the house, and left.

It had been a bad day, but it made him feel like shrugging.

He found the honeymoon woman sitting in his red pickup truck, her shirt on inside out, her hair a mess.

He drove her home. The air in the truck got heavy with quiet. Joe spent the drive debating whether to tell her that her shirt was on inside out.

"He's already home," she said as they pulled into her driveway. Joe felt drained and tired and wanted a hot shower. She got out quickly and Joe left. As Joe left he saw them in his rearview mirror. The hand of the husband around the shoulder of his limp wife.

It seemed odd to Joe to see both of them standing there together.

#21 Swarthmore

"Hey, if the Macho Man wants a piece of me, he can have it. Come Saturday night, it's all going down. And Lady Elizabeth, if you're listening, I've got my eye on you, sweet-thang."

—Junior Sociology major Rowdy Roddy Piper

The squared circle where the test of the man is how much of a man he is, where blood and sweat are the currency and amateurs are left home with the baby-sitter where they belong, professional wrestling—this is Swarthmore.

What else is there beyond the steel cages, the barbed-wire-covered baseball bats, and the championship belts? There is the glory. Pain is temporary, pride is forever. This is Swarthmore.

The 5 Most Hungry Tigers at the University of Maryland

1. Shee-Ra
2. Ghengis
3. Shere Khan
4. Slappy Joe
5. Randy

💪 Admissions

Each year nearly 5,000 students apply to Swarthmore; only 400 are admitted. The admissions process is based on a format known as a "5,000-man over-the-top battle royale," in which 5,000 prospective students gather in a large wrestling ring. After one hour, the 400 students still standing are declared the winners and instantly admitted to Swarthmore.

💪 Academics

Many Swarthmore students are already set on a career path, and preprofessional programs are among the school's strongest. "I ain't got time to bleed," explained senior Jesse "The Body" Ventura. "Medical school? Publishing? Banking? Figure-four leg locks? I don't know what I'm going to do when I graduate, but I know it's going to involve me going house on Hulk Hogan's puny little head."

According to the president of Swarthmore College, Vince McMahon, "Classes and lectures here are pretty much like they would be at any other college: They take place in a midsize minor league hockey arena, you've got like ten thousand screaming adolescents, people throwing things, the spotlights and the fireworks and the TV cameras and the ten-man, three-falls tag-team match going on in the wrestling ring, of course. And also the professor."

💪 Student Life

Because Swarthmore is located in a wealthy, quiet suburb of Philadelphia, students turn to campus sports to provide much of the action. Swarthmore's huge sports complex, the WWF Jumbodome, allows all students to take part in a number of athletic and recreational activities, from SummerSlam to RAW! Explained sophomore Ricky "The Dragon" Steamboat, "Wrestlemania is coming up in two weeks, and as student council president I'm in charge of all the preparations. Also I'm selling tickets, which can be purchased daily in the lunchroom."

#22 Denison University

"My boy spent some time 'round that old place. Ever since, he's never been quite right. I'd stay away if I was you."

Nestled far back in the wilderness of central Ohio, there lies a deep, dark forest. Folks in town don't quite know what to make of the crazy goings-on they hear tell of in the woods, but nary a mother neglects to lock her infants' door come sundown. Reports from trappers and woodland vagrants report of howls and screams, clanking chains, and the like coming from the old Denison place. That's the word, "Denison." No one 'round these parts ever says it. Because they hold in trust a secret, deep and dark, and they are sworn to never let the world find out the truth about their sleepy liberal arts college. "You'd best be on your way and forget you ever heard tell of this place," one crusty, coverall-clad man told us as he cleaned a spark plug with an oily rag. "Now get out of here before you start something you can't finish! Leave before it's too late."

☙ Admissions

But we found ourselves drawn to the village and its inscrutable inhabitants. We asked a group of ten- to twelve-year-olds playing by a fire hydrant to tell us about the admissions requirements at the ol' Denison University place. "Steve gave me two bucks to go up to that college in the woods and throw a rock through one of the windows. I ain't a girl so I said I would go. Now I won't tell you what I saw up there but"—and here he removed his baseball cap—"it turned my hair white as my granddaddy's and made me retarded until I flunked out of school. And I dropped those two dollars down a sewer grate, on account of being so scared. Do yourself a favor and go check out Ohio State or Case Western." Denison University is highly competitive and requires both an alumni interview and excellent SATs. Or at least that's what it said in the county records. We'd give the average GPA, but that page was mysteriously ripped out of the book.

☙ Academics

Details of the curriculum for Denison are hard to come by from talking to the citizens of Granville. One area farmer lent us some insight. "I live next to those woods and sometimes I hear all kinds of hollering. One night my dog started barking like judgment day. I went outside and all my chickens were beheaded and there was blood all over the place. There was a bloody set of footprints leading you-know-where." Aside from chicken slaughter, we have gathered that the students of Denison are also trained in stealing babies' breath, ruining crops, and making weird sounds and lights in the night. One man predicts a large contingent of Economics concentrators because "a boy from the college comes and helps with my taxes every April. But in a macabre and uncanny way."

☙ Student Life

Little is known about the lives or deaths of the students of Denison University. Townsfolk predict that student activities revolve around unholy rites and grave-robbing. Our greatest insight came from the deathbed confession of a Granville railroad worker, who heard about us college kids snooping around and called us up. We went to his ill-lit apartment and gathered in hushed silence as the rheumy oldster explained. "I can't tell what we did up there . . . it was twenty years ago, like it was yesterday . . . the evil needed to be stopped . . . we had to do it . . . but now it's coming back . . . it's got me first and it's stronger than before . . . the others . . . warn the others . . ." At this, the old man expired. This was when we decided to visit another college where we could go to some frat parties.

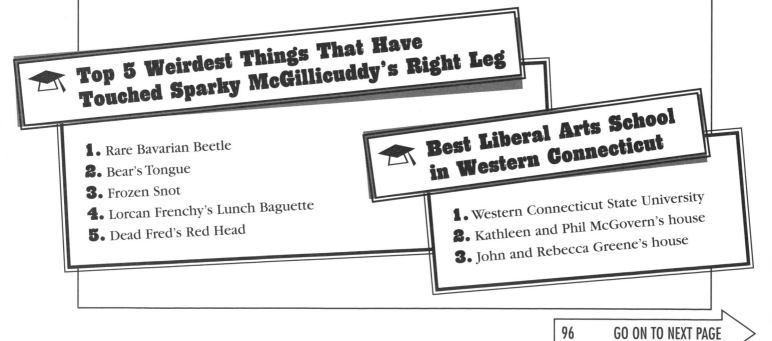

Top 5 Weirdest Things That Have Touched Sparky McGillicuddy's Right Leg

1. Rare Bavarian Beetle
2. Bear's Tongue
3. Frozen Snot
4. Lorcan Frenchy's Lunch Baguette
5. Dead Fred's Red Head

Best Liberal Arts School in Western Connecticut

1. Western Connecticut State University
2. Kathleen and Phil McGovern's house
3. John and Rebecca Greene's house

The Minneapolis School of NOISE

Do you enjoy loud sounds? Clamor? Din? Racket? Are you a fan of music, only without the rhythm and harmony? Atonal?

Then a degree from the Minneapolis School of Noise could be for you!

The Minneapolis School of Noise (MSN) is the world's oldest and most renowned noise conservatory. Founded in 1689 by an air horn, the MSN serves to provide its students with an academic understanding of noise—the history of noise, the social theory of noise, the literature of noise, the biology of noise, etc. But the MSN is about more than just noise . . .

❀ MSN Academics: MSN offers its students the opportunity to study over 40 disciplines, from noise-making, noise-listening, screaming, shouting, yelling, dropping pots and pans, blowing air horns, to setting off M-80s and listening to radio static.

❀ MSN Athletics: Although MSN has no athletic teams of its own, MSN students do enjoy attending pep rallies as well as cheering loudly and doing the wave in empty football arenas.

❀ MSN Campus Life: MSN has not had a fully constructed campus since its inception. From bulldozers to jackhammers to simple hammers pounding on nails, the constant reconstruction of demolished buildings shows that MSN cares about its students year-round.

❀ MSN Pride: Our motto: "Don't just make noise, make _loud_ noise." Our belief: "Without noise, the world would be a very silent place." Our hope: "That noise can bring together peoples of all colors and nations and create world peace."

Our graduates, never ones to be quiet (ha!), can attest to the richness of their collegiate experience . . .

"I came to MSN a quiet, silent boy who never said much. Today I'm a self confident, excessively loud man who isn't afraid of disturbing the peace with levels in excess of 140db, which I make every single day."
—**John Jones '92**

"[*Sound of an air horn blaring.*]"
—**An air horn '87**

"We came to MSN with a simple dream to make a lot of noise. I guess we got lucky and our noise ended up being considered 'music,' whatever that is. Anyway, to us, and hopefully to our fans, it's still just noise."
—**John Lennon and the Beatles '58**

"When I came to MSN in 1982 I had no idea what decibels were. Or sound or noise for that matter. Today I am knowledgeable about these sort of things, which will inevitably help me with my law degree."
—**Marty Senn '96**

"[*Screaming incomprehensibly. Stops, speaks.*] MSN changed the way I communicate [*begins screaming again*] as I have integrated [*screams, bangs pots and pans*] the way I approach [*blasts radio static*] talking with other people [*sounds air horn*]."

#23 College of the Real World

"I really am getting sick of (name). Yesterday he used up the hot water. He really is (derogatory adjective couched in vague terms). I'm not about (bad emotion). I'm about (good emotion) and (noun). Also, I think that (bisexual roommate) has a crush on (man/woman roommate)."

Do you yearn to enter the Real World? Looking forward to the time when you can find a spouse, pursue a career, and settle down into a beautiful house out in the suburbs? If so, the College of the Real World is *not* for you. Founded in 1995 by Eric Nies, former host of *The Grind* and an original cast member of MTV's groundbreaking sitcom *The Real World*, COTRW will give you everything you need to become a member of MTV's hit show. As current college president Julie (New York) points out, "Babbling about a second-rate dance career and hating your mother for no reason will only get you so far. There are certain things that will ensure your acceptance on to the show, and we at the College of the Real World are ready to teach you that. Did I mention I hate my mother for no reason?" Commented university provost and former supermodel Jacinda, "Good looks, contrary to popular belief, will not get you on *The Real World*. For example, I was also interested in talking and eating. And just look at Becky from the first season. Nice skin—NOT!"

Academics

The College of the Real World offers a variety of courses, including "How to Cry about Invented Problems," "Preventing Your T-Shirt Logo from Getting Blurred Out," and "Pretending You're Gay Because It Seems Cool." The College of the Real World also offers specialized programs that include "Writing Crappy Poetry: Is It Worth It?" and "Shaming Your Generation 24 Hours a Day." Part of the academic component will involve a yearlong seminar by Montana from the Boston season that will detail specifically how, through hard work and determination, Montana became the worst person in America but was still able to influence millions of MTV viewers. Throughout your entire time at COTRW, the latest MTV hits will be pumped through an advanced speaker system, such that every moment of your life can be accompanied by such songs as Shawn Mullins's haunting love ballad "Lullabye."

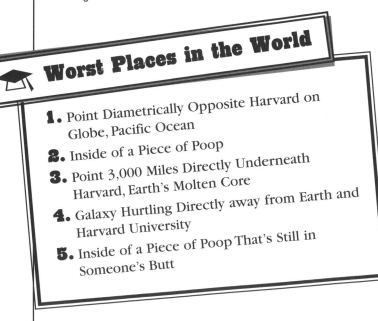

Worst Places in the World

1. Point Diametrically Opposite Harvard on Globe, Pacific Ocean
2. Inside of a Piece of Poop
3. Point 3,000 Miles Directly Underneath Harvard, Earth's Molten Core
4. Galaxy Hurtling Directly away from Earth and Harvard University
5. Inside of a Piece of Poop That's Still in Someone's Butt

Student Life

Students are assigned to dormitories with six other strangers. The deans of the college (Puck and Beth Stelarcheck) do their best to put at least one meek woman, one lovelorn man, one upset black, one gay, and one talentless poet/painter/singer in each room. The advising system consists entirely of video cameras in the bathrooms, where students can pour their hearts out in confessionals while doing their business. One of the most popular programs includes a ten-day vacation abroad, where students are treated to an expenses-paid vacation and shown how to say embarrassing things to the inhabitants of foreign countries. We're happy to teach you how to fake-smoke. Students are also encouraged to have late-night discussions in the college-owned Jacuzzis, where they are given the most basic information about world problems and taught to be judgmental through the use of rash generalizations. The College of the Real World will strive to make you adhere to the most common cultural and racial stereotypes so you too can become part of the free-form fun!

#24 Boston College

"The campus is splendid. The courses are intriguing. And the girls are pretty. Wicked pretty."

Looking for a great education in a Catholic environment? Hoping for a college experience that will nurture your spirit as well as your mind? Like an insanely disproportionate number of incredibly beautiful women? If you answered "yes" to any of these questions, or if you are a pretty Catholic girl, then Boston College, founded in 1863 by the Jesuits, may be for you.

BC has a nationally recognized academic program that is unique in its fusion of intellectual breadth, pretty girls from all-girls Catholic schools, and Jesuit philosophy. This is manifested most intensely in the Pulse course, where students take theology and philosophy courses for credit while simultaneously volunteering 10–15 hours a week. Somewhere, in the distance, a pretty girl howls.

BC students love their school and their time there, amidst the sprawling hills with pretty girls on them and winding streets where pretty girls walk in Chestnut Hill. Many find it hard to leave the College for Pretty Girls after only four short years. But fear not: The BC alumni are fiercely loyal to the BC alumnae, who are always pretty.

Admissions

Getting into BC is getting harder and harder. Last year's class had a median SAT of 1300 and a median high school GPA of 3.5, and female applicants averaged an 8.8 ranking on the International Pretty Index.

Think Boston College might be for you? Then a campus visit might be in order. It will help you make up your mind and see if BC fits you right with tons and tons and tons of pretty girls. Boston College has been described as the Best Place on Earth.

Most Popular MIT Majors

1. Electrical Engineering
2. Chemical Engineering
3. Electrochemical Enginecring
4. Chemoelectrochemical Engineering
5. Ele-chemo-ctric-istry-Elecgineering Engineering

Academics

Boston College's academic program is among the best in the nation. Indisputably, they have one of the highest numbers of pretty girls in the country. Many students study philosophy or theology; still more popular is economics. The pretty girls often study political science or biology (pre-med). About 10 percent of students go on to medical school, and about 17 percent to law school. Around 50 percent study pretty girls, and about 50 percent are pretty girls.

Student Life

Student life at BC is incredible. Students are known for their friendliness and their pretty girls, and it is easy to make friends as a freshman. Boston College manages to combine good times with social consciousness and an overwhelming number of pretty girls that by sheer probability makes it far easier for shy boys who went to all-boys Catholic schools to get dates. One of the most popular activities is attending Boston College football games in beautiful Alumni Stadium, built with money from graduates and often looked at by pretty girls. Each year, the Screaming Eagles valiantly lose to schools with far better football programs and far fewer pretty girls.

One of the most important parts of the BC social life is pretty girls/community service. Most students take part in some volunteer program in the city, and while many college students go to Cancún and Florida for spring break in search of a good time, many BC students spend their breaks with hundreds of pretty girls building houses in Appalachia.

"It was no time at all before I was good friends with my three freshman roommates, who I noticed bore an uncanny resemblance to me in regards to levels of prettiness."

"The thing I like most about BC is the sense of service. A close second is the pretty girls."

"I'm studying hard to complete a pre-med program. If that doesn't work out, I'll just work jobs I'm underqualified for offered to me by men who are made weak by my beauty."

#25 University of Notre Dame

Founded 130 years ago by Fr. Sorin and his fellow Holy Cross brothers, two sisters, mom, dad, and grandmother, the Notre Dame family has since grown to 7,700. Since its early days, Notre Dame has risen to become the producer of the greatest intramural teams this world has ever seen. Whether it be intramural football, baseball, showering, churchgoing, or chemistry, Notre Dame students take their intramurals quite seriously.

Intramural Admissions

Notre Dame has a rich intramural tradition. Every year, thousands of potential intramural champs apply, but only the best of the "pretty good" get in. Occasionally a mistake is made, and someone who is "amazing" is accepted. They are sent directly to Notre Dame's NCAA football team, a sort of farm team/minor league/feeder system for Notre Dame's intramural teams. Many of these varsity athletes are later "drafted" into the intramural league.

University of Arizona Sophomore Terrence McGovern's Favorite Cereals

1. Honey Bunches of Oats
2. Frosted Mini Wheats
3. Frosted Flakes
4. Frosted Rice Krispies
5. Frosted Cheerios

🐤 Intramural Academics

Notre Dame intramural academics are guaranteed to be a rich environment for learning. Here is a typical scene: Students solemnly file into a classroom, each pausing to touch the "Learn Like a Champion Today" sign over the classroom door. The guttural scratching of cleats crunching the classroom floor wakes up all the echoes in the hallowed Notre Dame classroom, and game-faced students prepare to tackle learning with vigor. Before class starts, the professor instructs the players to take off any watches or jewelry. The blue jerseys sit on the left side of the classroom, while the gold jerseys sit on the right side of the classroom. Halfway through the class they switch sides. Says one student, "This school prepares us for the contact sport of life." Another noted, "I was part of blue jerseys' winning chemistry team. We won 3.7 to 3.4 when Kathleen Fiona Kelly aced a late-semester exam."

Oui. Vous venez de la boulangerie?

Avez-vous rencontré mon amie, Michèle?

#26 La Sorbonne

"La Sorbonne était une expérience incroyable."

La Sorbonne est, peut-être, la meilleure académie en France. Les professeurs sont les plus savants, et les étudiants sont les plus curieux. Située en belle Paris, les étudiants ont l'opportunité d'expériencer tout ce que cette belle ville offre: les cafés, les bibliothèques, les musées.

Mais pour gagner permission d'assister à la Sorbonne, il faut compléter un portefeuille académique excellent au lycée. La Sorbonne ne voit pas de lycéens qui n'ont pas fait leur meilleur. Si on a de la chance d'être accepté, on peut compléter un programme dans une de beaucoup de disciplines académiques.

🐤 Academics

"La banque est en face du marché."

"Je ne veux pas manger mes légumes."

"Bof."

A. Translate:

Jean et Michel vont à la bibliothèque. Pourquoi est-ce qu'on va à la bibliothèque? Qui sait? Philippe? Parce que la bibliothèque a beaucoup de livres, et il veut lire les oeuvres de Hugo et Voltaire. Bien sûr. Alors, Jean et Michel sont maintenant très près de la bibliothèque, mais ils ont faim. Est-ce qu'il vaut mieux acheter des hot-dogs à la bouchère, ou des croques madames au café? Je ne sais pas; il faut demander à Henri.

🐤 Student Life

B. Complete the following sentences with the proper form of the verb in parentheses:

1. Je/J' _____ (voir) un cheval à la campagne hier.

2. Qui _____ (demander) s'il y a un examen demain?

3. _____ (manger) vos légumes!

4. Pendant que Marie _____ (finir) ses devoirs, Jean-Michel _____ (ouvrir) la fenêtre.

5. Il y a dix ans que je/j' _____ (habiter) en Rheims.

6. Pourquoi _____ (être) Philippe toujours dans la salle à coucher? Je lui/l' _____ (appeller) à 5h30!

7. Je/J' _____ (penser), donc je _____ (être).

#29 McGill University

"Eh."

Founded in 1984, only four years after Canada itself was discovered, McGill University is Canada's answer to the American Ivy Leagues. Ranked number one among all Canadian universities, of which there are three, McGill's school motto, "How's It Going There, Eh?" succinctly echoes the sentiments held by many McGill students. Current Canadian president Wayne Gretzky heads McGill's list of famous alumni, who also include Ray Bourque, Theo Fleury, and Geoff Courtnall.

In touting itself as the "University of Wisconsin–River Falls of the North," McGill aims to attract the top students from among Canada's nearly 700 high school students country-wide. In fact, the McGill bookstore even jokingly prints T-shirts like, "Princeton: The McGill of New Jersey" or "Stanford: The McGill of California" or "McGill: The McGill of Canada," etc. Although the bookstore may poke fun at other, less Canadian colleges, university administrators are quite serious about McGill's outstanding reputation as the best school in the world. As the president of the college, Dougie Gilmour, told us, "Harvard? I've never even heard of this place. What is this Harvard? Is it close to Medicine Hat? I do not understand."

America

There's a reason it's called "North *America*" rather than "North *Canada*" or "North *Mexico*." While McGill may be located in "North America," it certainly is *not* an American university, a consideration you should probably take into account as you enter the admissions process. But is there really a difference between Canadian universities and Americans? you query, like an ignorant Canadian . . . I guess not, unless Canada hosts the Blockbuster Bowl every December 25, the Duke Blue Devils play in Ottawa, or Toronto has its own professional baseball team! Not to sound biased, but don't go to college in Canada! My dad had an old saying: "The day they find a good Canadian university, I will graduate from high school, move to Canada, and attempt to go to college, something I have never been able to do."

Admissions

Perhaps you're expecting some inane joke here about how the McGill admissions process involves hockey or stupid Canadians or stupid hockey-playing Canadians, etc. Well forget it; McGill accepts top-quality Canadian students based on their grades, extracurriculars, SAT scores, and . . . *hockey!!!* Yes!

Academics

Although McGill's classes do tend to be a bit large, the caliber of professors more than compensates. Where else can you hear Mario Lemieux lecture on evolution, Bobby Orr talk about race in Canada, or learn sociology from Gordie Howe? At Princeton or Harvard? I doubt

Rankings of Colleges, Ranked by Depressing Features

1. Cornell University—most suicides
2. University of Kentucky—most eating disorders
3. University of Maryland—most man-eating tigers
4. Clown College—most people crying on the inside
5. University of Wisconsin-Eau Claire— just a bunch of fat, stupid, ugly people

it. Dartmouth? Maybe. As one sophomore told us, "I started out studying Canadian history, but after the first quarter of freshman year, when I had learned everything that had ever happened in Canada's history, I discovered my true academic calling: Canoeing!"

Student Life

McGill is situated in the heart of Canada's bustling capital city, the Yukon Territory, and boasts one of the country's most beautiful campuses: a frozen lake. Unmatched in its breathtaking barrenness, McGill's location is appealing to all prospective students, many of whom have only dreamed of attempting to survive in the middle of frozen tundra during their college years. But city slickers fear not! The Yukon Territory, world-renowned for its "artsy" scene, provides McGill students with the opportunity to sample from the finest in Canadian culture: whether pike fishing *or* ice hockey. And with a host of guest lecturers who visit the campus each year, from pro hockey coach Pat Burns to pro hockey referee Terry Gregson, McGill prepares its students for the often snobbish atmosphere of the Canadian cultural scene, historically centered in the Edmonton Oilers' Civic Center Hockey Arena.

Although every McGill freshman is guaranteed room and board, which consists primarily of an ice-fishing hut and a daily slab of raw lake trout, most juniors and seniors tend to move off campus, usually to nearby tents and sleeping bags.

McGill students, nonetheless, tend to love their school. In fact, wandering through campus one day I myself repeatedly heard the anthem sung aloud:

"Aruba, Jamaica, Ooooh I wanna take you, eh?
To Bermuda, eh?, Bahama, come on pretty momma, eh?
Key Largo, Montego, Baby why don't we go, eh?
To the, eh?, Kokomo, eh?, we'll get there fast, eh?, and then we'll take it slow
That's where I want to go, eh?, way down in Kokomo, eh?"

Most Important Factors in Choosing College

Prestige: 18%

Location: 15%

Dad went there: 6%

Oppressive dad went there: 3%

The hands-on educational value that Deep Springs has to offer: .002%

Love of butts: 4%

Free bubble gum, bubble gum in a dish: 5%

Pizza Hut was closed, registered at the college next door instead: 8%

Afraid of mice, admissions officer promises "no mice here!": 10%

Chocolate Heaven!: 17%

Less fat people: 2%

Better: 12%

#30 Gotham University

"Mphhhh! Mphhhhhh!!!!! Mphhhhhhh!!!!!"

Located on the seamy banks of the Gotham River, Gotham University is a respectable and affordable urban college community. Most GU students do hail from Gotham itself, but a respectable percentage of students come from states other than the state in which Gotham City is located. Despite its strong extracurricular program and talented faculty (such as noted psychotherapist Jonathan Crane), many students are discouraged from GU due to its status as the most crime-ridden college campus in America. Others are attracted to the presence of Gotham's dark avenger, the Batman. Last year alone, an entire Economics class was gassed to death by the Joker, and GU alum Two-Face '77 kidnapped eight sets of twins enrolled at the college, holding them ransom at the Gemini casino for $22,222. Fortunately, Batman and Robin were able to save four and a half sets of twins before Two-Face lowered them to their death onto a giant roulette wheel.

Admissions

Fully 72 percent of GU students have, at one time or another, been abducted or murdered by a supercriminal. An additional estimated 15 percent of students are supercriminals or masked avengers. GU is also 8 percent Asian. Financial aid is abundant due to the Thomas and Martha Wayne Memorial Scholarship Trust, for students majoring in criminal justice or criminology whose parents were brutally gunned down or died in circus accidents.

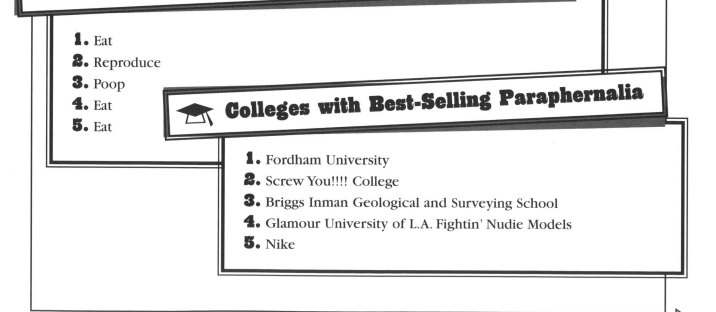

Top 5 Instincts of Rare Bavarian Beetle While It Was on Sparky McGillicuddy's Right Leg

1. Eat
2. Reproduce
3. Poop
4. Eat
5. Eat

Colleges with Best-Selling Paraphernalia

1. Fordham University
2. Screw You!!!! College
3. Briggs Inman Geological and Surveying School
4. Glamour University of L.A. Fightin' Nudie Models
5. Nike

☙ Academics

Most GU students are busy being held for ransom in warehouses and dockyards for most of their four years. We sat in on one of Professor Crane's famous psychology lectures, as he revealed to the class that he was the Scarecrow and wished to test out his new fear gas on us. After we spent fifteen minutes hallucinating that we were covered in rattlesnakes, Batman crashed through a fourth-story window and kicked the Scarecrow off of his podium.

"Crane, you're a madman," the Dark Knight growled.

"Flattery will get you nowhere, Batman!!!" quipped the Scarecrow as he was dealt a stunning blow to the solar plexus. The spindly professor lunged toward his last skull-shaped canister of fear gas as Gotham's avenger launched a batarang, knocking his hand away. The Gotham City Police Department arrived moments later to pick up Professor Crane and cart him off to Arkham Asylum. Professor Crane gave every student in class a D on their final.

☙ Student Life

The annual social calendar revolves around the Gotham Knights–Metropolis Monarchs football matchup in early November. Unfortunately for the fans, there has never been a game played to completion. Last year, for example, the Penguin had arranged with Lex Luthor for everyone in the stands to be frozen in time as the Penguin's goons looted them for jewels and cash. But for the uneasy alliance of Superman and Batman, the plan might have succeeded.

"I may not always approve of your methods, Bruce," offered the last son of Krypton, "but I valued your help today. Perhaps we can team up again someday."

"I work alone," replied the Caped Crusader, vanishing into the shadows to spend another sleepless night keeping his solitary vigil over the people of Gotham. GU has an active intramurals program.

"Criminals are a superstitious and cowardly lot. I will wear a disguise to strike terror into their hearts."

—John Silkovsky, GU Communications major

Popular Classes in Electrical Engineering at MIT

1. E-E 14632: Systemical Development
2. E-E 2062 (501): Systemical Development 2
3. E-E 613df: Programming H-44 IB Systems (excluding QV346011I Valve Disbursement Modules)
4. C-S (632)1-AVB5: C==(-C/35 lim——> \$\$&)!
5. Computers 1: Introduction to Windows 98

COLLEGE OF
Street Knowledge

- ■ *Are you tired of lacking the necessary "street smarts"?*

- ■ *Do you want to be educated in the ways of the back alleys and dark corners?*

- ■ *Looking for a strong Astrophysics department?*

- ■ *Hoping to strike fear in the hearts of naive country folk who wander onto your turf?*

Then a degree from the College of Street Knowledge could be for you!

The College of Street Knowledge (CSK) is a fully accredited four-year university with campuses in all of the nation's most prestigious ghettos, slums, and barrios. Originally founded as a classical music conservatory, CSK now specializes in providing its undergraduates with the necessary tools for achieving success in the competitive world of crime, hustling, research astrophysics, and pimping. But that's not all CSK is about . . .

- ⌘ CSK instructors: 98 percent have served hard time at some of the country's toughest correctional institutions, from Sing Sing to Alcatraz, and are truly world-class convicts.

- ⌘ CSK food: Is prison food!

- ⌘ CSK sports: CSK boasts over 30 Division I teams, from women's car-bombing to men's petty theft. Last year, the CSK women's golf team took home the NCAA crown with a stunning defeat over highly ranked Florida State University.

- ⌘ CSK academics: Over 97 percent of CSK students major in Astrophysics, and nearly 95 percent go on to do graduate work at the leading labs and research institutions in the world.

- ⌘ CSK pride: Our motto: "Let's try not to get arrested this time!" Our belief: "The only thing keeping you from realizing your dreams is *you*, and the police." Our message: "Look out world, I'm a college graduate with a 9mm,

thorough knowledge of theoretical astrophysics, and a strong desire to rob a 7-Eleven." Our school anthem: "F—k tha Police."

If you don't believe us, listen to what our students have to say:

"CSK has been great! I've met all sorts of great people, whether astrophysicists, convicted criminals, or Nobel Prize—winning, convicted felon astrophysicists."

"Although I took nearly all astrophysics courses and plan to study at Stanford next year, my one humanities course, 'History 1090: Carjacking, from 1780 to 1880,' really gave me an insider's view on carjacking in the nineteenth century, of which there was none."

"Coming into CSK I planned on studying astrophysics, like my parents. But after sophomore year I knew that my real love was 'Fire-Bombing Public Places.' Although I'm not sure exactly what I want to do after college, I know that it will involve fire-bombing, and that gives me happiness."

"I entered CSK a young, baby-faced, naive prep school student from Exeter. I leave CSK an Astrophysics major with three hijacking arrests under my belt and a scholarship to CalTech's graduate astrophysics program. Thanks CSK!"

#31 University of Pennsylvania

"The best thing about Penn, without question, is the friends you make. I feel like I have 12,569 friends at Penn. If there's one thing you can say about the University of Pennsylvania, it's that it's one big society of friends."

The University of Pennsylvania prides itself on being Benjamin Franklin's college. Indeed, "Franklin's University" was founded in 1740, and, due to a ridiculous technicality, is therefore the oldest "university" in the United States. Yet Harvard College was almost forty thousand years old when Franklin founded his school in Philadelphia. The "Fighting Quakers" are not without their spirit; one particular custom features students throwing toast on the football field before the fourth quarter. This tradition has neither a suitable explanation nor a desirable end result.

The University of Pennsylvania, or Penn, as most of its students call it, prides itself on a beautiful campus, a distinguished faculty, and aggressively mediocre students. Most of all, however, Penn prides itself on its founder, Benjamin Franklin. Just how much does Penn like to honor their founder? Consider: There are more than sixty statues of Franklin on campus; every building on campus is named after Franklin; all graduates must name their first-born Benjamin, regardless of gender; and all students must wear a Benjamin Franklin mask at all times.

Penn is also situated in West Philly, home of Fresh Prince Will Smith, the best cheesesteaks in the country, and horribly crime-infested neighborhoods prowled by, among other nasties, eight-foot rats. It is no wonder that students are not allowed outside of the campus after dinner hours.

The 5 Most Common Sounds Heard at College (University of Maryland Only)

1. "GRRRRRRRR!!!"
2. "He's hungry; be very, very quiet."
3. "ROOOARRRR!!!!"
4. "AHHHH! GET IT OFFF! HELP ME!!!"
5. [*munch, munch, munch*]

Best College Mascots

1. The Ohio State *Buckeyes*
2. The University of Arizona *Buckeyes*
3. The Alabama *Buckeyes Tide*
4. The UCLA *Eyeballs*
5. The UC-Berkeley *"Oh God, my eyes!"es*
6. The Northeastern *Eyesockets*
7. The University of My Eyeball *Fighting New Hampshires*

☙ Admissions

Non-Quakers:

Early Decision: November 1

Regular Decision: January 1

Quakers:

Decision by Committee of Friends: Rolling admission

Requirements:

✔ SAT

✔ 3 SAT II tests, including SAT II English or SAT II Friendship

✔ Must be a Quaker

☙ Academics

Penn's approach to learning is certainly unique, if not ineffective. Classes are scheduled as "meetings," as opposed to "lectures." Students sit in a circle, with the "professor" sitting in as an equal. There is no curriculum, assignments, or questions. Students are simply encouraged to stand up and speak when they feel they have something to say. Some meetings can go for more than an hour without anyone saying anything. This may seem frivolous.

But Penn students contend that this is the very heart and soul of their education. In fact, students have begun scheduling meetings where silence is not only common, but mandatory. How do students learn in such an atmosphere? The answer is unclear at best.

Perhaps the secret to academics at Penn lies in the design of an undergraduate's education. Each student must complete 64 credits before graduating. The breakdown: 12 credits in one of 6 core disciplines; 20 credits in elective credits; and 32 credits in Quaker studies. Then again, perhaps this is all an ill-conceived attempt to make the University of Pennsylvania appear to be an entirely Quaker school, a simple and all-too-unclever joke on the fact that Penn's mascot is the Fighting Quaker. Either way, Penn is for 'tards.

☙ Student Life

Penn students take their Quaker lifestyle quite seriously; it reaches beyond the classroom and into their social lives.

There is no social life at Penn.

Understandably, the provosts of U Penn decided long ago that evil temptations would lurk most prominently in extracurricular arenas. Students are allowed to participate in one nonacademic group. Unfortunately, school rules mandate that this participation is in the school butter-churning team. "Churn that butter, Ezekiel!" shouts one Quaker into the bleeding ear of another at 4:30 A.M., when team practices begin every morning. Quakers, of course, should not be confused with the Amish, who, unlike the Quakers, are known for churning butter.

🎓 Top 5 Students in E-E 14632: Systemical Development

1. Phil "Sparky" McGillicuddy

2. Scooter McNeely

3. Taylor Negron

4. Freezil Zipwad

5. Lorcan Frenchy

"Churn that butter! Like you never have before! Churn it! Churn it! The butter! Churn!"

That being said, fraternity life at Penn is unparalleled. That is, as Quakers, all students are considered "Brethren," and therefore Penn is one big, friendly fraternity. In addition, Penn has myriad frats and sororities, which often throw raging keggers and two-story bong parties.

"Yeah, it's kind of rough, not being allowed outside after dark, but it's best for all of us."

"Hey, Jedediah, could you pass the corn nuts?"

"Sometimes I just want to break out of these damned walls and run for the beautiful Philadelphia hills, which may or may not exist. Either way, Penn can be more than a little confining if you don't like small spaces and minimal sunlight."

"The Lord will watch over our meetings. He knoweth Chemistry like the Dickens."

"The only thing I've learned in my time at college is that Penn and Penn State are separate schools."

"Believe it or not, Wilford Brimley is actually not a professor at Penn."

> ## 🎓 Best U.S. Engineering Schools
>
> **1.** Massachusetts Institute of Technology (MIT)
> **2.** California Institute of Technology
> **3.** Carnegie-Mellon University
> **4.** Rensselaer Polytechnic Institute
> **5.** Worcester Polytechnic Institute

10,347 Yale University

"Yale is alright. I don't know how it is compared to other colleges because I haven't really gone anywhere else. I figure other colleges are more or less like Yale."

Ever since its founding in 1701, Yale has been considered one of the finest schools in the country, with a storied history of academic excellence. Nevertheless, Yale students, known as Elis, are always bothered by the lingering suspicion that their school is "not so good." Outsiders think the problem lies in Yale's natural inferiority to better schools like Harvard. But that notion is dispelled in the minds of many Elis because in 1997 *U.S. News and World Report* changed all their criteria and made Yale number one. That was the year they ranked Stanford 43rd and omitted MIT and Brown altogether. "But whatever," say some, "being better than Harvard is being better than Harvard." Being "not so good," however, is far more problematic.

Most of the time this notion of not-so-goodness is dismissed by the students of Yale. The extreme academic rigor of the classes and the general quality of the students make most people believe Yale has escaped the "not so good" badge it has carried from its first days as a converted circus tent in the middle of the New Haven Green. The beautiful, dark Gothic halls of Yale were built in an early attempt to cover up what was then called Yale's problem with being "a mere farthing gooder than ye olde pauper home." Some students claim the school is haunted by mediocre and unlearned apparitions, and that during the autumnal equinox the hallowed halls ring with their bloodcurdling, ghostly curse of the ages: "Of course, an excellent school. Maybe the best of its kind. But, perhaps, not so good."

Unfortunately for the Elis, Yale's storied history is still filled with legends about the not-so-goodness. Each of the residential colleges into which the school is divided has its own story about Yale's possible better-than-average mediocrity. Branford College has the bearded lady who got tenure on the novelty of her bearded female face. In the underground basement of academic egomaniac and jackass Harold Bloom can be heard what might be the cacophonous ring of four hundred graduate-student typewriters ghostwriting his bloated literary treatises. And it is rumored that you can see in a distant window of Yale's Silliman College a student called Robert "The Monkey Who Is Very Smart but Is Still a Problematic Acceptance Decision" Feigenson. All of these are merely speculation and half-truths, but their sum total makes people worry about the alleged quality of Yale and its Elis.

Yale student Matthew Lapointe echoed the sentiments of many fellow Elis when he commented on the shadiness of Yale's reputation: "I don't know. It's screwed up."

Admissions

If you call them up at their phone number they will send you an application and then you can fill it out and then they will tell you whether or not you can go to Yale. I don't know how I could state this any simpler without being condescending, brickhead.

Academics

Yale has made a concerted effort to eliminate any trace of its reputation for overachieving mediocrity. This is especially apparent in the Yale course guide where classes are clearly superior to classes taught at other schools. No math class could be more rigorous than Math 101: "Hypermath for Super Guys." Oxford and Cambridge offer no English class more difficult than English 1040a: "Hard English for Genius Ladies." And just added this year is a class that takes the teachings of the greatest German philosopher to the next level, Philosophy 8: "Philosophy for Shit-Kicking Immanuel Kant Killers."

The dean of the college, Amy Ozolowsky, commented on the extreme academic rigor of Yale: "I have one-half of a pool cue in my hand at all times. I will sometimes go into a class and find someone who is falling asleep or not paying attention, and I will hit them in the brain with my half of a pool cue. Sometimes I will hurt someone just because I do not value human life. What you got, Harvard?"

Student Life

At Yale there are 430 university-registered extracurricular activities, 423 of which are a cappella singing groups. A cappella music (which means singing without instrumental accompaniment) originated during the Crimean War by the Ottoman Empire as a way to torture dogs. In a recent *Yale Daily News* poll, there were fourteen undergraduates who were not elected into the "Elite 300" singing groups. This lack of normal, functional human beings poses great scheduling problems for the remaining 4,200-plus deranged a cappella drones who must find an audience for their infernal death Muzak.

It is often said that at Yale there is no dating. There is either just hooking up for the night or "marriage." In fact, Yale students are renowned for valuing long, committed relationships. Yale junior Frederick Ellickson expressed common sentiments among Yale students: "I only want to take your love and return it to you twofold. Hold me. Can't you see I am a bottomless well of love from which you can take and take?"

Elis love getting into long, emotionally involved relationships: "I just want to get hammered, see some breasts, and enter into a relationship that will fulfill me forever," said sophomore Chris Calarco. Yale senior Joan Kane offered some sage wisdom to incoming freshmen seeking a mate: "You'd better leave your noncommittal penis at home, baby. Wooo." She added, "No ring, no thang. If you know what I'm saying. Wooo."

Technical School: A Forgotten Friend

Along the college admissions journey, a different option might catch your eye: technical school. Don't scoff; refrigeration repair and its brethren are honorable scientific pursuits. Technical institutes are a throwback to a simpler, blue-collar era when men did science and women stayed at home and did women science (birthing). Within the confines of traditional colleges, science has become smug and bloated, like a gluttonous monarch who knows a lot of physics. A technical school graduate has hands that can tell you that they have done work, honest man's work. These are talking hands.

Forget about the highfalutin concepts presented in university settings, to be referred to from now on as Fancyland. Technical school offers all the utility, minus the frills. Metallurgy? Sorry, Generalissimo Miguel Fancy. In technical school, it's called welding. Medicine? Yeah, they still have that at technical school, but it is medicine/refrigeration repair. Do you remember the X ray? Those trained in medicine/refrigeration repair can repair refrigerators. And how about gravity? At technical school, they have lifting heavy things . . . in *space*. No, not in space: in a dirty garage.

And what about computers? In "university" settings, to be known hereafter as Mt. Dorkhouse, some say that computers are the horses of the twenty-first century. But let's not forget the horses of the twentieth century: horses. Whether it is welding armor for distended horse faces or repairing horse-related refrigerators, technical institutes deal extensively with horses. This is clearly good.

You're asking yourself: Should I go to a regular college or a technical school? Ask yourself this question instead: When you look into the crystal ball of your future, would you rather see a sweat-soaked rag inside a rusted oil can, or a physics textbook covered in popcorn butter? If you choose either, technical school is an option you should consider.

The 5 Most Useful Dorm Room Accessories

1. Tiger repellent (University of Maryland only)
2. Lamp
3. Tiger-killing pack of lions (University of Maryland only)
4. Pack of lions repellent (University of Maryland only)
5. A change of underwear

City College *vs.* Country College

Do you want to go to a college in an urban setting or more of a rural setting? Both have advantages and disadvantages.

"I never get bored here because there're just so many things to do."

"I never get bored here because there're just so many cows to milk."

"I can honestly say that I have never met so many colorful people."

"I can honestly say that I have never met so many horses while riding them to class."

"Crime? Sure, I worry. That's why I try to be safety-minded."

"Bears? Sure, I worry. But that's why I always carry Old Blue."

"I've definitely gotten more liberal and politically active during my time here."

"I've definitely gotten used to sleeping in a cave with bears."

"Good night, Mom. I'll call tomorrow."

"Good night, bear family. Please don't eat me as I sleep."

"So, this guy is like 'Nietzsche was just angry,' and so I was like 'That is so clichéd.'"

"So, this bear is like, 'Roarrr,' and so I wet my pants."

"Well, I better get back to my dorm before my roommate begins to worry."

"Well, it's late and I better hide before the bears come to eat us."

New York University Online Application

>Welcome to the NYU Online Application. Please enter your online application reference number.

>3336925

>Our records indicate your name is Fred Graham. Is this information correct?

>N

>Please enter your correct name:

>Sally Tryster

>I DO NOT UNDERSTAND "SALLY TRYSTER"

>Help

>Enter your password for accessing Help file

>?????????

>FATAL ERROR READING DRIVE C: (A)bort Application, (E)rase Application, (R)etry

>R

>SYSTEM OVERLOAD: (A)bort Application, (D)o Not Go to College, (O)ne Last Try

><ESC>

>GRAND MALFUNCTION. SERVER ERASING ALL APPLICATIONS IN TWO MINUTES: (O)ne Last Try, (G)ive Up

>O

>ONE LAST TRY.........................HAS FAILED!

>Erasing Accepted Applicants...<Done>

>Accepting Denied Applicants...<Done>

>Expunging All Current Students ....<Done>

>Deleting Medical Records for Oncology Patients at NYU Medical Center...........<Done>

>Razing NYU Medical Center...<Done>

>Erasing Internet ....<Done>

>SuperVirus Insertion into World Bank Computers ....<Done>

>Producing Sequel to *The Postman*....................................<Done>

>Poaching Bald Eagles ....<Done>

>World Accepting Half-Goat/Half-Man As Messiah ....<Done>

>Huge Comet Crashing into Goat/Man-World ....<Done>

>WOULD YOU LIKE TO CONTINUE?

>N

>Welcome to the Online Application to Goat-Apocalypse. Please enter your name:

>Sally Tryster

>YOU ARE DEAD.

Part Three

COLLEGE: A WHOLE NEW WORLD

Introduction

High school. That was the time you will treasure forever.

Do you remember Susie Donavan, the first girl you ever courted? How can you forget the innocent smile she gave you as you first put your arm around her? Or the stolen kisses in back of the field house that lifted the burden of your boyhood insecurities? Your scarred hand caressed the small of her back and the whole world seemed safe and warm.

And there was Matt Shamson, the lovable and awkward fellow with the patchy, unkempt facial hair whose sexual inadequacies could be washed away by your simple, feminine touch. You wanted to protect him in the comfort of your bosom from all toughness and pain in this hardscrabble, steel-working town. Because you understood like only a woman can, and he was just a boy. Just a boy.

Or Larry Tanner, the Tan Man, Tanny, or the Tanz-Manian Devil. He could drink a quart of drugstore scotch and tell you about a better place beyond the smoke of the refineries and the sweat-stained brows of men who earned their livings with callused, honest hands. And you listened because, beyond his uncontrollable alcoholism and violent vomiting, there was a good man.

High school is over. In college, Susie Donavan has given up her dreams of a career in nursing/social work to blight her smooth porcelain skin with black lipstick and five nose rings. In your college dreams, her eyebrow ring cuts you in a moment of passion and all the promise and innocence of your youth bleeds out into the university void. You wake up soaked in a cold, salty sweat and see that your roommate is watching pretentious French cinema with a stripper.

Matt Shamson sold the baseball glove that snagged the miraculous game-winning catch to win State in order to buy a bong made out of a water-cooler bottle. And in your lonely nights in your cold dorm room bed, you want to protect him from all temptations that have taken your Matt away. Late at night you hallucinate; you can pretend you are not alone and you can almost feel

Matt's rough, splotchy beard against your ample bosom. But you look into his eyes to see they are dead, useless, sucked out in the smoke of a hundred fraternity keggers. A single, desperate tear falls onto his face and you see that puppy-dog smile begin to form. But you look closer to see that this is the grin of an idiot. Your sweet Matt is lost forever.

It hurts too much to even talk about good old Tanner. He is still a good man, the most good man you will have ever known. But Tanner never made it to college, and sits amid the heat and coal fires of your hometown, taking deep, mournful pulls from his quart of drugstore scotch. You, his friends, have gone your separate ways to school and have forgotten him. Tanner has not forgotten you.

Welcome to college, asshole.

Section I:

Surviving the College Experience

Before you even move into college, you'll be faced with some difficult questions. What kind of roommate do I want? Should I party a lot? What should I wear? What sort of phone/message service do I want? First and foremost, you'll need to fill out a housing form, like the one on page 119:

Sample Housing Form

Name: _____ Nickname (required): _____

Address: _____ State: _____

Sex: M F

DOB: __/__/__

SMOKING

Are you a smoker?

    yes   no

Would you be able to live with a smoker, even if smoking is prohibited in the rooms?

    yes   no

What if there's a fan and you can leave the window open all the time?

    yes   no

Say the cigarette smoke smelled like fresh flowers? How about then?

    yes   no

What if your roommate drops ashes on the carpet and starts a fire? Would you still live with him/her if he/she was the only person in school with a fire extinguisher and there were none in the hallways and the closest fire department was 80 miles away?

    yes   no

SLEEPING HABITS

If your roommate lights up a sweet cig in the middle of the night while writing a paper, and you have an exam the next morning, is that going to wake you?

    yes   no

Pretend like you wake up in the middle of the night to go to the bathroom and your roommate has just chucked a butt on the floor, but it's still burning and you step on it and burn your bare foot. Is that okay?

    yes   no

What if your room is arranged in such a way that your roommate's ashtray can only fit on your face while you sleep? Would you do it?

    yes   no

STUDYING

Hey, have you heard the theory that if you stay up all night studying with caffeine, then you have to take the test on caffeine or else your brain won't work? What if it's the same case with cigarette smoke? Would you live with a smoker then?

    yes   no

What if I tell you that all the rooms at this school are unfurnished, and the only furniture you get is that which you make from empty cigarette boxes. Would you help your roommate smoke 10 packs a day, or just leave him to do it by himself?

    yes   no

Some housing forms include a little essay:

College Roommate Questionnaire

Please write a paragraph below about what you like to do for fun, what music you listen to, and what you look for in a roommate. Please be honest.

I really don't like country music. It is just so irritating. It reminds me of the time my cousin came over and slept the night at our house. This kid snored like a crop-dusting plane. It was louder than a mildly powerful dildo. I wanted to make fun of him and tell everyone, but that morning he caught me masturbating, and my mom narrowly escaped detection when he asked her what all the noise was and she said she was using a water pick to clean her teeth. After that I figured it would be best to agree to call it even.

I guess my favorite music is what you would call alternative. When I come home after going to my track meets and my band competitions, I play alternative music in the car on the way home. I tap out the rhythm on the dashboard but I am really hitting the dashboard out of anger because all the other kids in my high school are having lots of alcohol and sex while I live out my life in sometimes lonely and often solitary dignity. But they have girlfriends, and I don't. I figure that they are doing something right.

What is really infuriating about all those guys who have girlfriends, is that most of them have more zits than me. How do they do it? I think charm and self-confidence can often turn an ugly man pretty. And so can those little rubber yellow pills that the dermatologists are giving out like jelly beans on Easter. The zit wonder drug.

Classical music is okay. If I had a roommate that really liked classical I guess I wouldn't mind. Although I feel that people who listen to a lot of classical music take themselves too seriously. There is something necessary about letting go and listening to bad musicians and bad lead singers screeching out their angst. And there is something too perfect about classical music. And I am skeptical about anything that seems too perfect.

I want a roommate that is considerate, flexible, amiable, open-minded and Natalie Portman. And if that doesn't work out, give me anybody. Just as long as my home is always a place I can come back to and relax. I don't want a roommate who makes me feel insecure or stupid or not cool enough. I just want someone who takes me for who I am and runs with it to the nearest safe deposit box and puts my essence in it and protects it for me until I am old enough to protect myself, which may take a few years.
Sincerely,
Paul DeLaporte

Packing for College

The best advice about what to take to college is to pack only necessary items. One way to do this is to share with your roommate by arranging ahead of time what you each can bring. For example:

if your roommate brings:	*you can bring*:
a stereo	✔ a printer
a computer	✔ also a computer
a typewriter because she cannot afford a computer	✔ a laptop computer
an alarm clock	✔ three alarm clocks
crates for storage	✔ a construction crew that will install gold-plated shelves in your wall
a small refrigerator	✔ a full-size freezer to fit on top of that refrigerator, thereby crushing it
a television	✔ a microphone, and a karaoke machine
a white-noise machine	✔ a microwave, with microwavable pots and pans, and a helicopter
a halogen lamp	✔ a halogen lamp bulb smasher
her French horn	✔ a weighted death club
cookies her mom baked	✔ wealth and ostentation

What Should I Leave Behind?

Regardless of what your roommate brings, you need to know what's cool and what's taboo at college. If there's one thing the *Harvard Lampoon* knows about, it's probably not this. But we tried:

Bring	*Leave Behind*
✔ T-shirts of your favorite bands	T-shirts of your favorite scientists
✔ Teddy bear	Blankey and Elefun
✔ Poster of sexy supermodel	Poster of Yul Brynner
✔ Colorful posters	Colorful face paint
✔ Pictures of your family	Pictures of your roommate's family
✔ Pens, pencils, and notebooks	Pictures of pens, pencils, and notebooks
✔ Compact discs	Player piano
✔ Computer	Computer magazines
✔ Condoms	Modems
✔ Camera and film	Lion and tiger
✔ Toothbrush	Celebrity hair samples
✔ A few souvenirs from high school	A few bricks from high school
✔ Bedsheets	Bedshits
✔ Calculator	$600 protractor
✔ Your favorite pair of jeans	Your favorite pair of ascots

Defusing a Crazy Roommate

So how many times have you heard this one: A good, decent kid goes to college with an innocent excitement for the future, only to be placed with a freshman roommate who has major psychological and emotional problems which they dump on whoever is nearby, thereby ruining the entire year and making a bitter, angry person out of a once-friendly student? Well, it could happen to you too, so pay attention to see how to avoid letting them become dependent on you.

Meeting

You: Hi, you must be—
Her: Hi! It's nice to meet . . . [*begins sobbing*] I'm sorry, my just dumped me and my mom's mad about—
You: Which bed do you want?
Her: It doesn't matter, I mean, 'cause my mom is mad at me
You: Let's listen to some music. Loud!

Freshman Mixer

Her: I think that guy is looking at you!
You: I'm going to go talk to him.
Her: I wish I weren't so ugly! Then maybe a boy would look at
You: I hear you, sister!

The Cafeteria

Her: Do you think there's a lot of fat in this apple?
You: No. There's no fat in apples.
Her: Because I have a lot of self-esteem issues that make it easy for boys to take advantage of me.
You: Well, why don't you just stop having bad self-esteem, silly?
Her: Well, I wish I could, but when I was young—
You: Uh-huh. That is really interesting.

Studying for the Big Exam

You: So, can I borrow your notes from October 12?
Her: Did I ever tell you about October 12 when I was fourteen and my parents got divorced?
You: Did you ever.
Her: Did I mention the part about how my dad never came to visit me when he was supposed to?
You: . . . and how you began taking lithium when you were fifteen?
Her: Oh, you've heard that part.
You: It's hard to forget when you wear that "I Love Lithium" shirt every Sunday.

Falling Asleep

You: Good night.

Her: You're the only real friend I have.

You: We're not friends . . . sleepy-time.

Her: [*begins crying*]

You: Sleep tight!

Good-byes

You: So, um, whatever. Maybe I'll see you next year or something.

Her: I'll write you every day this summer!

You: Yeah, I don't know if you should, because, um, I . . . yeah.

Her: I love you.

You: Thank you.

Roommate Signals

Assuming your roommate is normal, you're going to need to develop a special sort of "language" for those . . . special moments. As a happening dude or lady with a happening roommate, you should be prepared to get "sexiled" from your bedroom while someone gets intimate. You'll need an elaborate system of signals between you and the roommate to avoid unfortunate collisions. Try these:

Door wide open: . . . ."Come on in."

Necktie on the doorknob: . . . ."Do not enter."

Door wide open with necktie on the doorknob: . . . ."Come watch me have sex."

Roommate wearing a necktie: . . . . "Do not have sex with me."

Roommate wearing something other than a necktie: . . . . . ."Do not have sex with me?"

Roommate having sex with you: . . . ."Weren't you wearing a necktie?"

Door engulfed in flames: . . . ."The room is on fire."

Necktie on the doorknob engulfed in flames: . . . ."The room is aflame with our desire."

Roommate and friend engulfed in flames: . . . ."AAAHHHHH!!! OUCHHHHHH!!!"

Roommate and friend engulfed in flames on your bed: . . . . "Sorry!!!! AHHHHHHH!!! I'll clean it up. OWWWWWWWW!!!! OWWWWWW!!!!"

Roommate wearing a cape and cowl: . . . ."I am Batman."

Roommate wearing a Batman T-shirt: . . . ."I need to do laundry and/or it is 1990."

Boata rockin': . . . ."Don't come a-knockin'."

Door rusted shut and covered in barnacles: . . . ."I died aboard the *Lusitania*. Don't come a-knockin'."

Advice for International Students

The challenge for international students wishing to attend U.S. colleges does not end with the admissions process. In fact, most students face an even greater obstacle in adjusting to American life. Here are some frequently encountered problems:

Dear International Office:
Hello. My name is Xiou-Xiau Ping from Taichung, Taiwan. I do not speak the English very well. So I have some bit of trouble communicating with my roommate from Texas. Sometimes we have many fights. Please help.

It seems to me, my foreign friend, that you are mainly having trouble because of your unfamiliarity with American slang terminology. Just remember that in our land, "biscuit" is actually a "cookie," and a "mate" is preferably known as a "friend."

Dear International Office:
I attend class without fail every day. But my professor speaks too fast and I cannot write sufficient notes. Furthermore, he has a strange regional accent, and I have failed my last three hourly examinations.

Ho-hum, foreigner! You see, what you must understand about American culture is that all different types of people are accepted into prestigious positions, even those with speech impediments or other medical ailments, which might I translate into your native tongue as "the plague"? Our nation has long since maintained "hospitals," which employ "doctors." Your city-state may soon come to know this word, "nation."

Dear International Office:
I am especially homesick because it seems like everyone around me goes home at least once a month to visit their families nearby. But it is inconvenient for me to fly 6,000 miles to Geneva for a weekend, and what to do with my Mercedes-Benz, for I cannot ship it home every time I have a vacation? Help, post-haste.

Not so fast, comrade! To overcome your problems adjusting, you need to first realize that America no longer has an extensive steamboat or covered wagon transportation system. Since our discovery of the road, our transport vehicles have added safety features such as seat belts, airbags, and front-wheel drive. We call these inventions "a pickup truck."

Dear International Office:

I have trouble with the American diet offered to me in the dining halls. Not only am I lactose intolerant, but my body does not respond well to the high amounts of fat and sodium. How can I get the university to accommodate my new-age vegan menu consisting of cosmopolitan herbs and spices?

Friendly beast, allow me to explain. We no longer hunt our food per family. Rather, we have large buildings called grocery stores, where food can be bought and prepared ourselves with something we've dubbed "fire." Furthermore, the woolly mammoth that you most likely seek disappeared in America eons ago, as did most dinosaurs and glaciers. The college may not be able to help you here.

Dorm Pets

So, let's say you go to college and after a few weeks you start to get real lonely. Let's also say that you're scared of asking someone on a date because you're scarred from four years of rejection in high school. And let's just say that you decide to get a pet for some long-needed companionship, and that the pet you settled on is either a goldfish or an endangered black rhino. Well, turns out that you wouldn't be the only one keeping an illegal pet in their dorm room. It seems you can't swing a dead cat on campus these days without hitting someone bringing pilfered cafeteria food to her puppy, stepping in an enormous piece of elephant poop, or having a tribe of Bushmen smell your shoes and discuss the scent of the poop on them through clicking and grunting as they track a bull elephant through the quadrangle.

Pet ownership among college students is at an all-time high, and more and more of the pets being kept in dorm rooms are not innocuous fish and the occasional kitty-cat, but wild, exotic species from all around the world. "I guess I've always tried to be different," said one wayward freshman who paid $2 for a rabid raccoon. "He eats garbage and bites everyone, but I was able to solve that problem by releasing a pack of wolves into my bedroom." Some students find out that caring for a pet is more responsibility than they can handle. As said by a freshman girl: "If there is one thing I learned about myself this year, it's that I know nothing about caring for a dolphin. And also I'm a people person."

So if you happen to be looking for a pet for your dorm room, what sort should you look for? A wild boar is a good choice. Hungry only for scraps of food, a wild boar is easy to take care of. "I love Herman," says freshman Sarah Edwards of UW-Madison as she strokes the razorback's tuft of silver hair. The only other things besides food a razorback requires are several acres of grasslands and an arid climate. "Huh?" says Sarah. "Snorrrt," says Herman. Another good choice is a shark. "Your best bet is a nurse shark, since they're tame beasts," says freshman Captain Beardy, peering with his one unpatched eye into the waters around his desk, which he is chumming with fish guts and blood, using his hook hand to hold the handle on the bucket.

Nobody seems to be able to explain this phenomenon, not even Crocodile Hunter. "Who could blame anyone for wanting to be near these beauuutiful creatures?" he yelled from the women's showers, where he was giving Matilda a washing. "Just look at these beauuutiful teeth," he called as he inserted his own head into Matilda's opened jaws. Indeed, nobody seems able to explain the recent surge in the popularity of wild animals on campus, and until somebody does, chaos reigns.

How to Wash Your Laundry

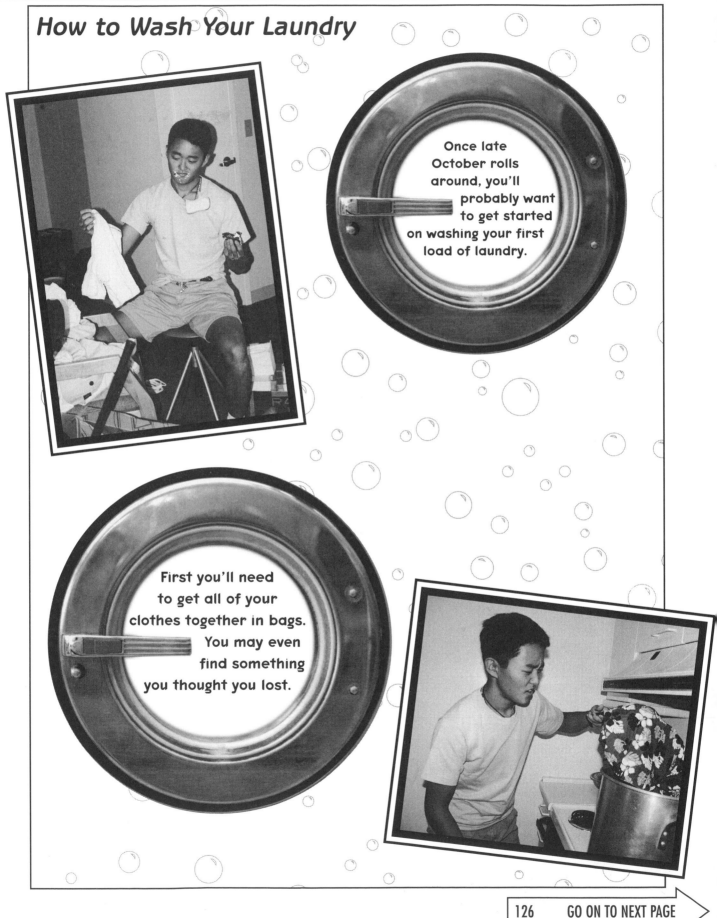

Once late October rolls around, you'll probably want to get started on washing your first load of laundry.

First you'll need to get all of your clothes together in bags. You may even find something you thought you lost.

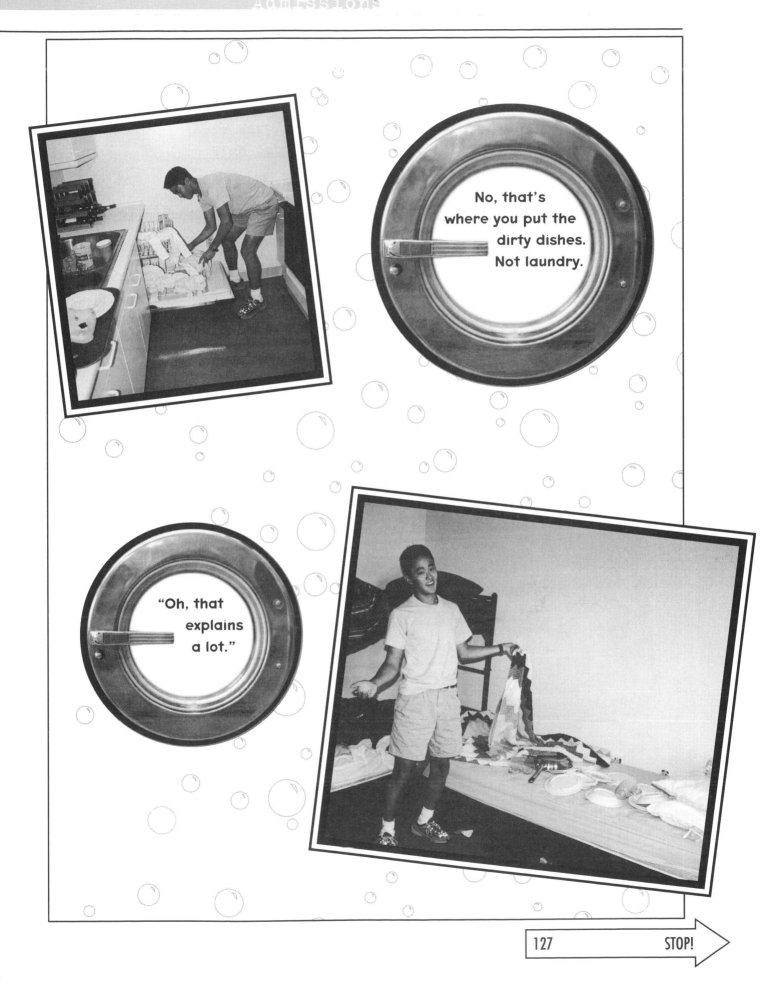

"Man, this laundry crap is easy."

"Sometimes I get so lonely [*hic*] . . . you guys are my real friends [*hic*] . . ."

STOP!

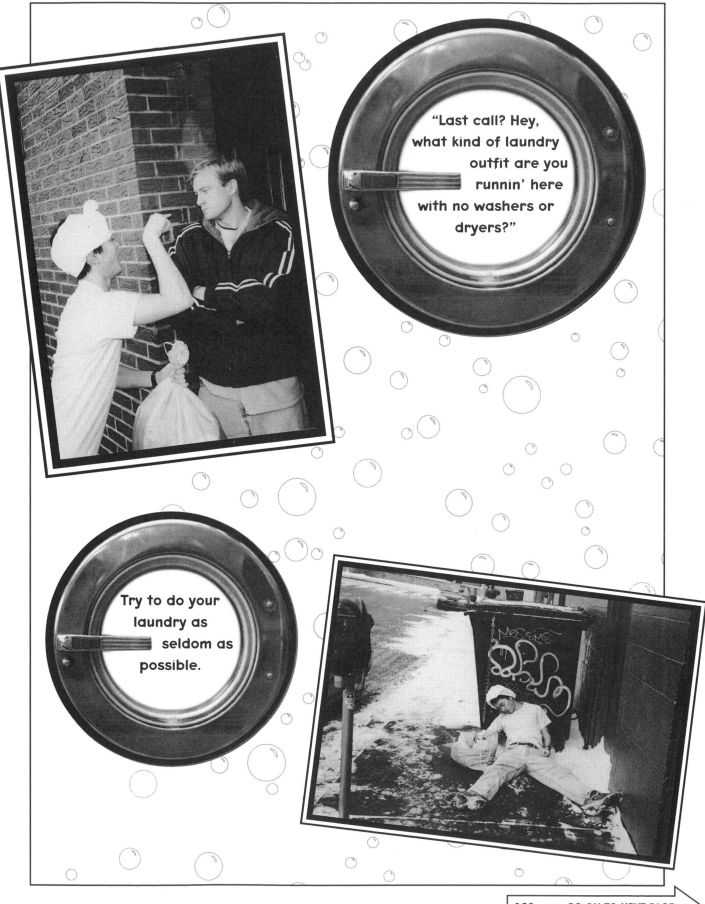

"Last call? Hey, what kind of laundry outfit are you runnin' here with no washers or dryers?"

Try to do your laundry as seldom as possible.

A Risk Worth Taking?

There will always be that varsity athlete who hurts himself in an intramural game. "What an idiot," you think to yourself as he limps by. "An intramural game is either a pointless ego boost for a real athlete, or a forum for washed-up nostalgic wanna-bes," you add as you kick one of his crutches out from under him and watch him fall. "Sorry," you say as you altruistically help him get up.

But someday you'll be playing intramural basketball and you'll hear your knee pop off your leg. "Ouch," you say as you fall to the ground. "It's not that bad," you tell yourself as you limp off carrying the bottom half of your leg folded under your arm like a businessman might carry a newspaper.

"I'll probably be able to run in my cross-country meet tomorrow," you tell your doctor as he accidentally sews your lower leg back on with the kneepit facing front.

"I'll run, Coach," you say to your coach the next day when he asks you why your lower leg is flopping like a wet sock in the wind.

"You won't catch me, I'm the gingerbread man," you trash-talk rival cross-country teams while you balance on your one good leg at the starting line and wait for the gun to go off.

"I'm winning, I'm winning," you scream joyously as you hop out to the early lead after the gun goes off.

"I'm falling, I'm falling," you say as you fall and all two hundred runners stampede over your lumbar.

"I can still win," you say optimistically as you paw at the ground helplessly.

"I think I was dehydrated," you say to your parents later that night when they call and ask how you did. "Or maybe I went out too fast," you say as you bend your leg upward and scratch your temple quizzically with your big toe.

Writing for Your College Newspaper

Listen in, Junior, and listen tight. Time was when jotting down a few notes in a scrawny pad made you a journalist, or a "J-dog." But these days, college types have lost the knickers and gotten into journalism—that's Journalism with a capital *J* for just about the toughest, most exhilarating, and toughest college extracurricular you can knicker into.

Horace Greeley. Colonel McCormack. Not too far back, these names meant newspapering, the way Tripp Cromer once meant baseball in certain circles. But times have changed. Newspapers aren't just low-budget roofing anymore—they're serious, respected, and hard-hitting. If you want to "make the paper" at Cub U, you're going to have to get in the game, get in the punches, and get the story. While you were laughing it up over a bottle of suds, Lil' Lucy in the corner just became associate editor of the *Daily Campus*.

So here's the "scoop," as we call it in the biz. Sometime in the fall, you, along with about a million other Benny and Betty Beanies, hit campus. But while those hayseeds are thinking of football and buttercups, you're busy typing out copy you bought on a rusty Vickers-Lytton you bought at a charity sale. Date, place, story, *action*—you're noting it all in prose that could sink a dreadnought.

Once the annual Activities Faire rolls around, you're out there with a sharp ballpoint to sign your moniker onto the ol' roster—it's time for newspaper tryouts. Have a quick look around, Newsprint Jimmy—that fellow in the raccoon coat is gunning for your seat at the Stories Desk. Eliza Muffin with the varsity sweater is ready to muscle you away from the ticking wire as she scrambles for a notch on the masthead. Better flex your thinking arm, Tiger.

You've now entered the manic world of the sweaty pressroom. While the gang is gathered around the editor, or "Ed," weasel your wormy way toward the action and get cracking on your first page one. Aces!

There are a variety of college papers—from broadsheets to flatties to old-time shimeyplates. But they all swim together in the brotherhood of journalism. With a twinkle in your eye and a gung-ho spirit for the "rag," you'll be sure to come up tops.

Disappointing Your Parents

Hey man. Yeah, you with the tight necktie and the keychain with the Ten Commandments on it. You're a college student now—no more parentdull supervision. Time to have some fun, disobedience-style! Naturally, some of the things you might do will be a tad irksome to them. Assuming that your parents aren't your RAs, you're no longer under their roof, so you have every right to disappoint them. Nothing is more satisfying than a little bit of letdown soup for Mom and Dad, believe me. If my parents weren't my RAs, I would have done all of this:

Expectation 1: Mom reminds you, "Make sure you get all your vitamins and minerals!"

Sorry, Mom, but your overbearing rules don't work anymore. Preach though you might, I'm gonna catch me some osteoporosis ASAP, with a little side order of scurvy. And you can forget vitamin D, too, because I'm going to cover myself in tinfoil. Take that, Mrs. Naggy Q. Nutrifacts. How sweet it is to disobey! Hope you enjoy paying for my intravenous force-feeding, Mother Dearest.

Expectation 2: Keep your grades up! We paid good money for your education.

Hey, don't tell me what to do. It's my life now, and if I want to fail all my classes, skip the academic probation meeting with the dean, get kicked out, live hand-to-mouth on the streets all semester, and fall victim to a hurtful, deceptive Hobo King, doggone if I don't go ahead and do it. How do ya like me now, my dear sweet mother? Revenge is so beautiful. Please send me any pocket change you can spare, bitch.

FDA
Food and Drug Administration

LOSING THE FRESHMAN 650

It is time to change your image. You have been constantly gaining weight since you went to college. You want to lose the weight, but you can't find the switch that turns down the gravity. There may be hope yet!! Follow this advice and you should instantly be lighter.

For starters, change out of that denim shirt and into this cotton silk shirt. That should at least give you .23 of a pound right there.

Take off your gun belt. I know the guns are plastic, but that should still be a few pounds.

Get a haircut. Your hair is long and unkempt.

Clip your toenails. Slowly but surely you are losing weight.

Take off your watch. You can draw a watch face in your watch tan that you can update every second. This type of watch is much lighter.

Pick your nose.

Cover your body with leeches, let them fill up with your blood, and then burn them off. Take the cooked leeches and poke straws into them. Drink blood. In this way you will get to drink a lot of liquid but you won't have to deal with all the calories. Alternatively, you can drink water.

Celery is minus three calories because it takes so much energy to chew. Eat enough celery to cancel out the rest of your calorie intake.

The gravity switch is in Cambridge, Mass., at 0 Freedom Square. Bring it down a notch.

Expectation 3: Bring home a nice boy/girl to introduce to your mom and dad.

Listen up, 'rents, meet Lesta Vilefist, my domineering and cruel girlfriend. She's just what you wanted—minus the sugar-coated wussy niceness! You wanted to meet a nice girl, instead I give you Ms. Vilefist, the Phys. Ed. major who beats me senseless every hour on the hour. Stick that in your pipe and smoke it. This shiner on my eye is my little symbol of the disappointment you must be feeling when you hear about how badly she kicked my ass last night. I'm a college boy now, time to let my hair down.

Expectation 4: Remember to call home every week!

Hey man and woman who gave me life, I'm eighteen now. Eat it. Those prepaid phone cards you wanted me to purchase? Oh I'm buying them all right, I'm buying them by the boxful—and then I'm flushing them down the toilet and/or breaking them in half! And then I'm pawning my belongings to buy more and not use them, too. Exquisite rebelliousness! Disappointment City! Your tyrannical rules are going down the drain much like the hundreds of dollars' worth of phone cards I have purchased and subsequently destroyed.

Expectation 5: Don't drink too much.

I won't drink, but darned if I won't imply that I do in my biweekly letters to home! "Hey Mom and Dad, I'll keep this letter short because I had a *late night* yesterday." They'll be afraid that I was out drinking, even if I was in my room writing this letter. Suck it, suck it, suck it!

How you all doing, Mom and Pop? A little disappointed, perhaps? I thought so. That's the college life for you—I'll try to take a break from my fun and drop in sometime. Or maybe I won't! Buy the tickets anyway because I probably will.

FDA

Food and Drug Administration

COLLEGE FRESHMEN: GAINING WEIGHT AND THEN GAINING MORE WEIGHT

A Report by FDA Nutritionist Meghan Simons

How many times have I heard this story before: A young beautiful girl goes happily off to college weighing a mere 125 pounds. One month later, she weighs 750 pounds.

That's right, the old freshman 15 has become the freshman 650. But why? Why do over 88 percent of all freshman women and men gain over 600 pounds during their first month of college? Is it the dining hall food? The obesity pills? The continuously administered IVs of pig and cow fat? The cosmetic surgery that adds hundreds of pounds of fat to their normally healthy bodies?

Sadly, we may never know.

Last month I toured America's colleges to see what was wrong with our students. I witnessed millions of students lying around in wheelbarrows, students who could bounce icebergs off of their gigantic flesh-trampoline stomachs, students who had to be transported on stretchers normally used only for polar bears, and also a lot of very fat kids.

So what did I do, you ask? Well, I did what any normal nutritionist would do: I took pictures, went sunbathing, had a massage, and I laughed until I cried, and then I laughed some more. Then I laughed again and again and again. It was uproariously hilarious. In a desperately tragic kind of way.

To be honest, however, our nation's universities have a problem on their hands. A "very obese" problem to be perfectly frank. But what are we going to do about it? Several parents I talked to don't seem too bothered by the phenomenon: "Hey, that's what college is for, right? You get drunk, fool around, go to class, gain 600 pounds, tailgate, become a sumo wrestler, and then graduate," explained sumo-wrestling champion Oko Bayashi, Yale class of '92.

But is that what college is really for? To prepare our youth for pro sumo wrestling? Do we truly want a country of obese, sumo-wrestling fatsos?

I don't see why not.

Send all questions, comments, and complaints to Meghan Simons at m_simons@fda.gov.

Section II:

Social Life

Ethnicity in College

A Serious Note to Our Readers

You hold in your hands a comedy piece produced by the Harvard Lampoon, Inc. Despite the ribald wit and japery that normally characterizes our creative processes, the laughs came to a halt during the production of this article, when we were forced to grapple with the issue of ethnic satire. Ethnicity certainly has been a topic that many formidable comedic minds have dealt with, and we felt it within our power to craft some jokes based around the serious issues that America faces; especially in regards to the waning (but still apparent) discriminations that are a blight across the American landscape. In our quest to find a joke that will at once bring a smile to the faces of our readers and offend no one, we consulted several organizations to which we owe a considerable debt of gratitude. Though naming them does not do them justice, they are as follows: the American Civil Liberties Union, the Anti-Defamation League, the National Association for the Advancement of Colored People, the Rainbow Coalition, Unity First!, the Society for the Prevention of Cruelty to Animals, the Please Don't Hurt the Taiwanese Group, Just Say No!, the Society for the Protection of Citizens of the Northeastern Quadrant of Oregon Who Are Half-Asian People, the I'm White and Right Society, the Montreal Expos, the World Wide Web, the cast and crew of *Family Matters*, and Tha Dogg Pound. Certainly the ethnic humor that follows could not have been possible without the help of the following contributors: Jesse Jackson, the Reverend Al Sharpton, President Bill Clinton, former president Benjamin Harrison, the Pope, King Arthur, Bea Arthur, Voltaire, Fatty Boombalatti, noted character actor F. Murray Abraham, Slopey the Bear, the night manager at Loews—Harvard Square, O'Callahan the Nice Leprechaun, and many others that space restrictions do not allow us to mention. If you have any questions about the legality of satire in the American discourse, the *Harvard Lampoon* would like to direct you to a helpful and informative Web site that will indeed answer many of your legitimate questions: http://www.whitehouse.gov/legal/1286/satire.html.

If you would like to pursue further inquiry into the nature of satire, you may want to examine the *Marbury v. Jackson* case of 1937. The transcripts of the trial can be examined at the Library of Congress (call number 1874.34.567.32.0000054). Barring that, we encourage you to examine Chapter V (subset 3b) of the American Civil Liberties Act. Particularly, we found Paragraphs III–VIII helpful. If you have any questions or concerns, we've set up a 24-hour hotline at 1-800-END-HATE. Call anytime.

Working together with these various organizations and people, a crack team of comedic minds spent thirty-five hours locked in meetings to come up with an ethnic piece that is tender, touching, and true. We thank you all. Without further ado:

The *Harvard Lampoon*'s Satire of Ethnicity in College

Rico: Ese, you got some cocaine?

Miko: Ching Chang Chong Chung Chen Ching [*translation:* no].

Tony: I don't-a-know-about-a-the-cocaine-a heyyyyyyy!! Where-a-the-pastafazoule did I put my pizza?

Leroy: I am in jail.

University of Alaska
N O M E

Dear Prospective Student,

Congratulations on being accepted to the University of Alaska at Nome! My name is Jenny Holowitz and I am the chairman of the Student Affairs Committee. We're sure that you've received quite a bit of information from the University regarding academics, advising, and rooming. We felt it would be great to tell you about some of the "HOT SPOTS" on campus. Take a gander, and we look forward to seeing you in the fall!!!!

Hot Spots at the University of Alaska–Nome

1. McKlintock Hall Boiler Room:
*It's almost impossible to walk back from the library to the dorms without suffering through mild frostbite and frozen snot on your nose. One of the best ways to avoid this problem is by sneaking through the back door of McKlintock Hall and giving Archie the Janitor $5 (if he's not drunk). The boiler room is at the bottom of the steps on your right. Make sure you don't touch the furnace—*__or have too much fun!!__

2. Steam Ventilator near the Admissions Office:
Populated by students at all hours of the night, the steam ventilator near the admissions office will give you everything you need to prevent unnecessary extremity amputation. Despite the preponderance of the Eskimos-without-igloos faction, there's still plenty of room to warm your windburned face. As a special for incoming freshmen, we are sponsoring a "Ventilate With a Date" night in March, in which every first-year couple gets to sit with their date for 10 minutes __right next__ *to the ventilator. Look out for it this spring!*

3. Dining Hall Dumpster:
Head of the Dining Hall Marcy Compson will dump a pot of warm dishwasher water toward the Dumpster every week night at around 7:30. One of the most popular student activities, a select group of "Dumpster dudes," congregates every night, praying that their numb noses will be healed by a refreshing splash from Marcy. Freshmen are encouraged to take part in the fun. Seniors often maim smaller first-years in a frenzied desire to prevent a cold, lonely death—don't say we didn't "warm" you!!!!

4. Gruberson Memorial Frozen Tundra:
If you are ready for the ultimate UA-N experience, be sure to trek the 13 miles to the Gruberson Memorial Frozen Tundra (PERMA-F.R.O.S.T.). It is said that seconds before freezing to death you feel a warm spot in your belly. Savor this experience as you drift into a cold-induced coma. Follow the lights, departed friend. If we thaw out your body in the spring and you are wearing a University of Alaska–Nome T-shirt, consider yourself the proud owner of a complimentary coffee mug!

5. Chingachgook's Hunting Lodge:
The wily Chingachgook often leaves his slain deer carcasses in a fire pit near his cabin. We've enclosed a __free__ *University of Alaska Fighting Elks nose clip in this envelope. Wear it proudly when you climb into the warm carcasses of the deceased deer to make your Friday nights caliente. Go Elks!*

Big Man on Campus

So you think college life is going to be the best? Well, don't get too excited, because you'll still be playing second fiddle. Nobody has a better time at college than the Big Man on Campus. Only a select few can attain this position, like these following dudes.

Eric Burns: Biggest man on campus at Penn State. Not only is he ripped (huge pecs!) and similar in the face to Jared Leto, he wears fly clothes and drives a Land Rover. He is also smart, getting A's and B's in his classes. Did I mention the size of his pecs?!? His nipples are like city-states!

Brian Whitten: BMOC at Tulane. He drinks like a thirty-pack a night, but he never says dumb things. I once saw him drink from a can of Aqua Net while wrestling two pythons. He has a butt that would melt the ice caps. This dude is so big, he once had seven fly honeys on his lap at one time and *still* had room for a laptop computer! (Don't worry, he was just using it as a coaster for some beer.) His immense body masks Whitten's true physical marvel: perfect symmetry.

Mighty Joe Young: Oh shiiiiiiiiiiiit!!! Big Gorilla!!!!!!

Me: I am the BMOC of BMOCs. Not only am I cool and envied, I also live in a giant water tank to support the weight of my organs. Consequently, I have not been to a party at college. Such is the price I pay. But as the BMOC, my whole life is a party. Sometimes my keepers put a boom box next to my ear.

But you may be wondering how you may become the Big Man on Campus. The *Harvard Lampoon* may know how . . .

How I Became the Big Man on Campus

By Ted Ripper

So you want to be the big man on campus, huh? Fine. But just think for a second, what do girls really love? Football players? Men in uniform? Handsome, caring, understanding men with looks like Brad Pitt and the compassion of Gandhi?

Don't be retarded!

Let me tell you a little story. Three years ago I came to Harvard a dorky, acne-ridden eighteen-year-old with a face like the Elephant Man and the body of a small infant girl. Today I'm married to nine brilliant Radcliffe grads-turned-swimsuit models and live polygamously in Maui where I have thirty-two children. So how did I do it? How did I wine and dine these beautiful women and cause them to fall helplessly in love with me? One hyphenated word: Monster-trucks.

During my sophomore year at Harvard I joined Harvard's D-1 Monster-Truck team. Believe me, there's nothing sexier for a woman than to see her man climb up into the cab of a monster-truck with its ridiculously large tires, huge, unnecessary headlights, and the word "Gravedigger" spray-painted in neon yellow across the front.

"Oh Johnny, watching you trample all those used Chevy Novas and then smash 'Big Foot' was so sexy," my first wife, supermodel Sally Jones, told me after the annual Ivy League Invitational Monster-Truck rally, as drunk men poured beer on our heads and spit tobacco juice in her hair.

If I've learned one thing at college, it's this: Monster-trucks are sexy; sexy in a distinguished, refined, New England blue-blood kind of way. Classy broads dig 'em. It's that simple.

Thank you.

Mathletes Beware!

The following is a warning from the NCAA Rules Committee concerning the recruitment and treatment of student-mathletes on college campuses across the country.

In 1989, when three members of CalTech's NCAA Division I—winning Math Team showed up at school with 8-karat-gold protractors, using graph paper made out of pages from a Gutenberg Bible and continuously accompanied by a coterie of promoters, prostitutes, and yes-men, school officials grew suspicious. It turned out, of course, that Math Team boosters had been illegally providing the mathletes with millions of dollars in cash gifts as incentives to keep CalTech a perennial Math Team powerhouse.

So an incident like that probably only happens once in a blue moon. Isn't that right, NCAA Rules Committee, you ask? Wrong. Each year college recruiters vie for the top high school mathletes country-wide, and these days the promise of a mere scholarship often isn't enough. According to Stanford Math Team coach Tim Fermat, "I had a kid last year who wanted me to *guarantee* him an endorsement deal with Texas Instruments. Texas Instruments! I told him the best I could do was Casio. He ended up at MIT."

Because recruiters will often begin the recruitment process as early as the third and fourth grades, prodigy mathletes get used to star treatment. In fact, by the time a decent mathlete has entered ninth grade it's a pretty sure bet he's snorted the purest Colombian cocaine off the tits of a $1,000-per-night hooker as he prepares for a front-page photo shoot with *Esquire*.

Not only are student-mathletes at risk during high school, but they often meet with temptation during their collegiate years as well, as demonstrated by the rise in gambling among mathletes. According to one student-mathlete, "I knew I had hit rock bottom when (Queens mob boss) Tony Fugliosiano told me before the NCAA quarterfinals, 'Your ass goes down in the fifth, during multivariable calc. and chaos theory.' I had no choice."

There is no two ways about it. College mathletics is a highly lucrative business that involves millions of dollars, hundreds of hours of TV air time, and corporate endorsements. But unless we ensure that our coaches, recruiters, and mathletes have at heart the principles upon which the sport of mathletics was founded—namely, calculus and linear algebra—then our problems will only continue to mount.

Thank you,
NCAA Rules Committee

📢 Lost Pants

Hi, my name is Kate R. Thomas. Although I'm a bit on the shy side, I'd like to make a small request.

Whoever stole my rumpless leather hot pants: I WANT MY PANTS! They have been in the family for several generations. My great-grandfather used to split rails and lay down track in those pants.

Hoping to join the Supreme Court when you graduate? Check out this sample cover letter!

Carrot Top
13 Alabaster Dr.
Los Angeles, CA 09874
342-CAR-TOPP (342-218-8666)

June 10, 2000

Sir William Rehnquist
Supreme Court Building
8 Pennsylvania Ave.
Washington, DC 09342

Dear Sir Rehnquist and other respected members of the U.S. Supreme Court:

I am a world-renowned prop comic and jokester who has performed at such venues as the Newark Laff-Factory, Des Moines' Comedy House, and Bismarck's Laff-nasium. I did not graduate from high school.

Yet I have always admired the U.S. Supreme Court. You are leaders in the field of Supreme Courts and I respect that. Being a prop comic, I know what it's like to have to make important decisions. Box of joke knives or hat with a pair of genitals on it? Wacky sunglasses or oversized comic shoes? Fake bloody hand or fake bloody finger? These are the kind of choices I'm forced to make daily. It'd probably be a whole lot easier if I had a panel of 8 other prop comics to consult for each decision, but not all of us have that luxury.

I feel confident that after reviewing my resume, you will see that I am a worthy candidate as a 10th judge on the Supreme Court. Not only could I weigh in on issues like environmental rights, free speech, and Internet restrictions, I could also provide light comic relief during tense trials. For example, if there was a trial about abortion, I could bring a baby doll with blood on it, and exclaim "Hey look, I just performed an abortion" and show everyone the bloody doll. That would be truly hilarious.

Moreover, if you do decide to hire me as the 10th judge, I will guarantee you all back-stage passes at my shows. It's not an easy ticket to get.

Thank you for your consideration. I look forward to hearing from you soon.

Sincerely,

Carrot Top

Carrot Top

"Coed Naked" T-shirts: What the Cool Kids Wear!

They've made us laugh. They've made us cry. And above all, they've made us think about the possibility of playing sports naked against girls. The "Coed Naked" T-shirt is a unique college phenomenon that deserves a closer look.

Bill Ding and Mike R. Tchecka knew two things. One, men and women naked together is funny! Two, men and women playing sports together naked is the funniest thing ever. And so it was born, the ubiquitous Coed Naked T-shirt. Although some of the earlier efforts were fairly uncreative, i.e., "Coed Naked Ice Hockey: It's Twice as Nice on the Ice," or "Coed Naked Basketball: It's Twice as Nice on the Basketball Court," and "Coed Naked Swimming: It's Two Times as Pleasing in the Water" more recent efforts have attracted nationwide attention. Last year's edgy "Coed Naked Football: Fourth Down on Your Knees, Toots!" drew protests from women's organizations nationwide. Admits cofounder Bill Ding, "That was a mistake. I'm just so glad we didn't run the 'Coed Naked Holocaust: Nice *Try*, but We Know It's All a Big *Lie*.'"

The last couple of months, however, have seen some of the funniest "Coed Naked" shirts yet, like the hugely popular "Coed Naked Baseball: Men and Women Playing Baseball Together While Not Wearing Any Clothes or Even Underwear," and "Coed Naked Oral Sex: Persons of the Opposite Sex Performing Fellatio on One Another."

But how do they do it? Explained founder Andy Bednarik, "We think of different sports, and then we think, 'What if men and women played these sports against one another. Naked.'" Genius? Perhaps.

Look for the team to continue to produce newer and wittier stuff far into the future. According to one writer, "We've got a couple new ones that should debut this fall. There's 'Coed Naked Fire-Bombing the Vietnamese Countryside during the Summer of '71: Man, That Was Some Fucked-Up Shit,' 'Coed Naked Wrestling: This Usually Turns into Sex Pretty Quickly,' and 'Coed Naked Life in a Nudist Colony: Dude, There Are Tits Everywhere!'"

College students nationwide shall continue to hold their breath in anticipation of what these artistic geniuses will come up with next. One thing, however, is for sure: It will involve naked girls and boys, as well as collegiate sports.

A Guide to Drinking Games

Binge drinking is a serious problem in college campuses across the country. To treat it lightly by discussing various drinking games would be socially irresponsible. Since the members of the *Lampoon* are serious about our social responsibility, we've provided a list of games that are dangerous and should be avoided at all costs:

Quarters: A game that should not be condoned by any responsible undergraduate. Two cups are passed around a circle of solid guys and pretty girls where quarters are bounced into the cups and then passed along. If the two cups meet at one of the solid guys or beautiful girls, then that person has to drink an ice cold and refreshing beer.

The Century Club: While you attempt to do one hundred shots of beer in one hundred minutes, alcohol will lift the weight of countless problems from your shoulders and all thoughts will pass into a mental fuzziness that makes everything safe and warm. Bad.

Beer Pong: Ping-Pong balls are bounced into triangular formations of beer cups at opposite ends of a Ping-Pong table. Sometimes the intoxicated members will get so merry with unsavory drink they will peel off their clothes and start writhing around to rock music in shameful nakedness displaying sweat-soaked bodies at the height of sexual flower.

The Lloyd Dobler game: While watching the movie *Say Anything*. . . participants will take a drink any time John Cusack's romantic protagonist, Lloyd Dobler, has his name mentioned. In the movie, Lloyd Dobler engages in romantic and emotionally satisfying premarital sex which is often the damning outcome of drinking during this heartwarming romantic comedy. How can you call drinking a game . . . this is life and death here, people.

Asshole: Intemperate things will happen when a deck of cards is thrown to the floor to make way for a private reunion performance of Led Zeppelin with Jason Bonham pounding the skins with the same genius as his late father. The transcendent, androgynous wail of Robert Plant and the sheer carnal virtuosity of Jimmy Page's guitar are the only positive things that can arise from this detestable game.

Where would big colleges be without school spirit? Take a look at this case study of how one school turned declining feelings of self-awesomeness into full-contact self-love:

The University of Southern Florida: A Revived School Spirit

In 1989 the athletic director at the University of Southern Florida, Tony Smith, decided that the school wasn't supporting their athletic teams as much as they should; attendance was down, school spirit had vanished, and the school mascot had just been arrested on heroin charges. As Smith put it, "Hell, when only 60,000 people are showing up for a late-season women's water polo game, you know you're doing something wrong." The school needed a shot in the arm, and that's just what Smith gave 'em.

"To the A, to the R, to the S, to the E! Stick it up yer arse, mates! Let's go U of SF!" comes the cry from the Southern Florida cheerleading squad at a recent home football game. The University of Southern Florida cheerleaders are today considered some of the best in the country. This, however, was not always the case. Whereas ten years ago the squad was made up primarily of beautiful, healthy, muscular, tanned young men and women who were enthusiastic about their school and their sports teams, today the cheerleading team is composed entirely of teenage British football hooligans with pasty white skin, leather jackets, and a penchant for "knockin' heads" if the outcome isn't to their liking.

And the school's students have taken to the British lads. Explained one sophomore, "I love the 'Oi! Oi! Sod off, ya' bloody rat-arses!' chant they do at every women's softball game. That really gets the crowd going." A U of SF junior concurred: "Last year, when our cheerleaders stormed the courts after the squash team's heartbreaking loss and they burned down the bleachers and lynched the umpire and ignited a city-wide riot, I could just feel the electricity, the spirit of *communitas* among my fellow students, running through my veins. That day, I felt really proud to call myself a U of SF student."

But the process hasn't been completely without its problems. For example, the university demands that all its cheerleaders wear the proper school uniforms when cheering. "Needless to say, some of the lads weren't too happy about that. But we had a reasonable conversation and it all got worked out," explained AD Tony Smith. According to cheerleading captain Danny Blair, however, "I fuckin' bloodied up his [Smith's] face and 'en I stuck a reyt' boot up his arse and spit in 'is puny li'l face. I says to 'im, 'I just fucked your wife, 'ow's that, you piece of fuck. I het these fuckin' unis and we hain't wearin' 'iss shite.'" Despite Blair's complaints, however, the university did eventually win the uniform battle, not, however, before having three top administrators stoned to death by the angry cheerleaders.

The squad travels next month to Arizona for the yearly NCAA D-I Cheerleading competition. "They says UNC's got a good squad, but I think they're a pile of shite," commented squad member Timmy Caullife on U of SF's competition. The team has been working out some new routines that they'll hope to try in Arizona. Explained captain Blair, "I wanna' do the one where we get reyt' blotto and then piss all over the floor. Oi!"

The University of Southern Florida cheerleaders: They do more than just lead cheers, they piss all over the floor. Oi! indeed.

Finding Your Ethnic Niche on Campus

Most students come to college from high schools that are much more ethnically homogeneous than their new surroundings. There are probably more Inuit words for "snow" than there are actual Inuits at your high school. And your school probably has about as many Apache Indians as there are Apache words for "Gatorade-flavored steak." But in college there will be 12 Inuits and 186 Apache Indians, so you need to feel comfortable around all sorts of people. A large part of this process will involve finding an appropriate social/ethnic campus organization. These are exactly the same at every college in America, and include the following:

The Asian American Association: Your college's AAA will most likely feature weekly Asian food-tasting or anime movies. The organization is a great way for Asian people to come together as a community and marry one another.

The East Asian/Indian Students Association: Your college's EA/ISA will most likely feature Indian food-tasting or Indian rug making. All should feel free to walk into such a meeting, but be warned that you will exit the meeting with a wife and two children.

The Hillel: For those of you residing outside the environs of New York City, a Hillel is a social and spiritual organization for students of the Jewish faith. Students in the Hillel are collected together during freshman year in a minivan. No boy is allowed to exit the van without a girl to whom he is immediately married. If there are an odd number of students, the last man in the van remains unmarried and becomes a Catholic priest.

The Catholic Students Association: This works more or less the same as the Hillel, except that all of the boys become priests and all of the girls are forced to marry one another. The Catholic Students Association is not endorsed by or connected to the Catholic Church.

The Hot Guy Students Association: Members of HGSA meet weekly to discuss issues like *Happy Gilmore*, ladies, *Billy Madison*, and guy stuff. They frequently hook up with good-looking ladies who like to have fun and hang out. If there are an odd number of people in the room, someone gets to have a sweet three-way.

The Campus Science Fiction Coalition: This is a great place for nice girls to come to meet and marry a sensitive guy who's maybe a little shy but is really sweet. Be prepared for a few weeks of sweaty and uncomfortable silence as the members decide by squirms and glances which of them has the least chance of crying while speaking to you.

Fake IDs

We at the *Harvard Lampoon* want you to have all of the privileges of an adult without all of the hassle (and marital infidelity!). So you can feel free to cut out one of these identification cards that you can use to purchase illegal fireworks or get you into a local nightclub, nursing home, or strip club. But don't tell the Five-O that we helped you out. Seeing your hands blasted off from a faulty M-80 is all the thanks we need.

This was our first fake and got several of us out of the Gulf War.

An Inside Look: Collegiate Fraternities

College fraternities: The word brings to mind images of oak halls, fireplaces, refined manners, dried vomit, and tweed jackets, as well as gentlemanly conduct and sexual assault. Indeed, most such organizations have existed since time immemorial, or at least 1985, and aim to foster respect for the importance of tradition. As one fine young Delta Chi Epsilon brother explained, "We've got lots of really, really old sacred traditions around here. Our favorites include puking on each other and biting off the heads of rats."

Collegiate fraternities have served for centuries as a meeting place for like-minded young men; a place where intimate bonds can be formed, where ideas and vomit can be shared and bounced off one another. "I feel like I have a home at Sigma Chi," explained one brother, "a home where I'm free to urinate in the VCR and then take a bowel movement in the microwave. It's the kind of home I'd like to provide for my own children someday."

Being admitted into a fraternity is no easy task. The selection criteria is long and involved and based primarily on one's social skills, community service record, ability to masturbate in a large group, and academic prowess. "We're looking for men of the highest caliber," explained Sigma Delta Epsilon president Deusche Baggy, "men who will contribute to campus life, men who care about their fellow students, and most of all, men who aren't afraid of masturbating onto a pizza or large crackers as other men look on and yell and cheer and shout encouraging slogans."

Most all fraternities have long and involved initiation rites and procedures. Explained one brother, who wished to remain anonymous, "Hi, I'm Joey Tortulina, a sophomore Delta Gamma at U of Florida . . . wait. Anyway, first, we put all the neophytes in a room and make them drink till they pass out. Then we do this seventy-five nights in a row. It's totally, totally secret. Wait a second . . . Shit." Added Sigma Chi president Peter Jones, "Our initiation rituals are ancient. In fact, our chapter was founded in like 100 B.C. or some shit like that, you know?"

The advantages of fraternal life? Honor? Respect? Camaraderie?

"No. I mostly just did it for the pussy," explained frat brother Tommy Jones. Millions of brothers across the nation echoed his sentiments exactly.

Marrying Right Out of College

I waited with slouching shoulders for my bride to meet me at the front of the church.

My family and all my college friends had come to see me get married. My first time. Her first time too. College sweethearts.

I had asked her to marry me six months ago, right after our senior year spring break. When I asked her to marry me I had three things in my pocket: wallet with thirteen dollars in it, an open pack of Life Savers that was brown on the top where the wrapper hadn't covered it, and an engagement ring.

I felt like I had asked her to marry me hundreds of times before. Only this time, instead of offering her a Life Saver, I offered her an engagement ring.

I read somewhere that the right side of a person's face is the most spontaneous responder to emotions, a built-in lie detector. And it's true. I can move my left eyebrow whenever I want, but the right one only twitches when I'm scared.

Yes, my favorite thing to do in the world is to read. I readily admit that reading is a solitary activity, but I think it has helped me study people. Like now for instance, I recognize something in my soon-to-be wife, an almost imperceptible tightness in the corner of the right side of her mouth.

I watched the tightness in her mouth and I did the math and calculated that if my life span equaled the life expectancy of a person in Ghana, my life was 51 percent over.

When the time came we exchanged rings. My ring had a little hinge. This is because my fingers are very bony at the joint, and extremely thin below the knuckle. The only way I could get a ring to fit was to get one with a hinge. I slid her ring on smoothly. She clicked my ring shut.

When the ceremony called for us to kiss, we kissed; it was a neat little kiss on the mouth. At the nadir of the kiss our teeth tapped quietly.

After this I stood up straight and tried to throw my shoulders back. My balance was thrown off and I almost fell. My wife caught me.

I was afraid. The limo hummed quietly along the road.

I don't know if I ever think twice about love, I just think one very long continuous time. I think in the counter-factual, in the made-up past and the made-up future, about the impossible and the nearly possible, the unlikely and the almost, and then I go back to the cold hard facts and try to piece them together to get a quiltlike mind-set of the woman next to me, my wife. Wife, spoken with a silent "k." Wife. Oh, but I know how she sees the world out of those blue eyes, those little light-collectors that oftentimes have my image pasted behind them.

I closed my eyes and slept on my wife's breast the rest of the way to the airport.

Section III:

Academics, or, How I Learned to Stop Worrying and Love the "C"

Choosing a Major

After choosing a brand of fabric softener and a favorite lite FM radio station, picking a major is among the top decisions you will make in college. Choose carefully, or you might pick a major that is impractical (Sanskrit), painful (Punches to the Abdomen), or overrepresented in the workplace (Punches to the Abdomen). Consider:

American Civilization

From the earliest days on this continent (excluding ten thousand insignificant years of Native American history), Americans have separated themselves from their brethren in Europe and beyond (Ireland) with a grand republican experiment that has lasted more than two hundred years. As hardy colonials forced to rely on no one but themselves and their effortless natural immunity to deadly European diseases, Americans expanded across the continent, spreading ingenuity and self-government from North Carolina to North California. From the moment that Daniel Boone said to Chief Wallum, "Here is this blanket that will keep you warm, and give you smallpox" to Molly Ringwald's prissy yet indelibly charming smile in *The Breakfast Club*, Americans have expressed a desire to be lazy armchair reactionaries protected by a resource-rich continent and a monolithic oppressive culture.

Students who study American Civilization will learn about all of America's wars, including the Civil War (win for the North), WWI and WWII (USA 2, Kraut-Huns 0), and Vietnam (tie). The Constitution will be emphasized, including each person's sacred duty to protect it from all those who inappropriately speak out against it, as will the Emancipation Proclamation, the Hawley-Smoot Tariff Act, and Amendment 45 to GATT regarding tariffs on potatoes and Velcro.

In conclusion, American Civilization is the greatest major on earth. Just ask the 1980 American gold-medal-winning hockey team.

Anthropology

Anthropology is the study of the Savage Mind. Ill-informed by his tempestuous desires, the Savage clods through the jungle on his leathern hooves, periodically feasting on his own kin. He marks the sunrise on a strip of bark secured to the bosom of his faithful squaw. From the seal-toothed fairy children of the tundra to the huggable Sasquatch, the Savage awaits "the dawn of the two moons," when the mantle of Civilization will be imposed upon his brow and the Bible tattooed on his chest. Lo, the Red Man, whose manly limbs rest but idly on the plough.

Biology

Biology is the study of anything you do not want to look at or smell. While normal people are *not* in a lab ripping through the intestines of a headless puppy, biology majors are. Fetal pig: creepy. Rat in formaldehyde: disgusting. Turd on fire: awesome but unrelated to biology. Despite turd on fire, biology is gross.

Classics

With the waning popularity of Greek and Latin studies, most universities have updated their Classics program to reflect a more modern interpretation. Professor Manfred Mann of UC Santa Barbara: "Classics has just come to mean something totally different in our society than it used to, so we've had to mold our curriculum accordingly. Besides, most college kids still like that old-time rock 'n' roll." Students who have little interest in the British Invasion will find their first year a difficult one. Adds Associate Professor Ray Davies of Clemson University, "If you don't cotton to the Brits, you might as well major in Bio." More advanced studies usually include the Kansas/Toto axis, a thorough differentiation between Styx, Yes, and Traffic, and a seminar dispelling the myths of Foghat. "Classics," notes tenured professor Gene Simmons of Wellesley College, "rock." Some of the most enjoyable theses in past years include: "Wall of Sound, Trail of Tears: The Phil Spector Corpus," "The Jefferson Airplane/Starship: Slick Yet Graceful," and "The Beatles."

Communications

Looking to control the world through various media outlets? Want to be the next Rupert Murdoch? Hoping to host the lottery show on the local news? Then a degree in Communications could be for you!

College course guides nationwide will often brag that, for example, "75 percent of our Communications majors become international media moguls within two years of graduation" (University of Mississippi–Jackson) or that "Nearly half of our Communications students instantly get high-paying jobs, model wives, and three sailboats upon graduation" (Texas A&M).

These statistics, however, can be misleading. "Nearly half"? "75 percent"? Let's be honest. Truth be told, fully

100 percent of Communications majors nationwide instantly become multimarket, multimedia, multinational, multitrillionaire media moguls as soon as they graduate. "It's almost as if they hand you this certificate that entitles you to world domination through media," explained BU Comm major Marty Senn '97, a check-out boy at Wal-Mart. "It's otherwordly, such a power trip for such young people like me."

As Rupert Murdoch once said, "Majoring in Art History was the dumbest thing I ever did. Not a day goes by I don't wonder what could have been if I had only chosen Communications."

Comparative Literature

What's worth more? Two florins or 35 million florins? I don't know the answer, but a Comparative Literature major certainly would. Students of Comparative Literature like to look at different things and compare them. For example, is proto-fascist Nazi literature any different from the writings of the American West? I don't know, because I'm not John Wayne, and I'm not Hitler. Speaking of which, who do you think would win in a fight between those two? The answer is Hitler. Or what if Batman and Spider-Man fought? I would say Spider-Man would win because he has super-strength, and Batman is just a normal guy. But the thing is Batman has all these cool things and also Robin. I guess Robin wouldn't be able to fight unless Spider-Man brought Spider-Boy with him, but does Spider-Boy even exist? Issues like these are the meat of Comparative Literature.

Comparative Literature concentrators also take classes on things that seem like they are the same but are different. These classes include "Affect/Effect: The Imbroglio of the Written Word" and "They're, Their, and There: What the Hell?" What would you rather do? Have a bucket of water fall on your head *or* Have a bucket of piss fall on your head but then get to kiss Cindy Crawford? These are the sorts of questions that require thought, scholarship, and time. If you are prepared to examine these issues study Comparative Literature *or* go back to masturbating.

Creative Writing

Just cut out this critique and you, as a Creative Writing major, can use it over and over again:

Dear Josh,

I found myself strangely sucked into your story here. When we got back from class I picked it up with the intention of starting it, and I kept going till the end and was late to practice. Don't worry, I didn't tell my coach it was your fault I was late.

But seriously, I will try to go through the story with suggestions and comments, and I'll address larger themes as they come up.

First, I just want to address confusing things. She starts with Eric as her boyfriend, and it seems that she wants something sexual with him, but he is hesitant to give her that. Does this story focus on a young woman becoming comfortable with her sexual cravings, are you showing a contrast in the purity of physical sports and the physical in the bedroom, or showing them to be one and the same? Logistically, it would seem that it would be hard for the trench coated flasher man to be heard over the crowd noise and through the glass and through her helmet unless he was yelling pretty loudly. What does the trench coated man come to symbolize, the Cheshire catlike smiling conscience, the thing inside that we look to when trying to decide if a thing is right and good or wrong and bad?

I don't know if this is a criticism as much as something to think about. Okay, hope workshop goes well and I hope the future of this story is a very good one. Thanks for the good read,

Terry
3-2707

East Asian Studies

Interested in St. Francis's excursions past the border between what is today Russia and Mongolia? Or Buddha's travels north from India through western China? Sorry, but I'm afraid those are *West* Asian Studies, a different major entirely. *East* Asian studies focuses on the rich history of Kushiro, Hokkaido, Japan's easternmost city at 144° E longitude. Or, better yet, Honolulu, Hawaii, with those people's humid clime and dark eyes. Or, still, the Bering Strait, where Indians crossed over to North America eons ago, culminating in the study of Mr. Wong's Tai Kwon Doh studio in Portland, Maine, where classes are held every Thursday and professional teaching is ensured.

Economics

The appeals of a major in Economics is clear: To study the ways of money is to know how to obtain money. To truly understand the complex mechanisms of global finance is to become a master of the universe. There are, of course, drawbacks to studying the dismal science. For example, have you ever met a guy that seemed sort of upright? Nothing special but just a solid guy or gal. You go out and have like seventeen drinks and just hang out because it's college, and you don't give a crap. But then for some reason you get a look into his eyes, and you are transfixed. In a moment of lucidity you see that something might not be right. You can see behind the glassy wall of his cornea into his dark places beyond his mind and his body. And you realize he is empty, his spirit made rotten and musty: He has no soul. Every person in your Economics classes is like that guy.

English

English is not only a universal major at all colleges, but generally one of the most popular. And it's no wonder, blokes. The four valuable years you spend learning the language of England will teach you the differences between a theater and *theatre*, football and *football*, *mathematics in quids* vs. *booze in pints*. The transition ought to be easy after the number of years you probably spent riding your penny-farthing past the Bobbies on your way to grammar school, and back home to do the chores your mum assigned, such as throwing the rubbish into the lorry, including that of the loo, then giving your mates a bell on the blower to ask 'em out to fish and chips. Or if you are a skirt, perhaps telling the wankers next door to piss off while you and your girlfriends watch a chat show on the telly and take tea and crumpets afters, discussing the 'andsome mates at the bloody school who aren't buggers or smart-arses, but accidentally throwing the spanner in the works and getting sod all of the squidgey. *Bollocks!* So, if you're interested in reading and writing theses on the works of Henry David Thoreau, F. Scott Fitzgerald, or Thomas Pynchon, you might consider majoring in American, *Yank*.

Film

Once in the early 1920s there was a man who said that there would never be a talking movie. What an idiot. That guy must feel very stupid/dead right now. Now film students across the country are making talkies. Here is an example of a talkie:

[*Starts with man at supermarket, slowly putting cans in the five-cent return machines. He is a good-looking man, but looks aimless and in need of an adventure/woman/conflict-resolution. A very pretty woman walks up.*]

Don: Hey, you want to go to the beach?

Kim: Yes. And I brought this.

[*Cue in sexy music as she displays a banana.*]

Don: Wait till I get enough money out of these cans to buy us a big house.

Kim: You should probably buy sunscreen too. You are pasty and white.

Don: [*taking off all clothes looking at pasty white body*] True. I am pasty white.

Kim: [*taking off all clothes looking sheepishly around the supermarket*]

[*intercourse*]

end scene.

Folklore and Mythology

"Well," said Zeus, clearly angry, "did you even read my application?"

"Yes Mr. Zeus. You are just not as qualified for the job."

"But I can throw lightning!!! Who else can do that?"

"Sir, that er, talent, seems irrelevant here."

"But the goddess of Wisdom burst out of my head a fully mature human reading at a twelfth-grade level! Who else could do that!!"

"That too proved to be irrelevant when we made the decision to not hire you here at Goldman Sachs."

"Is everything I've done irrelevant??"

"Yes."

Moral: Do not major in folk and myth.

Forestry

If a redwood tree falls down in a forest in California, will it take down all the rest of the trees around it because it's so big? You're damn right it will. How old is a 150-year-old tree in tree years? Yes, future forester, twelve years old is correct! What is the recommended method of chopping down a tree? "Take an axe and hack, hack, hack!" as any student will tell you as he wipes the enormous beads of sweat off his 50-foot brow, wearing only a plaid shirt with suspenders that hold up his real thick boots. If this sounds like it could be you, then you are a lumberjack, an Appalachian, and a student of forestry.

History

Well before 1548, Cicero wrote that "he who knows nothing of history forever remains a child." Our Latin friend didn't mean a lifetime of kickball, Legos, mittens attached to your parka, and chronic bloody noses. We're 95 percent sure he meant that those who never studied the works and words of people of the past would remain ignorant—*in the manner of children.*

But not being stupid isn't what drives thousands of people to study history every day. More likely, they're interested in having any manner of old things come alive (inside their brains). Japanese cowboys, samurai, shoguns, emperors, ham-fisted Yokohama fish peddlers—these are the sort of characters that fight with Vikings on the yellowing pages of history. But lest you think that history isn't very practical: wrong. Only studying history could prepare us for a world where viscounts administer justice at the end of a lash, Chinamen build themselves a Great Wall, and historical events duplicate themselves exactly time after time. History is also good for law school, I heard.

Some historians think history will end as it began—with the piercing cry of a lonesome baby, the first ever. Others think history will "end" in a cataclysmic ball of fire. Hopefully this brief introduction will leave a cataclysmic excitement-fire seething deep in your heart.

Hotel Management

Only one school has the balls to offer this major, and that is Cornell's School of Hotel Management. Also, the Holiday Inn, Ramada Inn, Marriott Inn, Sheraton Inn, Motel 6, and Harvard Square Hotel training courses. At these schools, one learns how to be the best concierge, bellboy, or maid in the entire world. Do you think managing an entire hotel is an easy job? Consider the required classes: "Hotel Studies 15: Making Sure There Is a TV in Every Room and Sometimes a Bible." Or "Hotel Studies 151: Continental Breakfast: Coffee and Doughnuts." Or "Hotel Studies 167: Do We Have a Pool?" Moreover, these students must learn how to record an automated message, take credit card numbers, and make beds. There is a reason hotels are either one-star or four-star, and that reason is the study of Hotel Management.

Marine Biology

Many living organisms in the world's oceans are becoming increasingly endangered. Luckily, most of these swimmers survive the briny waters of California and Miami and go on to become some of America's elite shark fighters at the U.S. Marines Biology Academy in Annapolis, Maryland. These silent heroes of the armed forces vigilantly protect our shores from the alarming number of whale invasions on our beaches. Not since Pearl Harbor have America's foes shown such audacity. Marines biologists spend hours both in and outside the classroom studying subjects from oceanography and sonar to high-powered weaponry, nuclear submarines and torpedoes, and taxonomy. Who do you think saves society from the armies of fish and birds who attempt to steal human oil under the guise of being poisoned to death by a "tanker spill"? Or seagulls who attempt to pilfer human beverage by drinking our six-packs and wearing the rings around their necks as a token of victory? Or the rest of the aquatic community that breathes, eats, sleeps, and poops in the 70 percent of our earth's surface that should be rightfully ours to drink? If not for the U.S. Marine Corps of biologists, we might not even have dry land to call home.

Philosophy

Philosophy is one of the oldest majors, and attracts the worst people in the world. Is your name Andre? Do you like belts? When people talk about things like football, action movies, and America, do you say, "What's that?" If any of the above apply to you, then you might as well major in Philosophy. If you are still unsure whether you should major in Philosophy consider this question: If a pale-skinned Philosophy major falls in the woods, does anyone give a flying crap? No. Or how about this one: What is the sound of one hand clapping against the drug-addled head of a Philosophy concentrator? It sounds like *Thwok Thwok Thwok*. Philosophy classes can be quite diverse, and you will examine topics such as personal identity, the mind/body problem, and How to Do the World a Favor by Killing Yourself. Philosophy was founded hundreds of years ago by Aristotle and his pupil Plato, or was it the other way around? Since no one cares about Philosophy, it doesn't matter. What's the meaning of life? I'll tell you. It's going into a sports bar in America, getting a Miller Lite, and shooting the shit with a member of the Steelworkers Union. What's *not* the meaning of life? I'll tell you. It's going into a jazz club in France, ordering a dry martini, and flirting with an unemployed artist named Pierre. If one more *goddamned* Philosophy concentrator comes up to me on the street corner and tries to get me to be a Russkie while I am trying to order a taco or watch my dog take a decent shit, I will go home and kill my mother in frustration. It's not like I haven't done it before. You should major in Philosophy.

Physics

Hey, maybe we're no rocket scientists, but these guys are!! The Physics major is constantly dedicated to making people's lives better. They have enormously difficult courses, but not so difficult that they don't have time to make dishwashers that run on toothpaste spit or robot dogs. The details are a little complicated for the layman, but it involves quarks. Whether it's learning how to make soda cans that can double as toilet paper or books that can read themselves to you, Physics majors never lack opportunities to better their fellow man. Do you know what a Higgs boson is? Me neither, but if it helps run my remote controlled telephone/basketball hoop, they're okay in my book.

Pre-Med

The curricula for most students interested in pursuing a career in medicine is known to be one of the most challenging tasks at any college. All students must take a full year of general chemistry, biology, organic chemistry, and physics, and there are only about a dozen slots open each year for new doctors nationwide. Half of these slots go to guys who were in a frat with dudes on the admissions committee, and another five are set aside for bad doctors from other countries whose medical school was a cattle slaughterhouse. So the competition among pre-medical students, or "pre-meds," can be fierce. About half of these pre-meds, or "assholes," will end up killing themselves. The remaining 50,000 have a giant study break to celebrate their increased chances of acceptance. At this study break, approximately 45,000 students will be either poisoned to death or tied up inside a trunk and thrown into the ocean. The remaining survivors are shipped to a desert island, to use their knowledge of organic chemistry and raw instinct to fend for themselves in the humid jungle darkness.

They usually form packs of roaming marauders who annihilate one another in bloody clashes. The last two gore-bespattered survivors are airlifted back to civilization to take the MCATs. Whoever gets the higher score becomes your doctor.

Psychology

Did you ever notice that, sometimes, people do stuff that's totally weird and you're like, "What was that all about?" Well, in the science of psychology, finding out what kind of stuff different stuff causes and stuff is what it's all about. Did we mention that this is science? Yes, we did. For example, maybe you noticed that pretty girls don't like fat guys with BO. In psychology, you could go up to a lot of girls and be like, "Hey, what's up . . . yeah? . . . awesome! . . . anyways, did you ever see a gross guy with savage BO? . . . Yeah? Was that really gross? Thanks!" And this will get published in the *New England Journal of Medicine*. It's all about the human mind!

And you learn all about Freud and all that. So he's like, "You love your mother or some shit and have sex with dogs or something," and you'll be like, "Whoa! This guy is messed up!" Exactly. When you major in Psych, you learn all kinds of messed-up shit. Like, did you ever hear about that guy in India with like ten-foot-long finger-nails? Messed up! If you like the sound of this, you should definitely *not* try this major. Psych!!!!!

Romance Languages

What's it like to have all of your classes begin with a song by the great Dean Martin? How can a walk on a black sand beach possibly count as a final exam? How does it feel to be served the world's best wine while you take notes? How can a university afford to pay for a box of chocolates for each female student at every lecture? What is *amore*? Is it better to have loved and lost than to have never loved at all? What do rose petals feel like against your cheek? How do you say "joi de vivre" in French? What does a seduction quiche taste like? What is the sexiest part of a woman's body?

One needn't even ask a Romance Languages major, for the answers lie in the piercing depths of their eyes.

Sociology

Although Sociology may, in the past, have gotten the rep of being an "easy" major, those days are gone. Sociology is the study of society; a rigorous discipline that is highly demanding, fast-paced, and often a bit strict. "I totally wanted to write my thesis about why people prefer the WCW (World Championship Wrestling) over the WWF (World Wrestling Federation). The department heads (at Dartmouth), needless to say, weren't too happy with my choice of topics. I ended up being forced to write the usual academic bullshit about why Randy 'The Macho Man' Savage is considered the most charismatic, and at times, most talented pro wrestler of the last two decades," commented Dartmouth Sociology senior Andre the Giant.

While Sociology may not be for the faint of academic heart, the rigor of receiving a Sociology degree often proves quite rewarding for the dedicated student. "I did a six-year research project on why people eat microwavable popcorn as opposed to the kind of popcorn that you pop in a pot or through means other than a microwave. I never set out to change the world, but it appears as though I have," explained University of Chicago grad student Orville Redenbacher on the results of his groundbreaking study.

Sociology: It's not just for retards anymore.

Dollars and Cents (Sense! Séance? Scents!): Majoring in Money

Studies have shown that there is a correlation between grades in college and later success in life. Here's a guide to the most wealth-creating majors.

Mathematics:

You know all that adding and subtracting you had to do in high school? Well, get ready for a lot more of it if you decide to major in Mathematics. Did you think you added some big numbers back in your AP Addition class? In the Mathematics major, you get to add *some of the biggest numbers in the world!* And after graduation, that's when the real adding starts . . . the adding of your salary, that is. You know, to your checking account. Never mind.

Communications:

This subject addresses such fascinating topics as media theory, and how to make millions and millions of dollars with these tiny classified ads. The potential here is enormous. Because people communicate all the time, just by making a little bit of money each time someone communicates, you could make millions of dollars.

Fine Arts:

Think there's no money in arts? Think again! You're still correct.

Applied Mathematics:

Take that math that you learned in college, and apply it. Or become mathematics, the concept itself, and apply for some scholarship or something. This major will make you rich, as Wall Street firms are always looking for people who can use protractors and inadvertently stain their clothes.

Computer Science:

There's no future in computers. If you choose this major, get ready for pay that's not much better than social work or library science. It's almost as bad as majoring in biomedical engineering Internet cell-phone technology cloning and cloning.

Classes to Avoid

All of us at one time or another have been burned by taking poorly thought-out classes. We have all felt the poison ivy itch of a crappy syllabus, the psoriasis-like burning of inadequate exam preparation, and the late-stage dementia of neurosyphilis. Consider the following guide to bad classes as a flu shot, which will hopefully prevent you from taking bad classes. Do not take these classes:

History 54: The Saga of Cheese and the Men Who Ate It: 1324–1800
English 12: Aninerak Anna: *Anna Karenina* Read Backward
Sociology 41: Your Dysfunctional Family
Poop 105: Eating Poop

Public Policy 40: Beating the Corrupt Local Government or the Tobacco Lobby As a Young, Inexperienced Lawyer with the Help of a Mentor Looking for Redemption

Political Science 202: Quit Yer Stalin: Bad Puns in Soviet "Agitprop"

Physics 115: How Anvils Fall on Your Head

Anthropology 905: Explaining the Teacher/Student Rift through Classroom Nudity and Unflattering Lighting

Botany 60: Smelling Stinky Plants

Music 703a: The Fleetwood Mac Canon: Origins to *Rumours* (Conference Course)

Philosophy 210: Who Needs a God When the World Has Burgess Meredith? (Seminar)

Computer Science 1204: Taking Your Shirt Off at the Beach

Staying Awake in Class

You stayed up until 5 A.M. You got up for your 10 A.M. class but, let's face it, your chances of staying awake through the lecture are slim at best. Those three beers you had last night and your chronic narcolepsy and addiction to sedatives usually restricted to wild game aren't helping. How are you going to catch some z's without the prof noticing, or stay awake through the whole class without distress? Ooh, ooh, we know!

▸ **Sunglasses**
Sure, wearing sunglasses yourself helps hide those resting eyes, especially if they're tinted extra-dark. But what about putting those same shades on your professor himself? Either he won't be able to see the class at all or he'll look so damn cool you won't be able to fall asleep.

▸ **The low-brimmed hat**
Wearing a low-brimmed hat, pulling it down over your forehead, and looking down is a virtually foolproof method of believably hiding your eyes from the professor. Make sure, however, that you don't draw a naked lady on the front of your hat to draw attention to yourself.

▸ **Caffeine**
Caffeine can be used (a) to help you stay up all night and/or (b) to help you get through class the next day without falling asleep. Unfortunately, no truly safe methods for ingesting this dangerous drug have been found.

▸ **Sleeping pills**
Give everyone in your class a few mickeys, and you'll look just like everyone else. Sweet dreams, English 103!

▸ **Elephants juggling pizzas through class**
Who could sleep through that!?

▸ **Roger**
That guy Roger who usually sits next to you will poke you in the arm once every three minutes for $12 a lecture. He also has an invisible sleeping booth you can use for free.

▸ **Not getting up**
The easiest thing to do, quite frankly, is to never get up in the first place, and just sleep through the lecture in your bed. Then you can dream about your classes instead of actually being there. "Well, hello, Professor Cindy Crawford!!" you might say. "Oh my God, I'm naked!!!!!"

A public service announcement from Andrew S. Weil, M.D.: America's favorite alternative health guru.

Procrastination:
How to Deal with It

Procrastination is one of the most difficult things to deal with at college. College students are given a large amount of free time to do a small amount of work, and this leads to wasting time. The *Harvard Lampoon*, after watching the movie *Mannequin* twice in one day, banged their heads together and came up with some ways to avoid procrastination.

Before we begin, however, it is often a good idea to put a CD on and listen to it while you prepare to sit down and read this piece. Have you ever heard of Smash Mouth? They are without question one of the most exciting bands to come down the pike in the last few years. But of course, that is getting off the subject. So go put on the CD. If you don't have the Smash Mouth CD, you might want to take a walk down to your local music retailer and buy it. It's probably in the modern rock section, or maybe even in the "hot new artists" section. Since you are already at the CD store, take a quick gander and see if there are any new Sugar Ray CDs. I've heard they're coming out with a live album!

Have you ever tried to jump up in the air and click your heels three times? Now I'm not saying this is something you should do at a party or something, but since you've got some time before reading this piece, you should try it. It's harder than it sounds. I did it once, but I had to jump off a couch rather than jumping straight off the ground.

Did you hear that Stanley Kubrick died? He is one of the most talented directors, and there are quite a few fan sites on the Internet that are devoted to that talented man's life and work. A good jumping off point is http://www.geocities.com/14678/kubrick.html. From this site you can view some clips of his movies, new and old. If you are near your computer with this essay about procrastination, you might want to check it out.

Sometimes we forget how important our friends are to us. Give them a call! You never know when unforeseen disaster might strike.

Alright, alright, back to preventing procrastination. "Preventing Procrastination" is almost a tongue-twister, but no more so than saying "toy boat" five times fast. It's always like "Toy boat, toy boat, boytoat, bo tat. Aw, heck!!!" It's not something that you should try right now, but I've never been able to do it.

I've also never been able to stand on my head or walk on my hands.

The longest I've ever been able to hold my breath is two minutes, and that was really hard for me.

Without further ado, Preventing Procrastination:

1. Don't wait until the last minute.

2. Go get 'em.

Writing a Dynamic College Essay

A college essay is much different than a high school essay. Take a look at the following two examples from an introductory English class on the major plays of Shakespeare. The first will get an F because it is very bad. Do not write essays like this:

Duffy Sasser
Literature and Arts A-14
Professor Tyler Chapman
Critical Essay #1
"To Be Or Not To Be"
A Comparison Between Romeo and Juliet and Hamlet

Romeo and Juliet and Hamlet are two of Shakespeare's greatest plays. Moreover, they are similar in a number of ways. However, in a number of ways, they are different. And yet on some level, they are similar in a number of ways. Let us examine this further.

Both of these plays feature an abundance of characters. A quick glance at Hamlet's Dramatis Personae shows fully fourteen different characters—and a closer look reveals three more. Romeo and Juliet goes even farther, weighing in at no less than twenty-three different characters. Significantly, both plays feature a number of characters who say things and a handful who do nothing.

Another striking similarity is the preponderance of implausible names: "Polonius," "Benvolio," and "Reynaldo" are all quite absurd, and I for one have never met anyone named "Gertrude." It seems clear that Shakespeare intended these fanciful names to evoke certain fragments of meaning. For example, Hamlet's name recalls the phrase "If you're not going to eat that ham, let your sister have some," while "Fortinbras" clearly implies "Hello, I am an eccentric old woman; I am looking for tinbras."

There is another similarity which it would be retarded not to discuss—the element of language. In both Romeo and Juliet and Hamlet, the characters are constantly speaking to each other, or listening to someone speak, or talking to themselves, or what have you. Here we see Shakespeare's characteristic penchant for words; more specifically, his habit of using words to signify things. One can clearly see how Shakespeare's growing up as a human boy in England may have influenced this aspect of his artistry.

Another obvious parallel between the two plays is the recurring motif of gravity. Both the Verona of Romeo and Juliet and the Denmark of

Hamlet are worlds in which objects are pulled toward earth by a force proportional to their mass. Thus, in Hamlet act II scene iii, as Hamlet and Laertes engage in a kind of verbal "jousting match," both characters remain firmly attached to the floor. Moreover, when Polonius drops his keys at line 187, it is implied that the keys then fall to, and make contact with, the floor (ground).

This seems clearly analogous to the moment in Romeo and Juliet when Juliet attempts (unsuccessfully) to pass her hand through a wall, and then Friar Laurence appears in her chambers, remarking that his feet "seem well stuck to the ground, as if't twere the very quality of nature." This in turn foreshadows the moment in act V scene iii when Friar Laurence remarks, "I dropped my keys on the ground." Thus, in Hamlet, as in Romeo and Juliet, no stable objects rise spontaneously into the air, nor do any dropped objects remain eerily suspended in mid-air.

Another major motif running through both plays is the concept of time. In Hamlet, Shakespeare depicts a tragic world in which time passes continually, such that, in act IV scene iii, Polonius remarks that "it..." is later than it was before. Similarly, in the balcony scene of Romeo and Juliet, we learn from Romeo that it is "...night," while Juliet observes that it is "4:36 A.M." With this recurring theme of the passage of time, Shakespeare weaves a thread of continuity throughout (and in) the play.

In conclusion, in both Romeo and Juliet and Hamlet, Shakespeare ironically suggests a tragic universe in which the real and the imagined coexist, and yet it is relatively easy to draw a boundary between them, such that, on some level, Shakespeare has written the greatest book of all time.

The *Harvard Lampoon's* Guide to College Admissions

This next essay is much better. Tim Durning here has apparently learned the most important rule of writing dynamic college essays: Use your thesaurus. Take a look:

Tim Durning

English 10a

12/15/99

Teaching Assistant: Nikki Westfall

A+

The Interior Reprisal in Hamlet's Revenge: To Garrote or Not to Atrocity

Hamlet is enlightened by an apparition to avenge his father's ghastly abrogation, but Hamlet stalls, vacillates, hesitates and then is laggard to action. High-brow Hamlet's discovery of the coexistence of blameless and flagitious, and his distinct belief in the momentousness of posthumous image after you are dead force him to delay his avenging his defunct father.

As the play extemporizes, we find that Hamlet is domicile during a hiatus from school in Wittenburg, where he had feasibly made the Dean's list. Indeed, his reputation as a cerebral scholar at Wittenburg had preceded him before he even got there. In high school, he had gotten penultimate place at the indigenous science fair. He had actualized a small solar-powered plaything airplane. First accolade was a vaccination for mumps and his mother prepared sweetmeats and victuals for his repast. It is clearly Hamlet's naturally adroit intellect that allows him to concoct the synergy of good and depraved within human temperament.

If Claudius were an integrally baneful person, Hamlet would have found it easy to consummate his onus to the ghost of his father and dispatch of his uncle. Yet, there is exemplary woven between the quilt that is an evil populace, even within the idiosyncrasy of Claudius.

In the equidistant middle of the play, Hamlet became cognizant of the ambiguity of bipedal good and evil. He has erudite that evil is not like a noxious plant that can be picked out. It is more an entity that is inextricably woven into the textile of our fellowship.

To desist, perhaps if we all initiate seeing the virtuous in ourselves we could cessation world hunger.

Picasso's *Guernica*

Dude, Do You Like Art?

Me neither. But did you know that a lot of art-shit is about college? Check it out . . . Pablo Picasso, although originally Spanish, actually attended the University of Arizona, where he pledged Sigma Chi. Picasso created his masterpiece, *Guernica* (pictured above) after the third night of UA's "BeerFest '89." Picasso explained, "I was f—d up on amphetamines and shit, and seeing like triangles. Everything was a cube and there were horses and shit. I just painted what I saw."

Don't like school? Like having the runs all the time? Screw school and your parents: Join the Peace Corps.

Joining the Peace Corps

Thinking about what to do after college? Think in the direction of the Peace Corps.

Everybody in the Peace Corps has a job to do. I build hospitals, says one woman in the Peace Corps. I teach English, says a lanky fellow. I watch football, says a third. It's a little joke. The men and women of the Peace Corps giggle excitedly. They are eager to start their new jobs.

The Peace Corps goes all over the world, to places like Africa and Senegal. The villagers there can't wait for the Peace Corps, which has been known to bring them candy and muffins. Local cats look about for treats. Some men and women in the Peace Corps find it so rewarding that they come back year after year. The genitals of these Peace Corps members are licked in fond remembrance by the local dogs.

One project the Peace Corps has long worked at is farming. A list of the many crops planted by the Peace Corps would fill a lot of space! Some of that space would be occupied by these words: turnips, beets, grain, carrots, potatoes, watermelon, vegetables, peas.

Do you think the Peace Corps may be for you? Don't be a hasty Harry. The Peace Corps is a twenty-seven-month commitment. Volunteers are sent to turbulent countries the world over, many of which are Guatemala. Although the experience is usually extremely rewarding, the reward is often a terrible experience. After serving in the Peace Corps, you will never be the same, which may or may not be a change for the better. It's something of a crap shoot.

Still, the Peace Corps has been around for well over several years. People throughout the world love the Peace Corps, though boll weevils and Communists don't like it one bit. Veterans of the Peace Corps never forget their time there. The taste of quinine lingers in their mouths.

The mission of the Peace Corps is to help people throughout the world. If you would like to help, then great. Awesome.

Is the pre-medical track wearing you out? Perhaps you should explore "careers" in writing. Take a quick look at what may await you at the most prestigious writing program in the country . . .

A Look Inside the Iowa Writers' Program

Each year a select group of writers heads to Iowa City, Iowa, to participate in the Iowa Writers' Program, the country's most prestigious writing colony. Although it may seem as though the epoch of arts and letters is dead, it's not. Take a look at this correspondence between two Iowa Writers' Program graduates . . .

My dear Bailey,

I must crave your pardon for not having written ere this. It may be said that we ought to read our Contemporaries, that McCannus & co should have their due from us, but for the sake of a few imaginative or domestic passages, are we to be bullied into a certain Philosophy engendered in the whims of an Egoist? When McCannus writes, "PERT PLUS Simply Great Hair. Simply." I revolt in the plainness of his prose, in the utter formality, the coldness of it all. Poetry should be great & unobtrusive, a thing which enters into one's soul. I don't mean to deny McCannus' grandeur, but we need not be teased with such grandeur & merit, when we all know Pert Plus is wholly inferior to Head & Shoulders.

Your affectionate friend,
Samuel Romslo

My dear Samuel,

I must take umbrage with your brutal slaying of McCannus' "Pert Plus" spot. When he states, "Pert Plus is gentle enough to use every day, even on permed or color-treated hair. And it's pH balanced," I am transported to a finer world. A world where everyone has "Simply Great Hair. Simply." Oh, such perfect pH harmony!

McCannus aside, I must say I thoroughly enjoyed your, "ISOPROPYL RUBBING ALCOHOL 70% Warning: Flammable, keep away from fire or flame." Although it begins somewhat lackadaisically, the later sun imagery burned a hole straight into my soul. You are truly a poet.

Yours most sincerely,
Bailey Jones

My dear Bailey,

I thank you kindly for your praise. I am, however, somewhat dismayed by your phrase "Although it begins somewhat lackadaisically." What nerve! I suppose your own latest work, "When used as directed, Johnson & Johnson Mountain Spray-Disinfectant is formulated to disinfect inanimate hard surfaces (such as bathrooms, basements, closets, attics, laundry rooms, and other areas) which are prone to odors caused by micro-organisms," far outweighs my "lackadaisical" treatment of rubbing alcohol? Your hackneyed prose, lack of mountain imagery, and dismal lyric cadence is nothing of which to boast. Upon reading your prose, I instantly picked up a competing brand, "Ida's River Valley Spray-Disinfectant," and was enchanted with its breathtaking label and far superior spray disinfectant.

Sincerely,
Samuel Romslo

Samuel,

While you may attack my prose, I implore you, never attack "Johnson & Johnson Mountain Spray-Disinfectant." It is, by far, the market leader in quality disinfectants. I treasure our friendship, but please speak nary again of "Johnson & Johnson Mountain Spray-Disinfectant."

Cheers,
Bailey Jones

Dear Bailey,

 I apologize for my ill-tempered, acerbic reply. I knew not what I wrote, emotion having so overpowered my mental faculties. However, while "Johnson & Johnson Mountain Spray-Disinfectant" may be a market leader, "Ida's," nonetheless, has posed a serious philosophical quandary for the informed consumer. Which to choose, "a Mountain Spray-Disinfectant which deodorizes those areas which are generally hard to keep fresh-smelling" or "a spray designed to kill Pathogenic Fungi, Staphylococcus aureus, Pseudomonas aeruginosa, and Trichophyton mentagrophytes." An existential dilemma indeed! To kill, or to deodorize? To take life, or to renew odor? Be they, perchance, the same?

Yours,
Samuel Romslo

Dear Samuel,

 I accept your apology. All in good fun. Your query, while in some manner mentally stimulating, holds no true weight in our post-industrial landscape. "Mountain Spray-Disinfectant" is neither, as you wrote, a "killer" nor a "deodorant." It is, antipodally, both, and yet it is each simultaneously. To kill is to deodorize, and to deodorize is to kill. And yet Mountain Spray-Disinfectant is not a killer deodorant. It is, as I have written, "designed for use in Homes, Nursing Homes, Hospitals, Institutions, Offices, Schools, and Motels." That is all that it is. Oh, also it is "Harmful if swallowed."

Your friend,
Bailey

Do you like beautiful college coeds?

Of course you do.

Enter the mystical land of **Blar** where the powers of the evil sorcerer **Zarn** are threatened by magical elves, undead knights, omnipotent mages, and tits.

This must be college!

- ✓ **Wet T-shirts and beer!**

- ✓ **Butt-naked sex party!**

- ✓ **Free access to our multiplayer Web site!**

- ✓ **Gonna get all freaky college style! Ass!!!**

ACKNOWLEDGMENTS

Ryan Koh thanks Mom and Owen.

David King wishes to thank: Mom, Dad, Mich, EAP, Jesse, Earce, the Boston Red Sox, T.J., and the summer staff.

Matthew Warburton would like to thank Bonnie and David Warburton, his grandparents, friends from high school, the cool dudes, NUMA special projects director Dirk Pitt, his roommates, the Depends Corporation, and Batman.

Summer staff and contributors thank:
Grandmaster Yu, Sun Yu, Anthony M., Judith J., and David M. T. DiGregorio, Chun family, Stroudsburg, Dave Papa, CYEP, Mary Crowley, Thomas Etten, Mike Crowley Etten, Ellen Crowley Etten, Mr. and Mrs. Lentz, Mr. and Mrs. Maher, the people of Minnesota, the one girl who said hi to Jake at 7-Eleven, Mr. and Mrs. Hely, DAO'D, Lillian, the people of Ireland, Nick Stoller, Eric Stoller, Phyllis Stoller, Kathleen McGovern, Maureen Katie McGovern, Brian Philip McGovern, Dan Mangiavellano . . . and Matt Hubbard thanks the following people for material: Mom, Dad, Erin, my grandparents, the Pickard family, LEN, Jeaner, Matt Ebbel, and noted character actor Taylor Negron.

The *Lampoon* thanks:
Joseph Hickey, William Oakley, Tom Beale, Rick Wolff, Dan Ambrosio, Eric Rayman, Tyler Chapman, Roland Ottewell.

THE
HARVARD LAMPOON
STAFF

Editors:
David King
Ryan Koh
Matthew Warburton

Summer Book Staff Writers:
Kevin Doughten
Kevin Etten
Matthew Hubbard
Jacob Lentz
P. Terrence McGovern
Jean Yu

Staff Contributors & Artists:
E. D. Bennett '97
J. D. Brancato '80
Amanda Burnham
Daniel Chun
Craig DiGregorio '99
Emily Harrison
Stephen Hely
Deirdre O'Dwyer
Elizabeth Phang
Chess Stetson
Matthew Stoller
Jed Wahl '99

Special Contributors:
Michael Colton '97
Adam Rosen '95
Michael Schur '97

Staff Photo
Back row, left to right: P. Terrence McGovern, Matthew Hubbard, Daniel Chun, Kevin Doughten
Middle row, left to right: Jacob Lentz, Stephen Hely, Ryan Koh, Matthew Warburton
Front row, left to right: David King, Ibis, Jean Yu, Elizabeth Phang

✓